The Truth Hurts
By
A.K. Scott

Copyright © 2019 A.K. Scott
All rights reserved.

ONE

Perhaps they are not stars, but rather openings in heaven where the love of our lost ones pours through and shines down upon us to let us know they are happy.

Eskimo Proverb

Chief Inspector Jim Barge hid in his Police car, praying for a reason to avoid visiting the family expecting him. The truth hurts when it's uncovered, but Barge was convinced this would sting a lot more coming from him.

LOCAL MAN DROWNS IN SHIPWRECK OFF ULLAPOOL

That was the headline The Southern Reporter ran in the end. Barge shook his head. How else would he die in a shipwreck? Forget the few hundred other poor buggers that died. The public would. The *local* man – who hadn't lived there for years, may I add – would sell far more newspapers than all the pensioners on board. They were almost dead anyway.

The local man was thirty-four-year-old Ronnie Macleod. Everyone thought he was a character. Never down. Never negative. He would always have a joke for you, whether you wanted one or not. People, only when you asked, would tell you his one purpose was to make sure everyone was laughing.

So, it was devilishly cruel the day he died. There was nobody to help those he left behind. There was nobody to replace that hole in their world. The empty space allowed hatred and negativity to bruise all that they touched. At least, that is how it seemed.

'I really am sorry to have to be the one to tell you this.' The police officer clasped his hands tightly and pursed his lips. He sat nervously on the couch, as though he should never have chosen to sit at all. 'I've come as soon as possible.'

'You're joking, aren't you?' The woman's beady green eyes stared back at the officer. She didn't blink, though she grit her teeth as her breath wheezed in and out of her lungs, catching audibly in the tar built up by years of smoking. 'You don't know where my son is. You don't even know what happened. You don't know even know when he died.'

'Well, we can guess- '

'Aye, exactly.' She was quick to interrupt. 'That's all you can do. Guess.'

'It's fair to assume-'

'Yeah, it's fair to assume you're a dickhead, pal. A fat one.' It was Ronnie's mother who barked first at Jim Barge, Chief Inspector, upon breaking the news. Now her only living son spoke. He was not shy to say exactly how he felt.

Jim stroked his round cheeks. They had grown over the years. He couldn't recognise his abnormal weight gain in the mirror. He had to rely on others, such as the Macleod family, to rudely inform him.

They all said it would never happen, and now it had. Only a year after one ship had battered into Lochmaddy Marina, ripping its hull, another was missing at sea.

'That captain knew exactly what the weather was going to be.' The brother bit his bottom lip as to try and stop his anger spilling over. He shook his head, with his eyes closed, and he sat on his hands to make sure that he sat still. He couldn't risk what he might do. 'It was windy, so they shouldn't have gone. He's the one responsible. Are you going to arrest the murderer?'

'The captain made his decision with everyone's interests at heart,' Jim spoke softly as he brushed his fingers through what was left of his wispy, brown hair. It gathered round the middle of his head. His eyes were bloodshot, stained with tobacco smoke. He wrinkled them with a fake smile as he tried to calm the family.

'He didn't consider my mother's,' the brother responded, coldly. 'Not mine either. You cock.'

Barge's smile vanished. It was difficult not to react. They were angry. Jim knew that. Yet it wasn't his fault. Not that they'd care. It wouldn't matter to them. He could tell them anything, but they would still attack him.

'When will he be returned to us?' The mother asked. She sat with her head in her hands and her elbows wedged into her knees. 'I want to bury my son.'

The leathered skin on the palms of her hands held back her tears. She was inconsolable, and between the gap of her teeth fell yellowed mucus. Her son sat inches from her, but he chose not to hold her. He stared at the officer and shook his head.

Jim was sure this was all an act.

'Ronnie died,' he said, taking a deep breath to let his mother shout out in pained cries to exaggerate what they felt the police officer was failing to recognise. 'He died for no reason.'

Outside, and I mean far outside, a storm brewed. Lightning crashed down into the open sea. The water was black. It was tainted now. It had all moved so fast. It was up, then it was upside down. In pieces. Dead. Blood strewn throughout the shards of metal and leaking diesel. It was difficult to make out any shape in the driving rain and wind. The swelling sea tried desperately to swallow the evidence from its crime.

Barge said all he could. There were no words to help. As he had had it put to him so elegantly, he was a fat useless balding prick. Instead of sitting in their house, he should drown himself in the sea and if he should be so lucky to find Ronnie Macleod on the seabed, to call them.

Days passed before the search officially ended and finally, the missing were presumed dead. People weren't happy, and many were outraged by the decision. *They might still be alive!* Yeah, sure. Out in the middle of nowhere, where there's no land as far as the eye can see. You think you'd survive out there? No. You'd eventually breathe in water. You'd feel the final silent moments before you drowned alone. You'd be as cold and as wet as every corpse out there.

Barge believed the same, albeit less aggressively. He had read through the investigation report many times. Then he read it once more. He couldn't work out why it was bothering him. He hadn't slept very well the night before, and he took extra caution to make sure he wasn't about to make a fool of himself.

'Hey Jan.' He thumbed through the final few pages. 'You've read this report?'

A voice mumbled yes from outside his door.

'Is anything odd to you?' He shouted.

The same voice mumbled no. Barge wasn't sure if she meant, no, there's nothing odd, or, no, please leave me alone.

In the same breath as he gasped at the error, he had picked up his telephone and dialled the Ullapool constabulary.

'Good afternoon,' said the voice. Barge was quick to interrupt the long and monotonous introduction.

'It's Jim from down south. I need someone who is working on the wreckage report.' He creased the page concerning him as the woman put him on hold. It annoyed him that the report seemed to blend between the past and present tense. It was poorly written.

The phone clicked, 'Tormod.'

'Funny way to say hello to a friend,' said Barge.

'Come on Jim, what is it?' The voice at the other end of the phone sounded tired already. Jim met him once at a conference. They had barely spoken. Or rather, the voice on the other end of the phone had barely spoken. Jim hadn't been silent the entire time.

'I'm hoping you can help me. The investigation report. It's finished?'

'Just this morning.' Tormod responded bitterly. Jim felt the force on the full stop.

'You're absolutely sure it's written in its entirety?'

'I checked it myself. What's the problem?'

'Page three. Open it.'

Barge heard the man fumble around his desk for the report, swearing once or twice when he picked up the wrong document. Jim wrestled a Fox's Classic from its wrapper and punched his desk when he threw the wrapper at the bin and missed. He had devoured the biscuit, but still found himself waiting for an answer at the other end of the phone. It took everything for him not to open another.

'Got it. I don't see what you're getting at,' said Tormod with a bluster around his sharply edged words.

'Nothing strike you as odd?'

'No.'

'The passenger list. Are you happy with it?'

'I took the list from CalMac.'

'You made sure not to miss any?' Barge began to tap his desk frustratingly. 'I am sure you see where I am going with this.'

'I assure you. I did this myself. Carrie checked it. We both read it two more times.'

'Well, it's not right.'

'It's been double checked.'

'I don't care how many times you've checked it. It is wrong.'

There was a long silence at the other end of the phone. Jim bit into a Blue Riband and shoved the wrapper onto the desk. He was disgusted at how much he had eaten that afternoon. It didn't stop him though. He would forget a few seconds later and help himself to another.

'How can you be so sure?' Asked Tormod.

'I know of information that isn't in your report.'

'Because it isn't relevant.'

'If I am calling you to ask if it is correct, it's fair to assume it is relevant.'

'Jim,' Tormod spoke softly this time. 'You know what assuming does to us both.'

'I'm not the ass,' Jim responded.

'We checked it over.'

'Are you winding me up right now?' Barge heard the other end of the phone shuffle, as though the other person had moved to whisper to someone else in the room.

'My boss is asking that you e-mail us your concerns.'

'My computer isn't even on, and I'm not sending anything.'

'Well-'

'Shall I just tell you?'

'My boss has already-'

'I am not, under any circumstance, sending anything.' Barge clenched his fist. 'Let me speak to your boss if he's so adamant.'

The phone shuffled again, and a gruffer, angrier voice came to the phone. Barge didn't even give him the opportunity to say a single word. 'I am sat with a major problem here, and you and your team are not helping me.'

'We will help you when you e-mail us.'

'I think this is more urgent than something which needs an e-mail.'

'I'll decide that when you e-mail me. Is that all?'

'Seriously?' Barge threw his notepad across the room, his temper flared. 'I can't allow you to take this stance on this matter. This could, realistically, cause a media shit storm if it turns out that you've avoided this.'

'There's always a conspiracy when Jim Barge is on the case, isn't there? You need to let it go… but, I can give you another ten seconds, if you can fit it into that.'

'Fine. There's someone missing from the passenger list that I have here on the missing person's list. Where the fuck is Ronnie Macleod?!' Jim wheezed heavily, his heart rate higher than his doctor warned was dangerous. 'Hello?' Jim shouted. 'Are you there?'

TWO

He rubbed his eyes and squinted in the direction of the burning red LED alarm clock. 5.34am. It was bloody freezing, he thought, throwing the duvet off the bed onto the floor. He had considered staying there, but his body odour was growing so strong now he felt the beginning of a headache.

His mouth was dry. Too dry. The bed and breakfast where he stayed had given him complimentary whisky. He washed that down with beer. Too many beers. He felt awful.

He got to the bathroom mirror and wondered if someone had come in through the night to beat him senseless. He looked terrible. Stubble growing unevenly, eyes dropping into the back of his head and greasy black hair. His skin was red and streaked with white. He touched his cheek, to find that blood vessels had popped and snapped leaving an oddly coloured complexion. He had been retching again.

'Jesus, Ronnie,' he said to himself. 'You look like shit.'

He decided not to punish his body any further and jumped into the shower, basking in the heat as it drained his body of the filth and debauchery from the night before and left him looking just over thirty again. He felt much better for it, but he twitched as he swigged a glass of orange juice left by his bedside. The toothpaste he had just used to scrub his mouth really ruined it.

He packed, he ate, he paid. Then he threw his bag into the boot of his car and started the ignition.

'The morning forecast is a rather bright one with no rain and few clouds on the horizon. Sadly though, it looks to be a cold one all day.' The radio coughed and spluttered. The signal was poor. Minus four, Ronnie thought to himself, bloody hell. The car had taken more than enough time to defrost and he was already very late.

He ploughed through the wilderness. A single-track road laid itself across the landscape as his car swallowed it, bringing him closer to Ullapool. The grass was straw-like. It fluttered across the landscape, colouring it lightly. The sun peered over the land tinting the edges of the world in warm yellows.

'It really is quite a simple question, minister.' Another voice boomed from the radio. 'There is obviously some concern about the funding that our ferry links are receiving. So why isn't the government considering this as a priority?'

'It's very clear that in difficult times, they are still turning over a surplus which is paying people wages and still attracting a service to our outlying islands.' The minister barely sounded convinced himself, as he stumbled over certain words and mumbled over others.

'Minister, are you aware of the ferry service's single largest income for the last financial year?'

Some bullshit answer, Ronnie whispered as he turned off the radio before there was any sort of response. He opened the car window to enjoy the ice air. It sobered him from the coffee coma he was suffering to mask his hangover. The beauty of the landscape was breath-taking. You could see for miles. The sea was calm. Ronnie was thankful for that. He had never made the sailing, but he had heard of it. That was enough.

Aye it's okay. Enjoyable, if you like spewing your ring for two hours.

Ronnie, for all his quirks, did not like to vomit. Ever.

He pulled into the petrol station in Ullapool. He picked up an aero and a can of coke and walked to the till, scrapping for change as the ham-fisted attendant mushed his items through the till.

'Five pounds ninety-eight.'

Ronnie looked at him blankly. 'You know I didn't buy fuel?'

'Funny. Five ninety-eight.'

'Is it extra for a receipt?'

The Truth Hurts

Not another word was exchanged. He couldn't afford his mortgage now, never mind a five pence plastic bag.

He climbed into his car and rolled it down the street into the ferry car park. He turned off his engine and pushed his seat back to relax. He rolled down the window to listen to the gentle approach of the Atlantic Ocean's remains.

'You can't park here,' said an accent that offended Ronnie's ears.

He looked out of his open window and admired the filth clinging to the luminous lime green jacket and previously white knitted hat. The man's eyebrows were close to taking over his face, and his distinct lack of teeth came off as a snarl.

'Isn't this the car park for the ferry?' Ronnie asked, raising one eyebrow into the air.

'Aye pal.'

'For people who want to use the ferry?'

'Aye.' The man grabbed a rogue crisp packet and jammed it into a black bin bag.

'And I'm not allowed to park here, even though I'm going to be using the ferry.'

'Naw. Need a permit.'

'Helpful,' said Ronnie through his teeth. 'Where do I park then?'

'There's spaces all along the wee streets about the town. You'll find one there.'

'Handy.' Ronnie revved the car to move and the man moved back, but he lifted his foot from the accelerator suddenly. 'How many people would you say park here daily?'

'It's empty.' He placed one hand on the roof of the car, and Ronnie immediately rolled the car backwards and looked up in disgust. 'Nobody parks here.'

'I think I might know why,' Ronnie started the engine and dragged his seat forward to reach the pedals. 'Fannies like you. Hang fire, I'm just going to drive into the sea.'

He hid his car in a side street and opened his boot three times before deciding he wouldn't need his coat. Instead, he picked up his iPad and threw it into his rucksack before marching back to the ferry.

The water remained calm. Too calm. It hadn't moved. He looked down the coast as he stood on the tip of the stony beach. Out to sea, it remained the same. It comforted him to know he wouldn't die. He didn't really like the idea of dying. If his mind was blank for a second too long, then his consciousness was obsessed by it. Why would he stop existing? That was his trauma.

The ship was in the port, but the port was empty. It was a lot smaller than the one he had found on the internet. It was missing the famous company logo, too. Ronnie was surprised. He had googled everything he could about the ship to Lewis. It was the largest in its fleet, mostly because of the waters were dangerously high. This one looked like it might be more of a rollercoaster.

The double doors to the ferry terminal hissed open as an elderly lady smiled to Ronnie on her way out, and he felt compelled to walk inside. It was vast and empty inside. There was little to attract you much further than the ticket office. Ronnie almost skipped up to it... until he realised who was behind it.

'Good morning,' Ronnie said in the worst Bristolian imitated accent. 'Do you work here?'

'Very good,' the man with the lime green jacket interrupted. 'I remember you from the car park. Single?'

'Sorry, I have a girlfriend, but-' The man quickly cut him off again.

'Single or return ticket, sir.' The man held onto the final syllable, as though he wanted to spit it into Ronnie's face.

Ronnie wondered if humour had travelled this far north yet. He had been born half an hour from the border between England and Scotland. When he left, he was concerned that he might have a nosebleed the second he got far enough above sea level. 'Return.'

'That'll be-'

'I mean, I hope I return.' Ronnie gripped hold of the desk and his eyes shot open widely. 'Should I just buy a single in case?' A smile burst from the corners of his mouth.

'Just insert your bank card... please.'

Ronnie entered his pin and the ticket chittered out of the machine. He looked up at the man, but he gave no response, so Ronnie broke a gentle smile. 'No, really,' said Ronnie. 'Have a wonderful day.'

The man scowled. What a dour place to live your life with such negativity. Ronnie turned around and heard the lime gentleman mumble. By the time, he had turned back, the man was smirking.

'What did you just say?' Ronnie asked in a tone different to the one he had woken up with. 'I'll regret what?'

'I didn't say that.' He took a step back further into the reception. His smile quickly disappeared. 'I didn't say anything at all.'

'You did.' Ronnie struggled with the decision - aggression or recession? Pick your fights, Ronnie. This isn't your battle. He harped back to his childhood, with his grandfather. He was bullied badly as a child, but his grandfather always had the best advice. Had that man not existed, Ronnie would be dead. A rope round his neck, as he had always dreamt in his sleep.

Ronnie walked off, muttering to himself. 'Gipsy.'

Minutes later, he had pressed the button on the machine for a cappuccino and completely missed his cup. Two pounds right down the drain.

He looked to the clock. It was still more than two hours until boarding. At least he thought it was. He suddenly remembered he hadn't listened to exactly what was said. He was bad for that. It was a spur of the moment idea to come this far north, so much so, he hadn't particularly paid attention to any of the details. In life, Ronnie let things take care of themselves.

The only problem was, everything was shut. Western Scotland was backwards. It firmly believed in the Sabbath. Everything remained shut, for the fear God would revoke entry to heaven if you didn't pause to celebrate him.

So, Ronnie didn't get his coffee. He turned to the bloke behind him and shook his head. 'Who do we have to crucify for a coffee round here?'

'I'm Catholic,' the man offered without much hesitation.

'Right,' said Ronnie, leaving quickly. He stood outside and felt the cold bite his neck. He shivered. Too much time still to pass. Not enough sanity to make it.

He lifted his phone from his pocket and opened the news. He wondered what headlines would drive him to tears this morning. Normally, he would open the sport section… but not today. He knew that his favourite football team had been beaten. He just didn't know by how much. How, as a Borderer, he had come to support Dundee United was anyone's question.

The main headline for the day read

MACLEOD, 48, MISSING IN STORNOWAY.

Great, he thought. Perhaps there was a hunt for the Macleod clan on the island. He hoped not. He was only going for the day. He wanted away from everything. He didn't often get that. Things hadn't been bad. He just liked time alone. Time to sit alone and know there was nobody judging him. He could wander amongst strangers. In his home town of Hawick, and where he was staying now in Burntisland, everyone knew each other. They were probably cousins.

'Sir, passengers travelling on foot have been asked to board.'

Ronnie looked up and down. Thankfully it wasn't his friend from before. This man was completely bald. He flashed his ticket and entered the steps to the boat. As he walked up the ramp, he realised that nobody else was following him. Uncertainty consumed him. Perhaps he was the only one on foot. The gate was closed, and Ronnie entered into the body of the ship.

It was small, yet large. More importantly, it looked strong. It wouldn't sink, Ronnie hoped. It was a fear of his. One of many fears. He didn't want to be on a boat when it sank, or a plane when it hit a mountain, or a car when it crashed. He just didn't want to die, if he was being blunt.

'Welcome, we will be departing shortly.' The Glaswegian

voice bellowed over the speakers. It sounded suspiciously like the man from the gate, but Ronnie didn't think too much about it. There wouldn't be many staff in Ullapool. They'd not have much choice for recording voices.

Ronnie walked to the front of the ship, climbed a few flights and sat down in the observation desk. He was the only one there.

...we will be departing shortly...

He was certain the next sailing wasn't for several hours.

'Is this seat taken?'

Ronnie looked up. An old man, almost certain to be at least ninety, shouted over to him from the other side of the observation deck with almost ten seats between the two of them. 'No sure pal.'

The old man nodded but sat down anyway. Ronnie laughed. It was a benefit he was looking forward to in his old age. Do *whatever* you want.

Nobody else entered the observation desk before the ship spluttered and began to chug forward. Ronnie wriggled about for the journey and finally set upon a position he found comfortable. The old man across from him had fallen asleep long ago.

The further they moved into the smaller islands on the coast, the weaker the mobile signal was. By the time, they were out in the middle of nowhere, there was barely enough signal to make a call. Ronnie had tried loading the news, many minutes previous.

However, he had now fallen asleep too. By the time he awoke, he had no idea how long he had been asleep for. Scotland had long left his view, and there was nothing but water from any window on the deck. Ronnie turned to see that it remained only him and the old man, still asleep.

He picked up his phone, forgetting what it was he was looking at. He stopped. The page reloaded. His phone was connected to WIFI. He did not ask his phone to do that. He was certain.

He read the title many times. He looked to his right, but the old man was still sleeping. For all intents and purposes, Ronnie was alone. He couldn't understand. It just didn't make sense. He needed more answers, but the signal on his phone had now completely disappeared. He read it one final time, this time, aloud, to make sure he wasn't imagining anything.

CALMAC ATTEMPT TO CALM FEARS AS SUNDAY MORNING ULLAPOOL FERRY VANISHES

Ronnie was on the only Ullapool to Stornoway sailing that day.

FLASHBACK I

Ronnie Macleod didn't really understand. He was only six. His brother was much older. He should have known better.

Everyone was upset. They were screaming at each other. They took no time to listen. Rain battered against the window. There was nowhere to hide from the noise. Silence did not exist. There was only anger.

'He wouldn't have!' His mum shrieked. 'Leave him alone.'

She tried to wrestle the handcuffs away from his brother's hands but seemed to slap the policeman instead. Immediately, she was in cuffs as well.

Ronnie cried. He didn't know what was happening. He didn't know what everyone was supposed to have done. He walked around looking for someone who would tell him everything would be ok. He wanted everyone to stop being angry, just so he could be happy again.

'Are you alright, son? My name is Inspector James Barge.' He was slimmer, and less greasy. You would be forgiven for not recognising him from the man he'd become. He placed a warm hand around Ronnie's small shoulder. 'I'm afraid you are going to have to come with us, but we will get someone to come pick you up, ok?'

Ronnie nodded. He still didn't know why. He didn't even know where they were going. Outside it was cold, dark and pouring with rain. The blue sirens spun in and around the house. Ronnie began to cry. He turned to try and go back into the house, where his family was. He was terrified of strangers. Terrified of everyone, come to think of it.

'Lewis!' Ronnie screamed.

His brother couldn't hear. He was too busy telling the police officer to leave him alone before he messed him up. Or something like that, anyway.

'Come here son,' Barge slapped his hip. Ronnie struggled over to him. 'We need to have a word with them. Nothing for you to worry about.'

Jim noticed that Ronnie had dropped a book just outside the front door. He picked it up and dusted off the dirt from the middle page upon which it hit the ground. An illustrated unicorn danced across both pages.

'Do you like myths?' Asked Barge.

'I like stories,' said Ronnie. 'What's a myth?'

Just then, Ronnie's brother headbutt the second officer trying to calm him down. She fell to the ground, screaming. Everyone, even Barge, got angry. Lewis was thrown to the ground and a knee slammed into his back.

Lewis tried fighting, but he couldn't move. Instead he shouted more foul words at the police officer. Something was said, young Ronnie didn't know what, but it did not go down well. The knee in his back dug deeper. His scream got louder. Everyone got angrier.

'Just calm down,' Jim barked. He threw both arms into the air and they came crashing down again, slapping onto his thighs. 'It'll be easier.'

He didn't calm down. He tried to spit at the officers. He only caught the officer's shoe. All around him, the police officers seemed to calm down. Lewis would not. He knew he was down and defeated. The police officers did too.

Ronnie looked at his mum who was crying and sliding down the hallway door. 'I'm telling you, I know my son and he would not rape her. Let him go.' She cried into her sleeve. 'Lewis wouldn't rape.'

Rape? Ronnie didn't know what that was. He was only six years old. His tiny mind could never conceive the horrific reality of such a crime. He would never know, until he was older, what kind of sick, bitter twisted monster would think to commit such an act. It must have been bad for them all to be this angry, he thought. He began to cry again. Barge came back. He grabbed Ronnie's hand.

'Listen son, don't you listen. I'm sorry you had to see that. Come with me.'

'Mister,' said Ronnie as he tugged at Barge's hand. 'What's rape?'

'Don't you worry about that, son. It's not something you need to worry about.'

Ronnie followed Barge. He seemed nice. Caring, almost. Stinking of cigarette smoke. Not quite as bad as the stuff his brother would smoke almost constantly. That made Ronnie's head feel funny. Barge didn't shout, and that comforted Ronnie. He wasn't angry like they were.

They walked out to the car through the rain. Neighbours stared out their windows and a few stood in the street. Ronnie felt shy. He didn't know why they were looking. He was only six.

'Is mummy coming?' Ronnie asked. Barge nodded. Ronnie's lip quivered. 'I don't want her to come.' Barge did not answer him.

In all the years Barge had been aware of the Macleod family, he was surprised how shy Ronnie was. He was drawn to his innocence. He reminded him of his friend, Ronnie's grandad and namesake.

'You ok?' Barge sat in the back, ignoring Ronnie's mother falling face first into the muddy garden, vanishing into the grass that had long needed cut.

Ronnie said nothing else. He looked around. He was so confused. He was so upset. His mind switched so quickly. Where was his brother? He heard his mum scream. Barge didn't look bothered. He just smiled at Ronnie. If everyone was so upset over what his brother had done, why did he choose to do it? He couldn't understand such an atrocity. He was only six.

'I'll be back in a second.' Barge got out of the car and walked right into Lewis' face. Lewis looked him in the eye and snarled.

'Fuck you.'

Barge gave no response.

'You wanker.'

'Listen here, Lewis. I have spent my whole night trying to keep calm with you. Don't forget, the only reason I am here tonight is because you committed a crime.'

'I didn't fucking rape her.'

Barge gave no response.

'She fucking wanted it.'

'I thought you just told me that you didn't do anything, Lewis?' Barge jotted words down on the notepad. He didn't bother looking into Lewis' eyes again. 'If you didn't rape her, why would you need to say that?'

'She wanted me to fuck her,' Lewis shouted.

'In broad daylight, Lewis? With someone she hadn't met until that afternoon? You must be out of your mind. Be real.' Barge took one step away, and then he turned back. 'Thank for admitting to the charge, though.'

Lewis spit in his face. Barge whipped his finger and the officer dragged him into the back of the van. His mum was loaded into the one at the back. Barge locked the house and climbed back into his car. Ronnie was asleep.

'Poor kid.' Jim sighed.

It wasn't long before he was at the station and by his phone. 'I'm sorry to be bothering you this late... Yes... Both this time, I'm afraid... He's here... Sleeping, yes... Okay, I'll see you soon.'

Ronnie's grandad was on his way. Furious. As Barge came off the phone, he could feel the temper from the end of the telephone. He got up and walked to another storm of anger - the cells.

The station was cold, but the cells were warm. Purely by the screams and shouts of the Macleod family. He felt sorry for the others. At least they were trying to sleep.

'Morag. You really need to calm down.' The cell door rattled and banged. Barge stood his ground. He looked through the window and she was stood, battering her foot off it repeatedly. 'You're forty-six Morag, for Christ sake. You're not getting out until you calm down.'

'Aye, what about Ronnie?!'

'Really? Ronnie? He's the only good one out of the two of them and it's a godsend that he hasn't turned out like that son of yours. He'll be going to his grandad and hopefully never back to you. You can't bring up a child like that with a boy like yours.'

The door came alive, louder and sharper than before. Barge left it to calm down. He walked down to Lewis. He was sat on the floor, staring at the hole in the door where Barge's eyes suddenly appeared

'I'm going to fucking kill you, Barge.' Lewis was almost toneless. He wasn't even looking towards Barge. He stared at the floor, not taking a moment to blink. 'I am going to make you bleed. I'll watch you die. I will enjoy every second of it.'

Barge looked around the corner, making sure nobody else was around.

'Is that what you said to her once you'd zipped up your pants?' Barge's nose was almost poking through the gap. 'Go fuck yourself Lewis. Rot in prison.' He slammed the metal grating upwards to lock Lewis in the cell alone. He walked out, ignoring the taunts. He was fed up. In any case, Ronnie's grandad had arrived. Thankfully, he had calmed down on the drive.

'Listen, Barge. I'm sorry you had to put up with this. I don't know where their heads are at. It's a crying shame you need to suffer them.'

'All in the pay cheque, Ron.' Barge shook his hand. Ron, Ronnie's grandad, shortened his name for convenience. He was an old man now, and Ronnie was a young man's name.

'Is the wee one okay?' Ron asked.

'Upset, scared. Asleep. He will be okay. He's a good kid.'

'A diamond. I've spoken to my boss. Packed it in. I should have done that the last time. He deserves to be happy. It's my fault the lad is in here tonight. Did he see much?'

'Most of it. All my fault. Sorry Ron.'

Old Ron sighed. 'Not your fault. Mine. For not doing this sooner.' He patted Barge on his shoulder. 'You're a good friend,

Jim.'

'You want to see them before you go?'

'Are you joking?'

'Suppose I am.'

Ron had gone to leave, then he paused. Something inside him needed affirmation. 'This claim of rape… I don't want to know what the poor girl went through, I can't begin to imagine… but, is solid? Is it certain?'

Barge didn't want to respond. He didn't want to close his eyes and relive it. Just like every other man on the case, he could not relate to what had happened. He could only feel sympathy to the woman and anger to a man who had felt he had the right to take away the rights of an innocent, equal human.

'It's all on CCTV. I don't know if he was on anything.'

'It doesn't bloody matter if he was on anything,' snapped Ron. 'He made that choice himself. Listen, the wee one needs to go home. I'll see you tomorrow.'

Many hours passed before Ronnie woke up to see his grandad at the foot of the bed, smiling at him. 'Grandad!' He exclaimed, 'Can I stay with you? Forever?'

'Yes lad. You can.'

A tear dripped from his grandad's chin. Ronnie hugged him tighter than he had ever hugged anyone before.

THREE

It had suddenly occurred to Ronnie that nobody had passed by to admire the view from the large window upon the observation desk. He was standing now, looking out into the water. It was so calm. Calmer than everyone had told him it would be. It was a lot sunnier too. He could feel the heat beating down through the glass all around him.

'It's an odd world, isn't it, Mr Macleod?'

Ronnie murmured a nod of agreement and gurgled in his throat. He shivered and turned. The elderly man was talking to him from his chair.

'How do you know my name?' Ronnie asked.

The old man just looked past Ronnie, as though he had never asked him anything at all. He continued to look out at the sea and smiled weakly at its beauty. As Ronnie looked at him, he realised he looked younger than his initial guess of eighty. He was a similar age to his grandad. His glistening silver hair swept over his head to hide any hint that he might be balding. His face was clean shaven, and his suit was in perfect condition.

'I know a lot about most things, Mr Macleod.' The old man licked his lips, then used a handkerchief from his suit pocket to dry them. 'I know everything about a lot of things. My business is knowing if I am being honest with you.' He smiled faintly at Ronnie. The legitimacy, or lack of rather, was telling.

Ronnie almost laughed. 'Isn't that what old people do? Retire and find out all the gossip?'

'My name is Charles,' he replied. His hand was outstretched.

'Just Charles?' Ronnie asked, shaking it gently.

'I'm the one who needs to know everything, not you.' Charles chuckled, and his wrinkles trebled, but Ronnie just stared. What was funny about that?

'There's a ship missing from Ullapool.'

'I know,' said Charles.

'We're on the only sailing from Ullapool.'

'Are we?' Charles asked, perplexed. Ronnie was certain it was all an act, but then it was all too much. How would an old man steal a ship? 'How's your grandfather?'

'You know him?'

'Of him, Mr Macleod.'

At this point, Ronnie had no idea what to say to him. The old man offered nothing back, and debate therefore felt very unattractive. Ronnie knew something didn't add up, but he didn't have the will, or want, to find out. He just wanted to know why he was stuck on a boat, which was alleged to have gone missing, with an old man. A bit creepy.

'He's alright. His illness has gotten the better of him, but in his head, he's still a charming old man.'

'And your work, Ronnie.' Charles cut him off, bored of his pleasantries. 'Do you enjoy it?'

'Not in the slightest. However, I'm good at it. It's easy. It pays for my grandad not to suffer. Given what he had to surrender, I don't feel too bad.' He stopped. 'Why am I telling you this? Why are you even asking this?'

Charles did not reply. He stood and watched a seagull swoop up into the air and drive downwards into the open water. Seconds later, the bird ripped out of the water, and with it, a fish in its mouth. Charles applauded that. 'Marvellous creatures. They'll rarely divorce the mate they choose. Very monogamous.'

'That's– '

'I have a job for you.' Charles cut him off and walked to the front window. 'On the island.' It appeared he had grown increasingly bored of trying to come across as if he cared. He had burnt himself out of being nice to get what he wanted. He was now blunt, and cold.

The Truth Hurts

'I'm not interested. In anything you want to offer me.'

'People always respect the opportunity I am offering, and they will always apologise for wasting my time.' Charles' frown appeared across his brow. 'Not you though Mr Macleod. Quite intriguing.'

'I don't even know who you are,' replied Ronnie. He reached back to his chair for his phone. Still no signal. 'We are both stuck on this ship. We aren't moving. We are lost. What time am I wasting?' Ronnie took a seat.

'I am a rich man, Mr Macleod.' Charles rubbed his suit jacket and placed his hand back into his pocket. 'I can afford it.'

'I'm pretty sure it's a discounted rate for pensioners,' Ronnie said as he sarcastically wrenched his receipt from his pocket and shoved it into Charles' face. 'Did you pay more or less than this?'

'Are you really dense, Mr Macleod?' Charles bit at Ronnie. Ronnie was surprised. It was very clearly a joke, but if he wasn't interested in Ronnie's jokes then *he* certainly wasn't interested in hearing his proposition.

'The only reason you are here is by my creation. I am friends with the man who owns this ship, and I borrowed it… for a price. A price I feel was worthy of my time and yours to set up this meeting. He needs the money anyway. You might have heard that in the news. The prices of these tickets certainly won't keep this company going.' The old man's breath was shallowing as his mood darkened. 'The only reason we haven't come ashore is my creation. I have asked you a question, and you haven't given me the right answer… so we sit here, until I do.' Charles sat beside him. 'I'm a powerful man.'

'And I'm a prick,' said Ronnie, shaking his head with his eyes rolled up under his eyelids. He sat for a moment and sighed. 'Alright, can we be on our way then?'

'How is Lewis coping?'

Christ sake. Ronnie couldn't believe he was having to listen to a pensioner show off how many people he knew. 'Are you for real? Did you google my family tree? Some of it you'll find in a prison. But you'll already fucking know that, Poirot.'

'Mr Macleod, there's no need to get angry at me. I didn't force your brother to rape.'

It took everything inside of him not to react. He had grown older and learnt exactly what it was Lewis did. He had written him off after that, living with him or around him for only as long as he needed to. His mother, for whatever reason, defended him. Ronnie packed his bags after that. He left. His grandad moved with him. He had had enough many years before. Ronnie was the only reason that he stayed.

Lewis spent his life after prison proud of his past. He told Ronnie that women didn't really matter. It was just sex, and any woman who thought consent was an issue was just a fucking feminist. It was a statement worthy of a beating, and Ronnie would have done it if he could. However, people looked up to Ronnie. They respected how he dealt with his brother, apart from that one time. His brother had been following a woman home, and Ronnie, late from work, had never moved quicker. His car, still in gear, rolled down the street. Ronnie, fist clenched, almost threw himself from his feet with the force that he had smashed his brother against the wall.

His brother didn't trust him after that. Called him a dirty grassing cunt. Ronnie didn't care. Why would he care what vermin like him would have to say?

'How do you put a boat in a busy harbour, and make sure that only I get on it?' Ronnie looked at the man. It didn't make any sense. 'This is a busy place. There are a lot of people who will have needed to get that ferry for their holiday, or their work.'

'Road blocks,' said Charles smugly. 'Unidentified for whatever I want. I know a lot, I told you that. I pay well.'

'Road blocks wouldn't be enough,' said Ronnie with deepening cynicism.

'You look at me like I'm a fool, Mr Macleod, but I seem to be stood in front of a man who boarded a ship which left port two hours before the scheduled sailing. Nobody was ever going to be that early. Nobody is as paranoid as you.'

'Very good.' Ronnie had heard enough bullshit. 'Listen, tell me what it is. I'll turn it down. We can both get on with our lives.' Ronnie moved himself from the old man's personal space.

'I need someone to investigate-'

'That is more than enough for me. No thank you.'

'But-'

'Please. No.'

Time rolled by as Charles asked questions, repeating his offer, and Ronnie turned him down every single time. He could see the old man tire, eventually running out of patience with Ronnie and ordered a helicopter to return them home.

'Why is it alright to sail your own ship in through the morning, but you wouldn't dare do it at night?' Asked Ronnie, throwing his bag into the aircraft.

'Roadblocks,' said Charles sharply. 'Get in or you can swim home.'

By eleven, Ronnie was back on the mainland. He clicked the button on his key and walked towards his illuminated car.

'Mr Macleod,' Charles shouted from his helicopter. 'I hope you understand I can't allow this to be our final meeting.'

Ronnie said nothing. He kept walking.

'I make deals that are very hard to turn down. I trust you'll contact me in time. My number is in your pocket. Call me when you... feel it's right.'

Ronnie opened his car door. He slammed it shut. His engine started. The car drove off, and the business card was dragged floating into the air with the force of the fumes from the exhaust.

'You'll regret that,' said Charles.

FOUR

Ron burst into tears when he watched Ronnie walk into his home. Ronnie hugged him as tightly as he had all those years before. He hadn't thought for a second of how the single most important person to him would feel.

'Jesus, I thought you were dead son. Left me here all alone with them.'

Ron hugged him tighter. They lived more than two hours away in a small town in Fife. Burntisland was hardly accessible by public transport, and given that his mother and brother didn't drive, it was the perfect destination that was too far away from them to bother with a visit. If they knew Ronnie was dead however, and money might be lying waiting for them, then distance would be no object.

'You never die before me, Ronnie. You never leave me with them.'

Ronnie could see the sincere tear in his eye. Another tear trickled down his chin. He wasn't too old, but he was frail. Osteoarthritis had crippled him. His eyes were swimming pools of wrinkles. He had all his hair, but it was white. His mouth had a constant ring of dry saliva. It had been there since the day he fell ill.

'Grandad,' Ronnie gripped hold of his greying hand and looked deeper than he ever had into his eyes. 'I've told you I will be here until you leave me. Have I ever let you down?'

'No,' he wheezed. 'That's what worries me. You're a good lad, but, awful things happen to good people. Your mother... she screamed down the phone at me like I owed her. I said, you haven't spoken to him in eight years-'

'Thirteen,' Ronnie barked.

'It's been that long?' His grandad's surprise was genuine. 'I said to her, why did she care anyway? She just wanted money. She hung up the second I told her I didn't know anything about your will.'

'That's not surprising,' sighed Ronnie.

'She was on something. She was slurring her words.'

'That's not surprising either, Grandad.'

Ronnie helped his grandad stumble back to his electrical reclining chair and made lunch. They spoke about everything apart from where Ronnie had been the night before. Anything apart from that, Ronnie prayed.

'Barge called me,' Ron sighed. 'He was the one who told me you were missing.'

'Missing?' Ronnie asked.

'Yeah. From the list on the boat.' Ron shook to reach a glass of water until Ronnie picked it up and let it flow into his mouth. 'Every sailing has a list of the people that were on it. All of them are accounted for, except you.'

Ronnie thought back, there was nobody else on the boat. Just him and Charles. 'What do you mean?'

Without speaking, Ron turned on the television. Live, on the news, was a swirling storm in the Outer Hebrides. The helicopter swayed one way and then to the other. Between the black rocks, the black water and the black sky it was almost impossible to make out what they were reporting.

'It was here on Sunday morning that the ship met its deathly end. Parts of the wreckage are still being recovered and reports in suggest that there were no survivors.'

'Apart from you, my son.' Ron tapped his grandson's shoulders. 'It's a blessing.'

There was no blessing. In a moment of panic, Ronnie wondered if the old man from the boat had set this all up. However, he could not control the weather and he could not wreck the boat. Ronnie sat at the edge of his seat as footage of bodies, parts from the ship, and cargo were pulled from the sea. The old man on the boat had said he could make things happen. Was this one of those things?

'You could have been in there, son. I'm so glad. So, so relieved.'

'I know,' whimpered Ronnie. 'It's scary when you think about it.'

Soon after, Ron fell asleep. Ronnie was left to watch some more television – avoiding anything related to the boat – and relax. Once he was bored, he stood up and wandered around his grandad's flat. It was warmly decorated in modern taste, but only because Ronnie had done the work himself before his grandad had moved in. Given that he would be spending so much of his time in the flat, he could not sit in a room sent rocketing back to the sixties.

Ron had a plethora of memories from his past sat right in front of him, just in case he should forget even a second of it. There was a single wall of his living room dedicated to photos of everyone he had met. Everyone but his family. Ron had always said this wall was for people he liked. He liked everyone. Everyone but his family. Ronnie wasn't sure if his absence meant a great deal to that statement.

He looked at the first photo and made his way up and down, left and right to look at every single one. None of the faces would mean anything to him, but it was interesting to see the life that his grandad had lived before his grandson became his obsession. He had been to different countries, all black and white, and met different cultures and societies. There wasn't a person or a civilisation that he hadn't seen with his own eyes. His work had taken him there. Everywhere.

Around the middle of the wall, Ronnie stopped. He stared at the picture in the centre of the wall. One of them was his grandad, and the other was surely a man he recognised. It was an old grainy picture; the two men were stood shaking hands to the backdrop of a coastline. Ronnie did not know which. They looked happy.

Clunky thuds smashed against the front door to the flat. Ronnie turned the corner, just by the pictures to look. It didn't open.

Ronnie walked towards it, but the door handle was down, and the door pushed open.

'Ronnie Macleod, as I live and breathe.' Jim Barge slid his police badge, that was around his neck, into his pocket. 'You're doing well for a man who died.'

'Breathing, Jim. That's about all I'm doing. How are you?'

The two men hugged, and then went into the living room. Ronnie woke his grandad up, and an immediate smile shone from ear to ear.

'Well Jim, what did I tell you? He's alive and he's back home with me.' Ron reached again to grab Ronnie's hand.

'Aye, Ron. What are you going to predict next?'

'Some mad bugger is going to get into the Whitehouse,' Ron said with a laugh.

'Not a prediction when there's two up for the job, is it?' Jim laughed with him.

The three men chatted about *almost* everything. Ronnie loved the friendship they shared. They met in high school and never had never fallen out. It gave his grandad someone to confide in, to cry at and laugh with. Ronnie missed that in his own life, so to see it in his grandad's old age gave him great comfort. He had no friends. A little by choice, but mostly through bullying. Why would you be friendly with the kid who's never done getting beat up?

'I was just saying to Ronnie, before you came in, that it's a miracle that he has come home.' Ron said, grabbing his grandson's hand. 'It could have been so much worse.'

'Certainly, Ron. The police are still investigating things. It's a bit of a mess.' Jim looked at Ronnie, and Ronnie knew he thought more than he was letting both men know. 'How are you feeling, Ronnie?'

'Yeah, okay.'

'What happened?'

Of course, it was always the first thing he would ask. Why couldn't he just fuck off and ask him something else, like how was work? Had he seen much of the Champions League? Was he embarrassed with the state of his football team sitting in the second tier of Scottish Football? Not that. *Fuck* that. 'I...'

'You know what, it's not the time or the place. I'm here as a friend, to catch up with you. That can all wait.' Barge smiled to him.

'I... thanks,' Ronnie had been scrambling around his brain trying to think of an excuse. Why was he so happy to just ignore it? He was sure it was a Police tactic. He'd comfort Ronnie into telling the truth. That was it. Barge would have all the information he needed to arrest Ronnie before he'd even be aware of it.

'Is everything okay, Barge?'

'I'm not sure, Ronnie. I'm not sure.' Barge smiled, but Ronnie left it. He didn't want to come across needy or make himself a concern to the man investigating what happened.

Much later, after many cups of tea, Ronnie was pre-occupied again by the picture on the wall.

'You alright, Ronnie?' Barge shattered his daydream.

'Yeah, sorry. Just trying to... figure something out.'

'What is it?' Ron asked.

'That photo on the wall. You're with a man, shaking his hand. Who is he?'

He looked to Barge, who looked to his grandad. His grandad shared his look.

'A friend,' Ron said sheepishly. 'His name was Charles.'

Ronnie froze. 'Was?'

'Died. Years ago, now. How long, Barge?'

'Oh God, many more than I care to remember.'

Ronnie looked at the photo, closing his eyes to think of the man on the boat and opening them to try and convince himself that this Charles was not his Charles. There was no mistaking that this was the same man.

'How did he die?' Ronnie pursed his lips, stumbled over his words and took large breaths through the one nostril which wasn't blocked. Barge was experienced in outing criminals, and Ronnie knew if he gave anything away, he would be in trouble.

'Good question,' Barge said putting his empty cup to the side.

The Truth Hurts

'We don't know. We never found his body.'

'So, he might not be dead?' Ronnie stared at both men longing for an answer. He was surprised that Barge hadn't as much as given him a second look.

'Well, my old gaffer, the bloke who had this job before I took it over, he had some funding issues back then and he thought rather than fire good men, he'd reduce the workload to reduce cost... He just kind of... he wrote cases off. It didn't work, obviously. But, Charles went missing, nothing untoward. Most people thought he was fed up of his other half. She was a good bit younger. You might even say she was old enough to be his daughter. Right cow though, wasn't she, Ron?'

'Well,' Ron choked on his scone. 'I guess she was. I never met her.'

'Neither did I. But the town talks, don't they? You hear it all.'

Ronnie nodded. He couldn't shit without the town knowing what colour it was.

'Anyway, we looked, and we looked. The whole police force was involved at one point. There was no sign of him. We tried to find out about his family, but whoever they were weren't for talking about him and they certainly didn't want to admit to knowing him. I think that dictated how long the force really did care about Charles. That point came a lot quicker than us signing him off as dead and that was only because of the legal mechanics behind it.'

'Why do you ask, Ronnie?' His grandad coughed, still getting over his near-death experience.

Ronnie considered telling the truth. There was a man, believed dead, who kidnapped Ronnie. Now there were many dead, lost forever in the depths of the sea. But then, how would he tell them? *Funny story, your dead pal... aye, the one in your photo... he kidnapped me and offered me an opportunity. I said no, and fortunately he let me live. Oh, and he knows all about us... owns a boat. He probably murdered everyone from the one on the telly. How mad is that?* Yeah, sure. What the hell were you really up to? That would be Barge's question.

'How did you know him?' Ronnie asked, almost biting his own tongue. He was paranoid that he was asking too many questions about a man he should not care enough about.

'We knew him from school,' said Ron. 'He was never really around, but I helped him out once or twice and that was enough for him to go up on the wall. I haven't seen him in years though, Lad, you weren't even born when I last seen him. Never worked a day in his life.'

'Well, what we would call work, Ron.' Barge mumbled and laughed.

'Aye. He just studied. He tried to learn as much as he could, when he could. Of course, he didn't earn a penny from it and lived off the handouts he could find. He must have done alright with them because he was never short on money. Then he was locked away reading and learning again. I wouldn't say it was odd, but he was. He would always say to Barge and I, wouldn't he... *knowledge is power, boys! The man who knows, wins.*' Ron laughed, Barge laughed too.

'Do you remember that night you asked him... Oh God, what was it? I can't remember. Not important. Anyway, you asked him a question and, as serious as you can be, he said, *I'm the one needs to know everything, not you.*' Barge almost spat coffee across the carpet.

The two men laughed as hard as they could. Ronnie's throat became sharply dry. How could this have happened to him? He lived a very empty, boring life. Now he was the centre of a dead man's life.

'What's wrong, Ronnie?'

'Who, me?' Ronnie almost interrupted Barge, as though he knew someone would ask why he was now as white as a sheet. 'Nothing. Well. It's... I think it's shock. I've had a bit of a tough weekend, and it's taken its toll. Grandad, I'll see you tomorrow. Barge, it was good to see you again. Take care. I am going to go lie down.'

He didn't even wait for Barge to ask if he really was okay. He got up, and he left. What had appeared to be a very suspicious, random event in his life had suddenly dug deep and rooted itself in the core of life.

He would ignore it. Yes, he would pretend it didn't happen. Wouldn't Barge want to know? Ronnie would worry about that later.

FIVE

It was Sunday. On any other, you would find Ronnie lying in his bed until the sun had risen and then gone back to the underworld. Today, he woke suspiciously early. So suspiciously, that when he opened the door to his grandad's flat, he was asked if he'd shit the bed.

'I think I did last week,' replied Ronnie. 'I've not checked.'

'Not funny,' said Ron, his brow down and his stare very serious. 'I really did soil the bed last week.'

Ronnie would make himself a cup of tea, and only just sit down before his grandad would go on to tell him that he hadn't been changed, washed or taken his medicine. Ronnie sat for a moment and stared at him.

'You can't be serious?' Ronnie asked, his voice highly pitched. 'You've had the same routine for three years. How do you mess that up?'

Apparently, Ron didn't want to bother his home-help on the weekend, so he sent him home with full pay.

'You're too kind,' said Ronnie.

'I don't want him wasting his time,' replied Ron, every part of him honest. 'Do you think so?'

'Yes, I think so. I bloody pay for him.' Ronnie sighed, and stood up. He looked back to the leather recliner where the mould of his body drifted outwards from the chair. He could have sat there all day, had he had the chance. His weekend had been ruined by his grandfather's complete generosity and kindness.

'Your mother phoned again,' Ron shouted through to the kitchen. 'I tried to get the fellow who was in to tell her I'd died.'

Ronnie dropped his pills over the kitchen floor as he suddenly heard Ron choke and ran through to find his grandad chuckling away to himself. 'He wouldn't even tell her I was choking on a piece of toast. He said I was in the shower.'

'Wow, he really didn't do anything when he was in, then.' Ronnie whisked his eyes in time with his biting sarcasm and walked through to blow the dirt off the pills. They would be alright, he hoped. He stuck them in a small cup and handed them to his grandad. He threw them down his throat without a second thought.

'I dropped those on the floor,' said Ronnie. His grandad's eyes opened wide and he stuck his tongue out, gagging.

'I bloody wet myself in there this morning, Ronnie. I'm medicating myself on my own pish.'

Ronnie's eyes opened wider. He shifted over to him, to make sure his grandad was ok. By the time he got to his side, Ron was laughing again.

'Only joking. I haven't wet myself for a week. You can't do one without the other, can you?'

'Must be a record,' said Ronnie as he returned to the kitchen and brought through two cups of tea. He sat down and scowled at his grandad. It was his way of saying, I'm not bloody moving. You're stuck now.

'Songs of Praise…' Ron mumbled to himself. 'Oh, look. It's in Galashiels. I didn't know they had churches there.'

The Macleods had been raised in Hawick, eighteen miles away from Galashiels. Though there was over half an hour away in distance, there was a minute distance in terms of who the people were and what they had in common. The only issue was, they hated each other. Passionately. It didn't even make sense. Hawick was dying, and Galashiels was thriving. It should only have been a one-way rivalry. Ron did not feel passionately about much, but if he ever felt the person he was speaking to was in bed with the enemy – that was, living in Galashiels – he would refuse to speak to them.

'Didn't they knock them down to make way for supermarkels?' Ron asked, highly aware that Ronnie had ignored his first jab. 'I don't think God ever looked down on Galashiels. He'd have destroyed it.'

'Alright,' said Ronnie, lowering the television magazine he was reading to spare himself from boredom. 'I'll bite. What is wrong with Galashiels?'

Ron gasped.

'What?'

'There's Teri blood running through you, son. You cannot be saying that.' Ron shook his head, forcefully labouring his breathing in protest. A Teri was the name of the Hawick born. 'There are no myths in the South. Those boys rode out there and they bloody took on the English and won. Heroes! Those Gala folk... those *palemerks*, they just piggyback on it.'

'I thought they were Border men who did it.'

'That's what history will tell you,' said Ron vehemently. 'They were all from Hawick. All Teris.'

'How did you come to live so far south, if we're from the Hebrides?' Ronnie wanted to change the subject before Ron started belting out his favourite song, *Teribus Ye Teri Odin*. 'Someone commit a crime?'

'Sort of,' answered Ron. 'Our family hasn't lived there in years. I think it was my great grandfather, Tam Macleod, who moved there. He married a Hawick lass. Her dad was the cornet.'

The Cornet was the lead figure of the annual Common Riding. Anyone from outside of the Borders would call it an annual Gala day, or fete. To *Teri* folk, the Common Riding was an annual reminder that they had once taken on the English and slaughtered the lot. That is to say a group of Scottish men ran over the border to steal a flag whilst the enemy slept. Hardly inspiring, thought Ronnie. The Cornet would ride the borders of Hawick every year, to ensure no Englishmen were on the way back to steal the flag.

'They'd probably just bomb us,' said Ronnie out of the blue.

'Who?'

'The English,' Ronnie replied quickly. 'I'm just saying if they wanted that tattered blue flag, they'd bomb us and nick it back that way.'

'It's yellow and blue,' said Ron, biting. 'You don't respect this.'

Ronnie chuckled as his grandad stood up in a mood and walked through to the bathroom. He was not as interested in his ancestry in the borders, as he had been of the same in the North. By that, he thought more fondly of it. He had never actually found the will to read up and learn about the people who came before him and lived on the island in the North.

Ron struggled back through to the living room and threw himself down on the couch. He thought about turning the television channel over – he hated snooker – but in the end, he put the controller down and stared at his grandson.

'You had a stroke?' Asked Ronnie.

'Why were you going to Lewis?'

Ronnie knew that his question would come, but he wasn't sure he wanted it to. Why couldn't people just let it go, knowing that everyone else died and he didn't. *Oh*. That was exactly why. He had somehow managed to escape from the middle of the sea, in a crash where everyone, even the lifeboats perished.

'A break,' said Ronnie. 'I wanted to explore.'

'You never told me that.'

'I did.'

'You didn't.'

'I definitely did.'

'Ronnie, I might struggle to hold a cup of tea without soiling myself, but I can remember everything. You never told me you were going for a break.' Ron shook his head. 'What happened?'

'I told you and Barge last-'

'The truth.'

'I-' Ronnie paused. What he didn't want to do, was lie. What he also didn't want to do, was tell the truth. 'I-' He paused again. In his head, his grandad was fully aware of what had happened, and he was certain that whatever he would say, would not be enough. 'I didn't go.'

'That wasn't so bad,' said Ron. He had finally escaped the urge to not turn the channel over. It was Bradley Walsh, and a particularly rotund woman. Ron laughed, as the woman guessed wrongly that Wales was the only home nation not to represent the United Kingdom at the European Football Championships. 'They got to the semi-final!'

They enjoyed the rest of the show in silence. Ronnie didn't watch it. He couldn't. He sat and thought how easily his grandad had accepted what he said. There were no other questions. It was almost as though his answer were the most obvious conclusion. Ordinarily it would be. He wasn't sure if his grandad believed him, or if he knew that he was lying, and he just couldn't be bothered arguing with him… he had long missed his afternoon nap.

FLASHBACK II

Ronnie was twelve. Six years had passed since his brother was arrested. He had been in jail for more time than Ronnie could remember. He was sat in his bedroom, watching the snow fall. Each time a flake fell to the ground, he was a second closer to Christmas. It helped him to blur out the noise of his mother screaming at his grandad.

'I am telling you, I am going to see Lewis and Ronnie is coming. It will do Lewis good to see his *whole* family!'

'Morag, if he wanted to see his whole family at Christmas, perhaps he shouldn't have committed a crime and gotten incarcerated. Ronnie is not going to a prison. He is far too young to be seeing things like that.'

'He's my son. He's coming with me.' His mother stomped through the living room. 'I do not expect you to think that you can decide what happens to my son.'

'That's the problem Morag,' Ron was muffled now. 'I can.'

Ronnie heard her slam an object against the wall of his room. 'Fuck you,' his mother's voice broke with the harshness of her yell.

'The court awarded me full guardianship,' Ron said with a brutal wheeze. 'That means I make the decisions for Ronnie, and when he's old enough he can then make them. Until that time, if you are going to be allowed in my house, you'll show me some respect, or I will phone the police.'

'Respect? Fucking respect? You're a bigger disgrace than his dad.' Ronnie heard his mother slap his grandad across his face. He then heard his grandad crash against the oil radiator in the room and moan in pain. His mother was a big, fat brute of a woman. She could sit on anyone and kill them. 'He's coming with me, and you can fuck off if you don't like it.'

'Hello, police please. Yes, it's Ron. Her again. Okay. Thanks.'

For a minute or two afterwards, Ronnie heard thuds and slams. He could hear the beg of mercy. He sat for as long as he could, before he couldn't take anymore and grabbed his coat from his door and walked into the living room.

'Okay,' said Ronnie. 'I'm ready to go.' His brow sloped to either side and a large breath fell from of his lungs.

'No! Back in your room Ronnie!' His grandad held his side and pressed against the side of his head. 'Please, son.'

'No Grandad. If I go with her, she'll stop hurting you.' He walked over and kneeled beside him. 'I'll be back soon. You know they won't leave me with her for long.'

Ronnie walked out the door with his mother, despite the pleading whispers from his grandad. He knew what he was doing was stupid, but he didn't want his grandad to die where he couldn't look after him anymore.

His mother, Morag, grabbed his hand and pulled him violently down the road. 'Come on, we're late.'

Ronnie had barely put his shoes on, yet he was being thrown up the road quicker than his feet could touch the ground. She marched him onto a bus and sat down as far back as they could, to prevent any onlookers finding them as the bus stopped in every street. They must have been on the bus for at least two hours, as they passed in and out of the countryside. Ronnie wasn't sure where they were, or where they had been. He had never left Hawick before.

'Don't you be listening to that grandad of yours, either. He is a liar.' Morag spoke, but she ignored Ronnie and continued to read her magazine. Take a Break. Someone was having a relationship with their mother. Twelve-year-old Ronnie wasn't sure that was okay. Given what he had seen in his short life, he wasn't sure it was the worst thing to happen though.

'I like grandad,' Ronnie whispered as he looked out of the window at the passing traffic. They were in the middle of nowhere now. There were only cars, and cows.

'He's a dick, Ronnie.' She threw her magazine down onto the ground. 'What he says about your brother is just to turn you against us. He didn't rape her.'

'What is rape?' Ronnie asked, looking out to an orange field.

'It doesn't matter Ronnie,' she spat. Morag had an incredulous look on her face, as though to exaggerate the irrelevance of his question. 'Fuck sake. What is rape? It would only matter if he actually did it.' She turned to a woman across from them and shook her head with a smile, as though Ronnie had just blurted out something ridiculous.

Strangers looked at Morag. Some were whispering between one another, but she was too self-indulgent to notice. One old lady murmured the word rape, looking to Ronnie. They looked angry.

'Ronnie!' She bellowed. 'We're here.'

Ronnie followed his mother, and as he got off the bus, the old lady gave him a concerned, sympathetic look. He wanted to tell her he was saving his grandad and that he was okay. He didn't want his grandad to end up like his dad, because he was dead.

They approached the prison, with the clouds flowing in ahead. The jagged wire ran across the top of every wall. It was a deathly looking place. Bars crossed every window. Ronnie did not want to be here. He turned, but there was nowhere he could go. He didn't know where he was.

'Are we still in Scotland?' Ronnie asked genuinely.

'Seriously?' Asked Morag.

Ronnie nodded.

'Shut up.'

Ronnie tugged at his mother's coat. 'I don't know where we are. I'm scared.'

Morag stopped and turned. She looked down at him and she could see her little boy shuddering. 'Shut up, you little cunt.' She turned and walked off.

Ronnie was confused as to what he had said wrong. He bowed his head and frowned. His favourite badge looked up at him from the ground. Brum. He bent down, picked it up and pricked his finger as he tried to pin it back into his coat. He didn't dare yelp. Morag would surely hit him this time.

Soon, he was in the prison and in a large room with lots of other people. Ronnie wasn't sure which of them were prisoners, and which of them had also been dragged along to visit relatives. Also, prisoners, then. Just not of the state.

Lewis wandered into the room along with the other prisoners. Neither man looked at the other, like they had never met each other. For this short space of time, they were not prisoners. They were home, with their families.

'Lewis, my love. How are you?' It was the first time that Morag had smiled and sounded warm in her words.

Lewis threw himself down on a chair and shrugged. 'Been worse.'

'You're looking well.'

'I haven't slept,' said Lewis as he rubbed his bright red eyes. 'It's awful in here.'

'I know sweetheart,' Morag grabbed her elder son's hand. 'I can write to our councillor again. I can tell him that you're struggling. He might be able to help you. Can I do that for you, my love?'

Ronnie's eyes wandered around the room. He looked to all the people that had come to live here and tried to work out what they did. They could have done anything. None of them looked particularly scary.

'Can I get a drink?' He asked. He quickly decided he shouldn't have asked.

'I'm going to hit him,' Morag said to Lewis. 'I wish I hadn't taken him. He's driving me round the bend.'

'Shut up, you little dick.' Lewis feigned a slap to the back of Ronnie's head. 'You're lucky I'm in here.'

'Don't let him annoy you my angel,' Morag spoke softly. 'This is our time.'

Lewis shrugged. He looked one way, and then the other. 'Business is picking up.'

'Good. How many?'

'Four new guys have come in this week. Everyone interested. I think we might need to increase stock.'

'That can be arranged,' said Ronnie's mum. She was rubbing her tattoo, it was Lewis' name in a love heart. She didn't have any for Ronnie. 'How much are we talking?'

'Double, minimum.'

'Okay.'

'Will he be able to get it so quickly?' Lewis asked, beginning to sweat from his brow. 'These guys won't mess around. They'll want it fast.'

'Listen,' Morag replied with a serious glare. 'If I tell him I want it, I'll get it. He has no other choice.'

Ronnie stood up for a second and took a step forward to his brother. 'What are you selling?'

'Fuck off, Ronnie.' Lewis scorned him.

'Shut your little fucking mouth,' spat Morag. Two guards by the entrance were suddenly aware of the situation. Morag noticed that too. 'Look what you've done now, you little cunt.'

Ronnie began to well up. He hated when his mother swore at him. All he wanted was a mother like all the other kids at school. They always spoke so lovingly of theirs. When Ronnie was asked, he just said she was working away. He had considered telling people she was dead, but that wasn't nice. He didn't *actually* wish her dead, he just wished she would be a better person.

He ignored his mother and his brother, it was the only way to avoid the impending tears. Across the hall, the two prison officers had taken even more of an interest in Ronnie and his family. There were two doors, and one of the guards now made his way over to the public entrance. He heard them use his name, he was certain of it.

'I have sights on the boy. What's his name? Ronnie. Okay. Lewis Macleod is a bit saucy so we will need to handle this right.'

Lewis and Morag were too busy discussing their business to be bothered by what was going on around them. Ronnie was too scared to mention anything to them.

'I'll handle it. You cover the door.'

The first guard, the bigger of the two, crept slowly to the table. He looked either side, as though he were merely monitoring the situation. Morag wasn't paying attention.

'Lewis, visiting time is over.' The guard spoke softly and placed his right hand on Lewis' left shoulder to be sure that Lewis knew exactly who he was talking to.

Ronnie had never expected it to go so badly. Firstly, Morag had stood to swear at the guard. Then Lewis, without thinking, smashed his handcuffs upwards. The guard crumpled, and the other inmates only served to create more havoc. Ronnie was knocked off his feet by his mother, who had noticed the second guard come over and stood up to push him over.

The inmate to Ronnie's left started cheering at Lewis, like he was a hero for standing up to the guards. Ronnie just lay on the floor, shocked by it all. He watched the entire situation play out before him. His lip was quivering. He should have stayed with his grandad just like he asked.

Minutes passed before the other officers burst into the room. They tackled the fighting inmates first, and then began to extinguish the chanting and shouting amongst the rest. One by one, everyone left the room. Except Ronnie.

Soon, he was in the room alone. He began to wonder if he was ever getting out, or if he had just been forgotten again. This time, it felt like the final time. His grandad didn't even know where he was. He would never find him again, and Ronnie would never be happy again. He felt his heart begin to break.

One of the guards, a tall, dark man, re-entered the room and briskly walked over to sit beside him. Ronnie looked up. His brown eyes sat as pins in his black face. 'Ronnie, is it?'

'Yes sir.'

'My friend called me, told me you'd ran off with your mother. That you shouldn't have.'

'Yes, but-'

'I know why you did it, Ronnie. It was a very brave thing to do.'

'Is he okay?' Ronnie asked quickly.

'My friend, Jim, said he's fine. A bit bruised, but he will be okay. Do you know my friend, Jim? Jim Barge?'

Ronnie nodded.

'Well, he's on his way to pick you up.'

'Already here,' Jim said as he walked from behind them. 'Ronnie, I can't believe you did that today.' Barge kneeled in front Ronnie as he sat on the bench. 'Your grandad was very worried. You know you can't go out alone with your mother. You know that she cannot be in the same room as you.'

'She was hurting him!' Ronnie shouted, grabbing hold of Barge.

'She was?' He wrestled the boy's hands off him subconsciously. He hated other people touching him unless he were first.

'Yes! She threw him against the wall, and she wouldn't stop kicking him.'

'Okay.' Barge tried to speak only to the guard, but Ronnie heard every word. 'Can you call the station? Get Jackson over to Ron. He's not told me everything.'

'I'm on it.'

'I mean it, Dave. I want everything.'

The guard stood up and left Barge, who grabbed Ronnie's hand and led him out of the prison. He sat Ronnie in his car and told him he would be straight back. The minute the boy was safe, Barge stormed back into the prison and into the room where they held Morag. As the guard left, Barge asked him if there was any recording equipment used. The guard shook his head.

The door closed, and Barge turned back to Morag who was handcuffed, by both hands, to the metal table cemented into the floor.

'You must be proud of yourself, Morag.' Barge crossed his legs. 'Not only have you assaulted your father-in-law, but you've almost started a riot in a prison. You must know that you won't get away with that.'

'I don't know what you mean, Mr Barge.' Morag smiled gently.

'You know that I know you too well to fall for that, Morag.' Barge tapped the table anxiously. 'What's going on?'

'With who?'

'You. Lewis. Ronnie.'

'I came with my child to see my son, I don't know what you're trying to say.' Morag pulled at the handcuffs. She was stuck fast. 'This place may be full of criminals sir, but I am not one of them.'

'You know what you've done.' Barge scorned at her.

'They'll give me community service, they always do.' Morag smiled. 'There's fuck all you can do about it. I'm a mother, with a child.'

'Well, you wouldn't be a mother without one, would you?' Barge smiled sarcastically, but Morag would never fully appreciate the touch of humour.

He looked down to the floor and let out a large sigh. There was an air of helplessness in the room. Barge knew that he would make no progress, but he would get angry talking to Morag. There was no helping her. He did want to help his friend, and his grandson. It was an almost impossible task.

'Morag, you can't keep visiting Ron just to beat him.'

'Tell him to give me my son then, and I might.'

'That's never going to happen. The court decided that Ronnie is safest living with him.'

'Nobody is safer than with their fucking mother, you moron.' She kicked the table. She stared into his eyes. She snarled. 'Let me out of here.'

Barge said nothing.

'He's coming home with me.'

'You're not going home, Morag. You'll be coming down to the station where you will be charged.'

'And let out.'

'Not if you're charged.'

'On bail.'

'Who is going to pay for you to be out on bail?'

'Ron,' she said almost without a blink.

'You just beat him into his radiator. Why would he pay anything to bail you out?'

'I'd kick his head in, Jim. It's that simple.' Morag clenched his fist and each of her five knuckles cracked loudly.

Barge sighed and shook his head. 'I don't think you're going to be offered bail anyway.'

'Aye?'

'Aye,' Barge said, imitating her. 'I think your luck has ran out, at long last. Finally, you might get what you've finally deserved.'

'You can't say that.'

'Can't I?'

'You're an officer protecting the law. You need to be impartial.'

'It's an interesting point you make, Morag.' Barge slouched in his chair. He stared past her. 'I never get emotionally invested in a case. In fact, most of the time, I really couldn't care about the ins and outs. I'll solve it, I'll find the guilty party and I'll move on. Sometimes, if I do a really good job, I'll get a message from my superior telling me so.'

'Thanks for the lovely story, Jim.' Morag tried to applaud him, then tapped the table instead. 'You're a real storyteller.'

'Then there's you,' Barge said with a real punch in this throat. His eyes now fixed on her pupils. 'You and your rotten son down the hall. I waste so much of my life with you. I can't think of a week, or a month, where I haven't had to mutter your name, or your son's, to a colleague. I really do deplore having to pick up the phone to find out that you or Lewis have purposefully gone out of your way to torment other people's lives, to only benefit yourselves.'

'Don't-'

'Shut up.' Jim even surprised himself at how loudly he shouted at Morag. He leaned forward and put out his hand to stop her words coming any closer. 'Don't interrupt. Time and time again, I have had to put up with the both of you scraping out of the punishment you deserved. I've tried everything, but you seem to always avoid it. Not only that, but I need to watch my good friend grow ill as he tries to stop you killing his grandson, or him. It's one thing to do what you do, but to physically hurt a man who is in a terrible situation, is not something I am going to take kindly to. Especially when he's my best friend.'

'Anything else?' She spat.

'Yes, just one thing. Are you aware of the sentence that supplying drugs to inmates in this prison can carry?'

Morag sat silent. 'Well?' He tried to force her for an answer.

'I don't know what you're talking about.' She stuttered, falling over her words. Her brow was now moist. Her eyes were wide.

'Oh, but you do.' Barge said, as he rooted around his pocket. 'Recognise this?'

Barge placed a large badge on the table in front of Morag. She looked at it, and then looked back at Barge. 'Ronnie was wearing it. So, what?'

The badge was very thick, and red. In the middle, sat Brum. A yellow car, who's famous adventures had made it onto the television. Ronnie loved Brum, and he wore the badge everywhere.

Well, not that badge. This badge was different.

Barge flipped it over and pointed to a slot in the back of it. He pointed at it, looking at Morag, but she was none the wiser. He slid the nail of his thumb into the slot, and the back of the badge popped open. Morag's face dropped.

'You fucking bastard.'

'Genius, isn't it?'

Inside the badge, sat a tape. It was still recording.

'It has everything,' Barge whispered. 'I don't know what you said, but I know why you went to see Lewis today.'

Morag tried to wrench her arms from the table. Barge sat and stared into her eyes, into her soul. He had finally gotten to her. She was always angry, but this was different. This was direct. Her anger was only for Barge. She didn't talk, not like she normally would. She knew that her entire life was about to crumble down.

'Shall we listen to it?'

'You can't. It's tampering with evidence.'

'Who would believe you, Morag?'

Barge pulled out a handheld cassette player and slotted the small tape inside a larger 'adapter' tape and placed it inside. He rewound it back to the beginning and allowed it to play. Morag became even paler. Jim thought she was going to be sick. After all these years, continually chasing after the two of them, he had finally found something to put her away and end this saga in his life.

'Tablets?'

'I have enough of those. It's wraps that I need.'

'I'll bring them in. Ronnie can come. He can sneak them in his bag.'

'Great. How much?'

'Charge as high as we can. Any smack heads?'

'One arrived today. Shaking all over the fucking joint.'

'You better have-'

'I was straight in there, don't worry. He's gagging for it.'

'Good.'

Barge clicked stop and looked at Morag. She was staring at the wall, right past him. He sat for a second trying to enjoy the moment, but she never looked back to him. He never got the sweetness in his revenge.

'Assault? Selling drugs? I suggest you call your lawyer.'

'We'll kill you,' spat Morag.

'Making threats to an officer is-'

'I'm not even joking, Jim.' Morag's head darted around so that she could make sure that her eyes were now staring into his. 'We'll get out someday. We will be out of the eyes of the law one day. When that comes, we will be ripping your throat out. Lewis told me he wants to end you. He wants your blood on his hands. I don't mind helping.'

Barge grabbed his tape, leaving the badge, and stood up. He had heard this thousands of times before. Only once had he bothered to act. 'Goodbye Morag.'

'We are coming for you, you fuck.' Morag's eyes were watering with the ferocity of her anger. 'We'll drink your fucking blood.'

SIX

Ronnie opened the boot of his car, launched his back into it and slammed the door back down upon it. It had been a very long day. He was glad to be home. Today was Tuesday, and that meant the night was his. His grandad played bingo with the others in his sheltered housing complex, so Ronnie could do whatever he wanted.

But he didn't go home.

He walked the other way into town. It was never something he did, but this wasn't a normal week. He was relieved that nobody had bothered to ask him about it. It was likely they didn't know, or if they did, they didn't want to ask. Ronnie was one of those people you avoided asking anything other than, are you okay? You'd only get something sarcastic in reply.

The night was peaceful. The sky was dark, there was no wind or rain. He looked down the street and admired the lights glowing in the soup of nothingness behind it. It had been a very long time since he had taken a moment to appreciate his new home.

Burntisland was hardly the first choice for homebuyers. In the last year, the house prices had dropped, and Ronnie felt the impact on his home and his grandad's.

'We don't need to live this far away, lad.' His grandad had been keen to avoid it. Yet he was wrong. They did need to move, and they needed to be far enough away that his family would not come looking. 'They're not interested in me now. If you're moving because of me, then please, don't. You have a good job here.'

Ronnie did have a good job. He was paid double what he was living from now. Yet he couldn't risk his mother or his brother taking an interest in his grandad ever again. He was sure part of his illnesses were caused by the violence and the mental torture he had endured just to make sure his youngest grandson didn't die.

Yet, despite all of this, he did like living here. It was quiet and the people around him tended to stay away because he wasn't from here and therefore, he could have been anyone. The locals here didn't like that. They didn't want to trust someone who they knew wasn't born here. It sounded all a bit too like Hawick, but it was what they needed. They needed isolation.

He stood outside a bar he frequented once, maybe twice. The Rule. It was modern. By that, the food was vastly overpriced and there were a variety of beers one had never, ever heard of. He had only ever gone in alone, to watch the football or have breakfast if he were hungover. Tonight, however, he fancied a beer. Just the one. Okay. Not just one.

'It's what, sorry?'

'Snake Venom,' said the barman, quite matter of fact. Ronnie wasn't sure if he was just distracted by his foot-long beard, or he genuinely just didn't understand the craze surrounding beer anymore. 'Quite sharp in taste, but it'll get you pissed if that's what you're looking for.'

'I...' Ronnie looked at the green label again. 'Two, please.'

Three pints later, Ronnie finally felt relaxed. The football was on the big screen above the bar. It was Celtic versus Borussia Monchengladbach. Ronnie dare not pronounce it. Someone had asked him who was playing. *Not sure pal, sorry.* He tucked into the rest of his pint in the hope the stranger would walk away.

For the next hour or so, he was left alone. He enjoyed the peace and quiet. He didn't like to think, but conversing was worse. He just didn't want to share any part of him and talking almost always led to that. People would talk, only about themselves, but they would ask a question – not to learn about Ronnie, but to tell him something else... about themselves. How boring.

'Ah, good evening Mr Macleod.'

For fuck sake, Ronnie thought. He came here because he knew nobody would know him. Nobody recognised him. Yet here he was. He looked up, and the feeling of utter desolation tripled. He didn't want anyone to speak to him. He certainly didn't want to see the man in front of him.

'You're supposed to be dead,' said Ronnie.

'No. I am supposed to be missing, *presumed* dead.'

'Still dead then,' Ronnie said, gritting his teeth.

Charles took a seat and placed a glass of red wine upon the table next to Ronnie's pint of lager.

'No, honestly, it's fine to join me. Don't even ask.'

Charles smiled. Of course, he still couldn't care for Ronnie's attempt at sarcasm. In fact, he felt as though Ronnie abused the term humour. He wasn't that funny at all, but he could pick where a joke should be.

'You have a very beautiful home. From the outside, I mean. I didn't go inside, before you shout at me. I presumed you would be very unhappy for me to go inside. Do you own it, or rent it?'

'I would say guess, but you probably already know.'

Charles smiled again, this time genuinely. 'You do know there are much cheaper interest rates outside the Royal Bank of Scotland, Ronnie. I could help you if you-'

'You might be surprised by this Charles, but I'm still not interested. In anything. You helping me, or me helping you. I don't even want to know why you decided you would be dead... sorry, missing, *presumed* dead. I just want you to take your red wine, stick it right up your arse, and leave.' Ronnie sipped his pint.

'The type of work I am involved in, it is easier to be dead than alive.' Charles took a large mouthful of his wine and closed his eyes as though he were enjoying it to an uncomfortable level. 'I enjoy what I do, Mr Macleod. It is very rewarding.'

Ronnie pretended that he wasn't listening. He watched the football. Moussa Dembélé had just scored a penalty to level the game. Ronnie fist pumped. He was never the biggest fan of Celtic, but overall supporting Scottish football was better than supporting nothing. That is at least, what he told himself. Dundee United would never hit such heights. He would never see his beloved team maintain their undefeated streak against the mighty Barcelona.

'I have a job for you, Ronnie,' Charles swirled the wine in his glass, and his eyes then moved from that to Ronnie's face. Ronnie did not return the glance. 'Do you remember?'

'I said no. *Do you remember?*' Ronnie scooted an inch to his right to see the large screen better, and to remind Charles that he was not interested.

'I need you to find something for me.'

'Find someone else then.'

'Nobody has what you possess.'

'I don't care.'

'I can offer you more money than you'd earn in a year.'

'Really?' Ronnie exclaimed, sarcastically.

'Yes,' Charles replied, ignoring the sarcasm.

'Still no.'

Ronnie drank the rest of his beer in one long gulp.

'I am afraid, Ronnie, that I cannot take no as a final answer.'

Ronnie paused, and then he laughed. He slid his glass along the table towards the wall. 'What are you going to do if I don't say yes?' He waited for a response that would never come. 'Just like I thought. You going to fight me, hard man? If I say no?'

'No, I won't.'

'Then piss off.'

'I have my means of getting what I want.'

'That's smashing for you. Are we done then?' Ronnie stood and went to grab his coat.

'It could be very painful for you, Ronnie. I can make things happen.'

Ronnie smirked. 'I've had far worse threats from far worse people than you, Charles. You'll forgive me if the last thing I do is shite myself.'

'I-'

Charles had gone to speak but Ronnie held up a single finger. Each time he opened his mouth, Ronnie wiggled it. It became tedious and annoying very quickly. Charles patience ran out.

'Very well, Ronnie.' Charles stood up sharply and ripped his coat from the back of the chair. 'Just remember, when I tell you your life is about to get very uncomfortable, that it is because you said no. Your misfortune will all be my making.'

'So, if I have a dodgy curry… you made it?'

'Well, no. Of course, not.' Ronnie could see Charles' confusion and irritation that he was just saying things to annoy him. Ronnie's small laugh did not help anything.

'Not *all* my misfortune then.' Ronnie tapped the table with a smirk. 'You sound like a prize wanker making these Hollywood threats, when you and I both know there's fuck all that an old man with a big wallet can do to me. I have nothing to lose. You, being the man who knows *everything*, know that just as well as I do.' Ronnie grabbed his own coat from along the bench upon which he sat. 'I think I'll be going now, Charles. I'm steaming. It was lovely to see you again. Let's meet up again?'

'I'm-'

'That was another joke. I never want to see you again. Goodbye, Charles.' Ronnie took one more look at the man and walked out of the door. He hoped that it would be the last time he would need to meet him. He hoped that very much.

FLASHBACK III

Ron held promises with the highest regard. He was always careful making one with his grandson. He wanted Ronnie to respect the importance that a promise created between two people. It was an unbreakable vow. That way, when Ronnie was older, he would value a promise and bloody well keep it.

Around a week before they were set to move from Hawick to Burntisland, Ronnie was working hard. He barely noticed his mobile vibrating across his desk because, well, nobody ever called. His grandad was the only one who knew his number, but he refused to ever use it. He explained once that he would never need to call him, because if such an emergency happened, he would probably be dead before Ronnie could ever do anything anyway. Ronnie still hadn't worked out a response to that one.

'Hello?' Ronnie waited several seconds before saying anything, but it became too awkward even for him. He had opened his mouth to talk again before a button clicked on the end of the line.

'Good morning, or should I say, hang on... Good afternoon. It's five past twelve now. How are you doing?' The voice on the other end chuckled. 'I'm always doing that. Good morning... what an idiot. You work one nightshift too many and you're not even sure what decade you're in.'

'What have they done this time, Barge?' Ronnie sighed.

'Why is it that every time I call you or your old man, that's how I'm treated?' Barge feigned a sigh himself. 'I just feel like nobody cares about me.'

'You can beg for sympathy all you like Jim,' Ronnie took a break to flip a finger silently at his laptop. It had just crashed again. 'When your majesty doesn't pay you to lock up my family and then call me to let me know, despite the fact I could not care less, then I might ask how you are. Until then…'

'You could have given me a second at least,' Jim's continued chuckle was awkward now. 'You're no fun.'

'Did my grandad tell you to say that?' Ronnie paused and considered the possibility for a second. He wondered if his grandad did want to move. Of course, he'd promised that he did want to leave, but… people break promises all the time. 'He's never done telling me that these days. How can I help?'

'Odd request,' Barge said. Ronnie could sense the uncertainty. 'I need to chat with you. Can I take you for a pint?'

It was odd for Jim to ask to see Ronnie on his own. Their only interactions had been with his grandad. 'Are you asking me on a date, Jim?'

'I arrest scum. That doesn't mean I want to date it.' Ronnie's eardrum almost collapsed at the thundering roar of laughter which came unnecessarily down the phone. 'Sorry Ronnie, this line is bloody recorded too. If the gaffer listens to this, I'll be struck off.'

'Good job you are the gaffer.'

'I've never said I wouldn't sack myself.' Barge composed himself. 'In fact, if this place doesn't fucking improve then I might just do it.' Barge never swore. Unless he was particularly emotional. 'Can I meet you at the Melgund? Eight o'clock?'

'With fucking bells on, Jim.'

Ronnie worked late that night, but he didn't mean to. He was due to handover all the work to a lady starting the following morning. He originally set everything out within a complex excel spreadsheet until his manager informed him that she didn't even have the software installed on her computer. 'It needs to be simple,' she said. 'Don't you just have it all in a notepad?'

'Doesn't every computer have Microsoft Office installed as standard?' Ronnie asked.

'What's that?' She looked at him, puzzled.

'Wow. Well, that's me finished.' She could lock the office up by herself. 'Night.'

She tried to call him back, to at least pretend she was thankful for all the changes and revisions he had made to drive her company's performance from concerning to exceptional. Though it made him happy to know he made a difference, he couldn't give a fuck what she thought.

It was half past eight when Ronnie burst through the pub doors. Men and women of all shapes and sizes lined the walls, tables and chairs. There was little room to stand, or think with the terrible racket, and the smell of sweat and beer was already beginning to give Ronnie a dull thudding pain behind his eyeballs.

'Wrong side,' a voice bellowed. Jim was waving, sipping a pint from his other hands. I've got one for you too, come over, before some walloper steals my table.' He seemed to look at the thin lady beside him, who glared back with venom.

Ronnie tried to turn, to move back through the crowd, when a hand rested upon his. It was soft. He could smell the perfume through the beery smog of the pub. 'Hiya.'

'Seonaid.' His heart froze. The sounds around him faded out as his face began to grey. 'You okay?'

He couldn't shift his stare from her brown eyes. They had glistened once upon a time, but they were dull now. Long ago, she would smile through her eyes. Tonight, nothing sat behind them. The longer he watched, the more certain he was that they were filling with tears. He knew why. He could never forget why.

'You don't need to answer that,' he blurted, trying to retract his question. 'It was a stupid thing for me to ask, I'm really sorry. I can't imagine how you're feeling.'

'It wasn't,' she whispered, reluctant to let go of Ronnie's hand as it fell from her grasp and disappeared from the bar. 'Nobody asks me how I am anymore. They're too scared to upset me, just like you. But, since you asked, I am doing okay. It's hard sometimes. Mum is there for me every day, but Dad is distant. I think he's still trying to understand what happened, but... he still loves me. At least, he says it every day.'

Ronnie knew that it wasn't normal to tell a distant friend this much from a simple, how are you? At the same time, it would be disrespectful of him to consider himself a distant friend. Yes, this was their relationship now, but, not then. To give their past no respect was an afront to friendship.

'Are you still staying with them?' Ronnie could have hit himself. Why was he asking more questions? Why was he making the entire situation worse? Why was he not breaking this off, to go sit with Barge?

'They haven't been together since it happened, Ronnie.'

The same questions ran through his head. What a stupid thing to ever ask her.

'You're looking great,' Ronnie tried to say. His voice quivered. Seonaid didn't really hear him. Yet, he small red lips curved at the edges. It was the first time, in a very long time, that she had even tried to smile. It did not fool Ronnie, or any of the people who glanced between the two of them. It was fake.

'It was never your fault, Seonaid. I should have done more.'

'We shouldn't blame each other, Ronnie. What could we have done? What could you have done? You can't see the future. You can't see anything other than what is right in front of you. I don't blame you.'

Ronnie still blamed himself. He hated to think about what he had caused to happen. It was obvious, to Ronnie at least, that her life ended when he didn't help her. She could kid the two of them on and tell him every day for the rest of his life that nothing he could have done would have made anything happen any differently. It was an uncomfortable flashback for the two of them, that they would be required to endure for eternity.

'I heard whispers round the pub that you're leaving. Is it true?'

'Next week.'

'Because of what happened?'

'What? With us? Oh gosh, no. Never. I promise.'

'Where to?'

'I'd rather not say.'

She bowed her head.

'It's not you,' said Ronnie. 'It's just safer for my old man if I don't tell anyone where we're going. Once we're settled, though, I would love for you to visit. It's a nice part of the country.'

'That would be really lovely.'

They were both lying. This would make everything easier. They would never have to bump into each other by accident. They would never need to remember what happened between them, and how it ultimately shaped their views of themselves, of each other, of friendship and romance. They could try and pretend that it never happened for the first time, because the thing dearest to them would not be there to tear open the scars.

'Do you work here fulltime?' Ronnie asked, changing the subject.

'No, I'm at college.' She wiped the bar, but she couldn't take her eyes from Ronnie. 'I'm studying counselling. It's going well. It's even helping me out a little too, so I can't complain. Do you have a job where you're going?'

'I'll worry about that when I'm there.' Ronnie shook his head subconsciously. 'I'll worry about everything when I'm there.'

'If you ever need someone to talk to-'

'Ronnie!' Barge shouted from his table. 'This pint is about to go out of date, are you going to drink it or am I going to down it?'

He smiled to Seonaid one final time as he began to work his way through the crowd. 'I'd better go over, I'm already very late and he asked me to meet him at eight and… I hope you get what you want in life, Seonaid. I really do. See you later?'

'Goodbye Ronnie,' she said firmly. They both knew this was the final time they would talk to each other. 'I love you,' she whispered, just out of his earshot.

Ronnie threw his jacket over the remaining barstool and bumped onto the bench beside Jim. He picked up his beer and took a long pull, closing his eyes as the alcohol dripped down his throat and began to ease his overclocked anxiety.

'How was your afternoon?' Jim asked.

'An absolute fucking nightmare, yours?'

'I got to have a day without hearing your surname, so it's been okay.' Barge punched Ronnie jokingly on the arm. 'How was she?' he asked, nodding his head towards the bar.

'How do you think?'

'I don't know, to be honest with you.' Jim wiped his sweating palms down the outside of his jacket. 'Her dad won't talk to me anymore. We used to get on well. It was a tragedy, Ronnie. I wished I could have done more. We've made big changes because of what happened to her. Poor lass.'

'At least the next person won't need to go through the same thing,' Ronnie looked up to the bar, but she was gone now. 'She seems better though, Jim. I wouldn't worry too much.' Ronnie was lying again. He wanted to protect Jim. He was a good detective. He needed protecting.

'Don't move,' said Jim.

'What?'

'Don't move.'

'I don't know what you mean,' said Ronnie. 'Is there something going on?' He looked behind him and around him.

'No,' Jim said, shaking his head. 'I am asking you not to move home.'

'Why?' Ronnie's scrunched face gave away more than he intended. He was almost offended by the suggestion that Jim felt he could have some sort of input into the decision. 'We need to move, Jim. You know that.'

'I know, you've both told me everything and I know more than anyone what he… they have put you through. I don't want you to take Ron away.'

Ronnie sat his pint down onto the table and spun it until the large red T looked back towards him. He pondered this sudden vulnerability from a man who had always been the reliant safety barrier in his life. 'I'm not taking him away from you, Jim. You know why we're going. You can always come visit.'

Jim didn't know what to say. He felt that if he just kept begging, he would strike across the argument that would change their minds. This was perhaps the first time in his life where logic had been forgotten. 'You know my relationship with your old man. He's been my best friend since the day I met him, and I've never gone a day without seeing him unless he was on travelling for work. We've shared our lives together.'

'I...' Ronnie wanted to be sure these next few words counted. 'We're not going far, Jim. Fife's closer than you think.'

'It's really worrying me that he'll be so far away. I know he needs me. What if something happens to him, and I don't know about it?' Jim rubbed his palms together. He was nervous for the first time in a long time. 'I'd never forgive myself.'

'I'd be there,' Ronnie whispered. 'Are you sure this is about him?'

'One hundred percent.'

'We can't stay here, Jim.'

'I can protect you.'

'Not when they're both out of prison, Jim. They're too much.'

'I don't just mean the Police, Ronnie. I know people inside the service and out of it. You don't get to where I am without knowing the people who make things click on the other side. They've given me assurances. I *can* protect you.'

'First things first,' Ronnie spoke more brashly. 'Don't be fucking stupid and get yourself into bother with the fucking idiots in the Higgins family. I went to school with them. They're not protecting anyone. They'll fucking ruin you quicker than my family will, Jim.'

'They promised-'

'Don't you dare say another word, Jim.' Ronnie shook his head. 'How could you be so stupid?'

'What else am I supposed to do?' Barge's raised voice brought eyes from around the bar. 'The man I have relied on for my entire life is moving away and I don't think I can cope.' His words were slurring now. 'I'm fucked without him, Ronnie. What do I do?'

'You don't go to people who have seen a desperate man and

promised him the world. How many of them have you jailed?'

'That's not the point,' Jim scowled.

'That's exactly my point. You've jailed them all. You even jailed their granny. You think they're going to do you any sort of favour? Christ, Jim. You and I both know he's dealing with my brother. They'll stab the two of us quicker than they'd help you.'

Jim's face fell into his palms. His shoulders jumped ferociously as the man let out a loud cry between his forearms. It all felt a bit desperate. Ronnie's grandad had mentioned to him that Jim wasn't himself, but Ronnie never expected it to come out like this.

'You know I've protected you since you were a boy, Ronnie. I've seen a great deal in you since you were six years old. I would never endanger you or my best friend, but you know that taking him away from me would leave me all alone here. I don't know how I'm going to cope with that.' He wiped his face with his sleeve. 'This is my worry.'

'No.'

'No?' Jim asked, an air of confusion around him.

'This is our problem.' Ronnie put his hand on his shoulder and lowered his voice. 'How many times have I needed you to save me, or him? You're as much of a guardian angel as my grandad ever was. He needed you just as much as I needed you. If you've got a problem, you come to me.'

'You've got enough on your plate. I appreciate, but…'

'Jim, you and I both know how much nonsense he talks. You know how long I will last up there by myself.' He gripped down on Jim's shoulder. 'If you need me, for anything, you phone me.'

'I will.'

'Look me in the eye,' said Ronnie.

Barge stared into his pint.

'Look me in my eye, Jim.' Ronnie gripped his hand tighter.

Barge was defeated, but he had to respect Ronnie. He raised his glance just enough to meet the eyes of the determined young man.

'Never mind these childish gangsters who have made you promises. When he's out, and he's calling you and making threats again, you only phone one person. He's not going to listen to anything anyone has to say to him. He's going to come out of that place thinking he's the most important man in the world. You know that Morag is going to sell that to him. You don't tell anyone other than me. You never go a minute without telling what he's doing and where he is doing it. I will make sure he doesn't bother you.'

'Ronnie,' Barge wiped away his tear. 'You're a good kid.'

'I'll be here for you, Jim. No matter what. I promise.'

SEVEN

The silver iPhone buzzed and buzzed, but it was the thud against the floor which finally woke Ronnie up. He checked the time and groaned. It was far too early. 'Hello?' He murmured.

'Good evening my pal,' Barge's voice and an overwhelming warmth. 'Or it might be good morning. I haven't checked the time, just noticed it's still dark outside. How long does it take to drive from where you are to where I am, keeping to the speed limit?'

'Too long,' Ronnie said, coughing into speaker.

Despite his pleas that it was his day off, and it was far too early to be up when he wasn't working, Barge told him it was out of his hands – Ronnie had fobbed him off too many times already. As much as Ronnie knew that was a complete lie, given Barge was in charge, he told him he would be down… only if Barge had a bacon roll waiting for him.

By the time he had gotten dressed, the rain was smashing against the windows of his home. Ronnie hated driving in the rain. Not because he feared it, or because he wasn't very good – everyone drove so slowly, and badly. There was almost always a smash too. He breathed a sigh of relief then, when he travelled from his house in Burntisland to the Police Station in Hawick relatively quickly. There was no other traffic on the road.

Ronnie parked up and entered the police station reception. 'As I live and breathe, Stacey.'

The blonde haired, blue eyed receptionist turned around and grimaced. 'Ronnie.' She was Seonaid's friend. He had never been sure how she felt towards him.

'You're looking well. Have you been ill?' Ronnie smiled, encouraging her to enjoy the joke.

'I'm just back from the all clear for breast cancer.'

'Right. Well, Barge... he... You shouldn't really be offering that sort of information out to strangers.' Ronnie felt sweat suddenly amass like floods around his collar. The lights became bright. Ronnie's cheeks blushed brighter than they had his entire life.

'Please take a seat.' Stacey was completely unimpressed as she picked up her phone. He had never been so sure of her opinion.

Ronnie sat down, cringing to the point of death. Why, oh, why did he even ask that? He could have made a joke about anything else in the world, but he, and his terrible luck, chose to joke about the one thing that would make the entire morning awkward.

Minutes passed before Barge arrived down in reception. He was smiling, as though he knew something that Ronnie didn't. 'You'll never change, Ronnie... but you are looking well.'

The two men had laughed about it by the time they had climbed the three floors to Barge's department. Ronnie stepped inside the interview room and sat uncomfortably inside the cold, prison-like cell. He fiddled with the buttons on the recording unit which sat at the side of the table. His eye then lurched to the camera in the corner, and he stopped. He was in enough trouble already.

'Now then, Ronnie.' Barge opened the door, and accidentally slammed it shut with his foot. He jumped a little with fright. 'You're not in trouble, you'll understand that. I just need to ask a few questions about the ship. I don't know how I've managed to be the one investigating this. I made one phone call, and the big man up north told me to deal with it. You can't question anyone on their work, honestly.'

Ronnie smiled. He didn't know what to say. He looked at Barge and couldn't decide if he had put on slightly more weight in the last few months. He had lost more of his hair. Ronnie also noticed he was trying to grow a goatee. Ronnie didn't like it.

'The problem I have, Ronnie, is this.' He handed out a copy of the report which was produced at the time of the ship's crash – the one which Barge himself questioned in detail. 'You can read the report in its entirety, but your name is never mentioned once.'

'Okay,' Ronnie said nervously. His heart rate increased.

'Now, there could be a variety of reasons for that. My initial thought was that the office up north had just made a mistake, but they assure me they haven't. So, then I think it's the ticket office, but they have all their slips in date order and for the date in question, your name doesn't appear. Not even once.' Barge sniffed rather loudly. 'That leaves me with no explanation as to why you're completely unaccounted for. It means that you cannot have been on that boat.'

'I didn't do it,' Ronnie interrupted.

'Didn't do what?'

'Wreck the ship.'

Barge burst out laughing. He attempted to stifle it once, but he couldn't, and his loud chuckle roared through the room. Ronnie stared. Eventually, Barge calmed down, but not before tears ran down his cheeks. 'Thank goodness. I've been worried you were a terrorist.'

'Really?' Ronnie sharply inhaled and gulped.

'Goodness, no. It's a good thing too, I've forgotten my handcuffs. For the tape, Mr Macleod, can you please confirm your whereabouts on the night in question?'

Ronnie couldn't look Barge in the eye as his mind raced to think what to say. He was sure Barge knew. He was sure that he had taken the time to investigate it, and he knew the truth. He wouldn't ask otherwise. Yet, Ronnie wasn't about to tell him the truth. He did not want to be involved in whatever the hell was going on with Charles.

'I slept in at my bed and breakfast, a few miles from Ullapool. It was-'

Barge's fat finger slapped the stop button on the recorder. He ripped the tape out and jammed it into a box. Upon it, he wrote the time and the date as he mumbled both under his breath.

'Is that it?' Asked Ronnie, his face screwed up.

'Case closed, I'm afraid. Normally love a drama, but I cannot be bothered dragging this out. Ron told me the truth, that you'd never made it to the ship. Why not just say that? Could have saved the trip. Well, not really.' Barge sniggered once more, before opening a brown folder in front of him. 'You're pretty lucky anyway, Ronnie.'

'Why?' His heart skipped a beat. The long breath Barge took seemed to be the longest Ronnie had ever heard. 'The boat, right?'

'No,' mumbled Barge. He was ticking boxes and signing spaces with his scrambled surname. 'Much worse.'

'Worse? How could it be any worse?'

'They're struggling, Ronnie.' It was frustrating how little attention he was paying. 'They cover miles upon miles of nothing and they've had cuts after cuts after cuts... now people are going missing.'

'People are going missing where, Jim?'

His eyes shot up and his pupils opened wide.

'I can't tell you this,' he slammed down his pen. 'I've told you too much. You can't tell anyone outside of these walls.'

'Well, if I can't tell half a story, you may as well not let me tell the whole story.'

'The Isle of Lewis,' sighed Jim. 'There are a number of people having been reported missing. They just don't have the manpower to investigate. I think there's one guy investigating four disappearances.'

'Jesus Christ, Jim. Four people have gone missing? Why aren't you doing anything?'

'Me? I'm too busy interviewing criminals like you.'

'Very funny,' Ronnie said as he rolled his eyes.

'That's not the craziest thing, lad. They all have the same thing in common.'

'Really?'

'Yes.' He closed over the paperwork. 'You do too.'

For a second, Ronnie was sure that Jim had been building this up to prank him. He was always trying to wind up Ronnie. When he was younger, Ronnie would believe anything. Barge had convinced Ronnie that the world was flat. It was funny until one of the bigger kids hit him for it. Barge stopped after that, until Ronnie was big enough and ugly enough to solve his own problems.

'They're all Macleods.'

'Nobody is going to become a serial kidnapper over people with the same surname.'

'No,' agreed Jim. 'I think they're killing them.'

'Stop.'

'I'm not lying,' Jim frowned. 'I am being serious. Nobody outside of the Police force can know. Like you said, why would someone be kidnapping people based solely from their surname? And stranger yet, how do they know?'

'I...'

'Coffee?'

Ronnie nodded. He took the sign that he already knew too much. Anyway, he didn't plan on going to the island anytime soon.

On his way out the door, Jim stopped. His thigh was vibrating. He pulled out his mobile, put one finger up to Ronnie and answered the call. 'Hello. Yes, Jim Barge speaking, how may I help? You're kidding me. Really? For Christ sake. Never ending. You're bringing her in? No, that's fine. I have someone here who may be able to help me. If there is any helping her.'

Barge pointed at Ronnie and smiled. Ronnie knew it could only be about one person. One of two very good reasons why he never came to visit. Jim hung up and came back to sit beside Ronnie. 'I have a few more questions, but they'll need to wait for another day when I'm not scanning or filing. Which is never. Your mother is here. She's been arrested again. Care to join me?'

'I can do that?'

'Of course,' Jim said, smiling. 'Who's going to stop me? I'm the boss.'

Ronnie nodded, and stood up. 'Why is she here? I thought her order was finished now.'

'Oh, it is. It finished yesterday, so she's decided to celebrate.'

'What's she done?' Ronnie asked, anxious if he truly wanted to know. 'Who's she beat up now?'

'It's worse than that, my boy.' Barge stood up and opened the door, inviting Ronnie out of it. 'She's only gone and bought herself a gun… to kill me, apparently.'

Ronnie's pupils exploded.

They made their way down to the ground floor, and Barge explained Ronnie was with him. Everyone knew Ronnie. Only because his family was so well known to the police. They were very courteous to him, given the hassle his blood gave to them almost daily.

'Morning Ronnie,' said one police officer. Ronnie wasn't sure who he was. 'Give my best to your grandfather. I haven't seen him in the longest time. Is he alright?'

'He's surviving. I'll let him know. He likes to hear from people back home.'

'You do that, thanks pal.'

They weren't five feet away before Barge chimed in. 'Just tell Ron that Fat Craig said hello.'

Ronnie turned back to the man. He was so thin, had he turned to his side he might vanish. 'He's not fat.'

'Not now,' said Barge. 'He was bloody huge until this year. His wife had had enough. Probably realised that she wouldn't do any better than a fifty-eight-year-old man who loves wrestling. She told him to slim down before he died. So, he did. Eight stone he lost. Unbelievable. Now he has type two. You'd never bet on it. Lose weight, gain diabetes.'

They made their way further into the station. Ronnie was only six the last time he had been this far, and at that time he was asleep. It made him feel uneasy to know that his family had spent so much time in the cells. It disappointed him that his kin, the woman who raised him, lived such a horrid life and enjoyed it.

'I imagine she'll be angry, Ron.' Barge said as he buzzed into the secure part of the building. 'I haven't told her you're alive yet.'

'Oh Jesus.' Ronnie's feet became stickier, as though his gut were trying to find a way out.

'Tell me about it. I tried to get anyone else to give them the bad news that you were missing, presumed dead, but nobody else would take it. I said, you realise they've threatened to kill me? They despise me. I'll be the next one to go missing. Nobody cared though. They'd rather it was me than them. So, I go around, and she's shouting abuse from the second I'm in the door,' he paused to wave to the officer behind the desk. 'They're reminding me I'm fat and bald, like I didn't already know. They didn't care you were dead. They just seen it as a good opportunity to kick me and slag me off. I tried phoning them, but the one time I answered she told me to go and choke myself in my garage. Do you know what's the worst part about that?'

'There's a lot wrong with that, Jim.' Ronnie answered sheepishly.

'I don't own a garage,' Barge laughed again. Ronnie, normally the lover of humour, was again lost at his joke. 'I mean I have a parking space, but what would that do? I could lie naked in it and catch pneumonia, I guess.'

Ronnie wished he could rinse out his eyes. He had the hairiest, filthiest image in his mind of a man he did not wish to imagine nude. He slid into an interview room whilst Barge walked further down to collect his mother.

'I'm fucking telling you right now, get your hands of me! HELP! He's raping me!'

'Very good, Morag. There are cameras everywhere and officers through the door.'

The door flung open, and Morag stared directly at Ronnie. He wanted the world to open and swallow him immediately. Thirteen years had passed since Ronnie last seen his mother. He was a teenager. She was screaming at him, telling him how much she loathed him and how much she so very wished he had never been born at all.

She had not aged at all well. She had always been fat, yes, but she now had wrinkles and her wrinkles had gotten fat. She looked like an obese CD rack. Her hair had no colour. You could say grey, but it wasn't. It wasn't blond either.

'Take a seat, Morag.' Barge nudged her gently to the metal chair across the table from Ronnie. 'We'll get onto the pleasantries in a minute.'

'You little wanker,' Morag hissed to Ronnie as she sat down. 'Pretending to be dead so I wouldn't come after you? Well, here's some fucking news. The day you walked out on me and your brother, you were dead to me anyway.'

'I thought I had always been dead to you, Morag. So, that's an improvement.' Ronnie kept eye contact with his mother for the first time in years. He would never dignify her title of mother. After all, she hadn't brought him up. She hadn't treated him as a mother should. 'I'm very much alive.'

'Fucking half-breed.'

Barge and Ronnie looked to one another, both having the same thought. If he was a half-breed, then she was surely insulting herself. Neither of them chose to speak, for the fear of giving her a reason to kick off again.

'Morag, you were arrested today as you were in possession of a gun. Can you confirm this to be true?'

'No.' Morag stared at the ceiling, mouthing numbers as she badly counted the foam tiles above. Ronnie peered at her, wondering what she was doing. Her behaviour didn't make sense.

'Well Ronnie, we're doing well. You were found with the gun on your person. My colleague took this from the coat you were wearing. Can you confirm the reason as to why you were carrying this weapon on your person?'

'No.'

'For Christ Sake, Morag.'

'No, Ronnie,' Barge interrupted. 'Let me.'

'Sorry.' Ronnie sat back in his chair.

'For Christ Sake, Morag.' Barge smiled to Ronnie.

Ronnie could see his mother only focused on one thing – him.

Clearly, the disappointment that her son wasn't dead was too much. She was written out of every penny she could gain from him. The fact he no longer existed was sweet enough for her, no doubt.

'Morag, my colleague overheard you say that the sole purpose for owning this gun was so that you could attempt to kill a police officer. You understand the seriousness of this offence?' Barge took a CD from the folder he had brought in with Morag and placed it beside the audio player.

'I don't know what you're talking about,' her eyes darted back to Ronnie. 'I never liked you. I never wanted you. It was all your fucking dad's fault. He can't have kids, but one shag and I end up with a fucker like you. Unbelievable.'

Barge didn't have a chance to talk before Ronnie jumped in front of him. 'You talk like Lewis isn't one of his too. Yet you love him.'

'He's not his son.'

'What?' Barge and Ronnie both asked at the same time.

'Lewis has a different dad,' Morag said with complete sincerity. 'Everyone knows that.'

Barge's look to Ronnie suggested that nobody knew that, and to the man that had spent most of his life enforcing the law upon the Macleod family, this was very much a new development in his file of Morag and Lewis.

'What?' Morag barked. 'The only thing you and Lewis have in common is that you popped out my fanny. That's it. That's why you're a waste of space. You're not the same. You never will be like my Lewis. I wouldn't want you to be. Thinking of you and that stupid father of yours makes my skin crawl. He had a tiny-'

'Okay, Morag.' Barge interrupted. 'That's enough. We're not here to discuss that.' He could see that Ronnie was shaken by the news.

'What happened to my dad?' Ronnie interrupted, and Barge began to realise that he had made the wrong choice. 'I don't get why he would be with someone like you.'

'Okay, Ronnie,' Barge tried to talk but Morag interrupted

him.

'Me and your dad were high school sweethearts, but then I realised I haven't got time to be fucking nice. We broke it off, and he came back thinking I was still that silly cow. I had sex with him, aye. I needed a cock deep inside me. Every woman does. He left, and I don't fucking know what happened. He died. Stupid dick.'

'Enough,' barked Barge at the two of them. He did not want Ronnie upsetting himself any further for the sake of his own wrong decision.

For minutes afterwards, Barge interrogated Morag as to why she had decided to kill him. Ronnie, meanwhile, sat in disbelief at the revelation he had learnt, almost at random. He had spent his entire life, since the age of six, wondering at what point he would unconsciously start to act like his brother, but he couldn't understand why it hadn't happened yet. There it was, though. He was nothing like his brother. They were, at least, half different.

'Who's his dad?' Ronnie asked, breaking up the interview once again.

'Ron-'

'I know who his dad is, but I'm not telling you.' She flipped the middle finger to Ronnie. 'He was a great man. A powerful man. He made me feel alive. He knew just how to treat me. He knew exactly what I wanted.'

'Heroin?' Ronnie asked, to which his mother began to violate the table with her fists and feet. Barge knew now, without doubt, that he had made the wrong decision, and he had let it run on long enough. He grabbed Ronnie and dragged him from the room.

'I'm sorry, I shouldn't have done that.' He patted Ronnie on the shoulder. 'My colleague will show you out, oh, and Ronnie. I didn't know. Honestly, I didn't. I would have told you if I did.'

Ronnie smiled, and let Barge know it was okay. It had been good to learn the things he had. He followed the other police officer to the front door. It was sunny, and warm. Ronnie took off his coat and enjoyed the winter heat. As he walked down the steps, a familiar face appeared from the corner.

'Alright wanker,' Lewis shouted. He was steaming drunk.

Ronnie continued to walk past him, ignoring his loutish behaviour.

'You're going to ignore your brother?' Lewis shouted louder this time. 'I mean it's only been nine years since I saw you last. Not like I don't fucking matter, do I?'

Ronnie stopped. 'Thirteen,' he responded. 'It's been thirteen years since I saw either of you, but nobody remembers that, do they?'

'Exactly,' said Lewis.

Ronnie turned. 'Exactly what?' He stared directly at his brother.

'You act like you're better than us.'

He thought for a second about what he should say. There were many things he wanted to say. For once though, he could not decide.

'You think you're better than us,' Lewis spoke almost immediately after to hide the silence.

'No Lewis, I don't. What I do is I act like I don't want anything to do with you.' Ronnie thrust his hands deeply into his pockets and tried to walk on, but he knew that his brother would not let him have the last word. He stood for a second, facing away. He should have just left it, but his ego kept his feet planted to the ground.

'Seriously?' He took one step to his right, and then three to his left. He hiccoughed. 'Bro?'

Ronnie stared into the distance and took a deep, long breath. He held it, trying to calm his frustration. He wasn't angry, he just couldn't be bothered having to deal with the situation in hand. He turned, just to see his brother fall against the wall, bruising his shoulder.

'This... I don't want anything to do with you. I haven't seen you in years, far less spoken to you. Every single time I see you, it's because you've done something wrong.' He had raised his voice, and his hand to point to the Police Station. 'This is a fucking godsend, that it's not you who broke the law.'

'Don't act like you're the angel of this bloody family. Don't think I don't remember the time you-'

'Shut up.' Ronnie took another breath. 'We've gone in different directions.'

'You're a fag,' spat Lewis as Ronnie turned to walk away.

Ronnie stopped for a second time and turned back. 'I said shut up, Lewis. The only reason I'm here is because of your stupid mother, and she's as good as in jail again after getting caught with that gun.' He turned, walked a few more steps and then turned back one final time. 'Oh, and by the way, you don't fucking matter. Morag just told me the good news. We have different dads. We're only half-brothers. In my book, though, it's as good as nothing.'

Lewis scrambled up the wall with his half-bitten fingernails. His eyes cocked from one side to the other as he tried to formulate some kind of comeback.

'No,' said Ronnie. 'You keep out my life now, okay?'

EIGHT

He threw his head onto the pillow and groaned as his phone began to ring one more time. The vibrations against the table made his eyes roll into the back of his head. It stopped, and he picked up his mobile. There were five missed calls from Barge. Presumably, he had forgotten to ask Ronnie something, but Ronnie couldn't be bothered answering him. The rest were from his grandad and he sounded very upset.

'Jesus, Ronnie. Why haven't you been answering your phone?'

'Calm down, grandad. What's wrong?'

'Lewis! He's... he's out of control this time. I can't believe it. He's gone too far this time. I told you we should never have moved. We've caused this Ronnie. This is all our fault.'

'Okay, Lewis.' Ronnie forced a break in the conversation. 'What's Lewis done?' He was slightly concerned that his comments the afternoon prior may have had more of an effect than he'd hoped. Then again, he thought to himself, what could he possibly do? Kill someone?

'He's stabbed Barge.'

Oh.

Ronnie was in his car now, racing towards his grandad's home. He hoped so very much that it wasn't true. They weren't sure if he would make it through the night. Something about losing a lot of blood from an artery. He hoped this was after the missed calls. He had always told Barge to call him if something was going wrong. It was hard to see why he would escape any blame this time.

'Ronnie, he might be dead!' His grandad was screaming down the phone. 'I can't lose him. I cannot lose Barge. He's too good to me. He's a good friend. You know that! Please, we need to go and see him. He doesn't have family. Just us. Please, Ronnie, please. Oh, I think I see you now. Goodbye.'

Ron held onto his walking stick for dear life as his carer held his entire weight to keep him upright. Ronnie arrived at the complex apologising immediately to the man who looked less than impressed at having to shelter Ron from the battering rain. As they walked to the car, Ron explained that he was one of the 'good guys'. Ronnie took that as he was the only one willing to be paid to listen to him.

As they raced home, Ron's attention was drawn to the changing colours of the fields. 'There's a trainline down there now.'

'You know there is,' Ronnie groaned. 'You gave me daily updates on it being built.'

'It's nice to recognise someone's work, is it not?' Ron smiled. 'It's nice to be remembered for what you did.'

The A7 twists sharply through the Borders. There are two types of drivers; those who know the road and move, and those who don't and... don't. Ronnie was the former, and he risked their lives a number of times to overtake nervous drivers on blind, dark bends.

'I'd quite like to just visit Jim, not move in with him if that's okay?' Ron smiled, but inside he was still deeply upset. 'The carers at work tell me everything has changed these days, but I don't see it. Why would they lie to me, Ronnie?'

'It has.'

'Like what?' Ron asked, exasperated.

'Grandad, you sit and watch the news from the moment you wake up until you go to bed. If you don't know what is going on in this world, I'm going to have to tie you down to a bed.' Ronnie panicked and hit his break. A car had pulled out of a junction in front of him. He held his horn, blasting it at the driver. He got two fingers out the driver's window.

'Ronnie,' spat Ron. 'Be careful, for Jim. He's a good guy. He looked after you and me when we lived back home. I almost had a direct line into that Police Station because he knew that neither of them would stop calling us. He's the one who put them both away... Oh goodness, and now they've plotted together to kill him.' Ron feinted a cough to hide his tears. A roll of snot rocketed back into his nose as he sniffed it violently.

Ronnie was very aware that his grandad did not know about Morag being arrested. 'What do you mean?' He asked, pretending he wasn't aware.

'They'll have been sat in that dirty little council house in Burnfoot, planning how they would kill him. They told him countless times what they were going to do. He's taken the kitchen knife and just decided to do away with him. Oh, Jesus Christ, Ronnie. Why are we tormenting him?" Ron wept into his sleeve. Ronnie left him alone.

'I think you're worrying about everything, now. Barge will be okay.'

'He might not be, either.'

To calm his grandad, Ronnie made a call to the hospital. The overnight staff member answered the phone, and Ronnie wasn't sure if she was hungover, angry, or just not enjoying her job.

'Good morning,' Ronnie said.

'Only just. How can I help?'

Ronnie squinted at his grandad, wondering if he had made the right move. 'Our friend, James Barge, was admitted through the night. We were hoping you could give us an update as to his condition?'

The nurse on the end of the phone rustled through some papers. Ronnie nudged his grandad calmly, as if to say silently that they were about to receive good news, and everything would be alright.

'Mr Barge was rushed to theatre around an hour ago. We have yet to receive an update from the surgeon.' There was a long silence on the end of the phone, as though Ronnie were hoping for more news and the nurse was hoping for the end of the call. 'Hello?'

'Smashing,' Ronnie spat sarcastically. His grandad was now in tears. He wondered how he could make it worse for him. 'We will be in soon. He has no family. My grandad is his next of kin.'

'You won't be allowed in until-'

Ronnie hung up before she could utter another word. His grandad was in pieces, almost as bad as he was when Ronnie came in from the ship disaster. He reached over and grabbed his old, cold hand and squeezed it. 'Jim will be okay, grandad. Do you think he's going to want to let Lewis win? Not a chance. Barge is winning that war. He'll be there to see him sentenced.'

'It's not that, lad.' Ron sniffed rather loudly. 'He's spent his whole career trying to make a name for himself in the police, and it's been my family that's taken up his time. Think for a second Ronnie, where he would be, if he didn't have to always clean up after us?'

He was right.

The two men sat in silence until they reached the hospital. Ronnie had flown past it, and it was minutes before the two of them realised. Ronnie, recklessly, did a three-point turn in the main road connecting the countryside to the city and pressed hard to make up the time he lost. By the time they arrived, the sun was beginning to rise, and the car park was empty. Ronnie rolled into a space, and helped his grandad to the nearest wheelchair.

Borders General Hospital sits midway between Galashiels and Melrose. Ron would be forced to ignore he was within touching distance *palemerk* territory, even now. It sits on its own piece of land, raising up in square blocks. It's moulding skin is beige, and moderately old for a hospital. Behind the building, smoke rose to the east. Ronnie was fully aware of what part of the hospital lay there – the incinerator. Someone's leg was going up in smoke. He just hoped it wasn't Jim's.

Ron wheezed as he fell into the wheelchair, exhausted. He wasn't used to staying up all night. He closed his eyes as his grandson wheeled him inside, hoping for some good news. The lights flashed above them as he ran through the hallway. A cleaner jumped out of the way, pulling his mop as Ronnie narrowly missed tripping over it. Shutters remained down, and everyone else in the building was asleep or drinking coffee in the staffroom.

There was no good news.

Barge was out, but he was back into high-dependency. There was a single officer stood by the door of the ward, but neither Ron nor his grandson recognised him.

'Please, you must know Jim?'

'No,' replied the officer. 'I'm here from Edinburgh.'

'I need in to see my friend, you see, we have been friends since we were young and I am really the only person who cares for him.'

'Are you family?' The officer asked bluntly, his face expressionless.

'No, sir.' Ron's head dipped.

'I'm going to have to ask you gentlemen to leave now.' His oversized finger pointed down the hallway.

'We need in.' Ronnie cut his own sentence short. 'You know from his file that he has no next of kin. If you haven't read it, then that's your fault. Don't let my grandfather get more upset than he already is just because you're not doing your job.'

Even Ronnie's heart was beginning to sink. There was no way that they were getting in here, whether he pleaded or argued with the office.

'I don't need to answer to you, but I have read the file. James has a next of kin who can visit him.'

'Who?' Both men asked, surprised.

'Ronnie MacLeod.'

'That's me,' his grandad shouted, accidentally.

'I doubt you were born in the eighties, sir.' The officer smiled childishly.

'I'm his next of kin?' Ronnie gasped. He couldn't understand why Jim would record that. Perhaps, he felt his grandad was now too old and Ronnie would be able to manage any crisis on his behalf. 'Since when?'

'Are you wanting to see him or not?'

'You've changed your tune,' said Ronnie sarcastically as he

entered the ward.

The intensive care unit was eerie. Nobody moved, nobody made a sound. The machines, connected to poorly souls, popped to one another down the room as though they were trying to encourage each other to get better. Lights flashed across the hall as they made their way down to bay nine, where Jim Barge was sat fighting for this life.

'He's awake, but he's weak.' The young nurse handed bibs and gloves for both men to wear. 'He won't be able to speak to you this early on. It's too late to say how he will react to the operation.' She caught Ron's jolt forward as he began to cry. 'He did brilliant. The doctor is really hopeful.'

'Thanks.' Ronnie smiled.

They pulled back the curtain, and both men winced. Jim was covered in blood and tubes. His eyes flickered, as they came closer to him. He outstretched a hand and squeezed Ronnie's as he slid his own between the bloody fingers. He felt the cold squelch.

'I'm sorry, Barge.' Ronnie sat down beside him. 'I think this is my fault. I caught Lewis outside of the station and I told him what Morag said. He was annoying me. I shouldn't have even spoken to him. Then I get home and...' He was careful not to mention the missed calls in front of his grandad. 'I can't believe he's done this. It's one thing to threaten you, but to try and take a life... your life... I don't even think an apology would be enough.'

Ronnie and his grandad looked to each other, they were certain Barge was shaking his head. He tried to lift his oxygen mask, but he was too weak. His body was conserving too much energy to fix itself. Ron took his other hand, and squeezed it.

'There's no point telling us there's nothing to apologise for, Jim.' Ron was near tears again. 'We are just as responsible. We ran off, we hid from our responsibility as his family. We left you to tidy up the mess, and this is what happened. Jesus, Jim. You're such a good man. It should be me lying there, or Ronnie.'

Ronnie looked at his grandad. 'Really?' He almost swore, and had to hold himself given the company. 'Thanks.'

'You know what I mean!'

'Aye, you'd rather it was your grandson stabbed than your pal. I feel fucking fantastic now.' He realised that he had sworn now, and his grandad looked at him gravely. Ronnie turned to Barge. 'Look Jim, I'm not saying I'm happy with you lying here but I would rather it was none of us than one of us.'

Barge smiled.

He fell asleep not too long after, and Ronnie sat holding his hand as he watched the time tick by on the monitor beside the bed. Barge's heart was strong, even he could see that. The nurse who came in earlier to do a few tests, said that he seemed to be in a serious, yet stable condition. A second nurse entered shortly after, reached into his pocket, and pulled a syringe which he injected into Jim's drip.

'What's that' Ron asked the nurse, but he received no reply.

'Do you think he might be able to speak soon?' Ronnie's eyes didn't move as he waited for an answer. 'Sorry, did you hear me?'

There was no response. The nurse just shook his head. Ronnie nudged his grandad, but Ron simply whispered to him, 'probably procedure.'

'Any results back?' Ronnie asked.

The nurse checked the sheet by the door and left, his old face wrinkling as he smiled behind the mouth guard.

'Why do you think Lewis did it, lad?'

Ronnie shrugged.

'Jim didn't have anything on him. He always told me if he did," Ron finished talking, yawned and then rubbed his eyes. 'There's no reason for Lewis to attack him. Two rapes are unforgivable. He wasn't a killer though.'

Ronnie found it odd that his grandad tried to quantify what sort of criminal he was. Twice he had been convicted of forcibly ruining a woman's life. Twice he had been found guilty of forcing himself upon someone else, and using them for power... the sex was an afterthought. Lewis liked to punish people, just like his mother taught him to.

'There was no reason for him to rape Seonaid, but he went and did it anyway.' Ron shook his head. Seonaid was the second girl on Lewis' criminal record. She was very close to Ronnie. Lewis had been convicted of sexually assaulting her, despite her inability to provide a solid testimony to the event.

'He's sick in the head. He was probably full of drugs, he was when I saw him.' Ronnie desperately tried to think of things to quantify the situation and prove to Ron that neither of them were to blame for the whole drama. 'Morag puts ideas in his head that Barge is out to ruin them. That'll be why he did it. No other reason. Remember, Morag is in there too for having a gun. She was the one to try and kill him first.'

'What?' Ron asked confused.

Ronnie froze, he hadn't meant to tell him about that. He didn't need to know. He shook his head, bit his knuckle and sighed. 'Oh yeah, I didn't tell you about that.'

He then filled his grandad in on the day's events previous. The further he went; the greyer Ron's face went. He almost passed out at one point, and Ronnie was forced to hold him until he felt better. Towards the end, Ronnie cut some of the details short. He needed to know what happened, but not everything. He didn't need to know that Ronnie had decided to tell Lewis that his dad was not his dad.

Barge groaned.

The two jumped over, stretching over to see that he was okay.

He groaned again. His voice was masked by the oxygen flooding into his nose and mouth. Ronnie pushed his ear as close as he could, but it was no good. He was just too quiet.

'Jesus, Ronnie, take off the mask! He could be telling us something.' Ron tried desperately to stand, but his legs gave way each time.

Ronnie looked outside, but there were no nurses around. It was dark, and there were no prying eyes watching the room. Ronnie jumped over and ripped the mask from Barge's face. His eyes flicked, he took one breath, the largest that he could take and then he hissed.

His eyes shut, and he went back to sleep. Ronnie placed the oxygen back over his face, and looked to his grandad like he had no idea what it was that he had just said.

'What was that?' Ron asked.

'I couldn't make it out. I was hoping you did.' Ronnie replied.

'From here?' Ron spat. 'You must be kidding.'

'No,' replied Ronnie sheepishly. 'I'm sorry.'

However, Ronnie did know. *Charles.* The same man was again interrupting Ronnie's life. What link this had, Ronnie wasn't sure. Did Barge know about Ronnie's true whereabouts the day the ship was wrecked? Or was he just aware that Charles was not missing, presumed dead?

'Gentlemen, it's time for you to leave, if you wouldn't mind.'

Ronnie and Ron weren't out the door, before the nurse – who had allowed them in originally – sprinted back into Barge with several her colleagues, including a doctor. Every alarm in the room sounded. Ron was too weak to move. Ronnie took one step forward, and seen blood cover the room. It looked as though Barge had suddenly haemorrhaged everywhere.

'Is he alright, son?' Ron asked.

'I think so, grandad. Let's go. We're just taking up room, here.' Ronnie continued to lie to his grandad until he was home. He was sure it was for the best. His grandad would be paranoid that lifting the oxygen mask had killed him. If it had, he didn't want his grandad telling anyone. He could see the headlines the next day; Ronnie the murderer. After all, Barge knew about Charles. So he also had to know the truth. He had to know that Ronnie was involved in all of this.

Despite his tragic passing, the papers would not report it. Nobody would care that he was murdered. For all the work he put into enforcing the law, to be killed by a notorious local criminal, it was as though he had never existed. It was sad, really. James Barge died that night, and nobody gave a fuck.

Nobody, except Charles. His plan was going slightly better than expected. He sat with a glass of red, and watched the fire before him smoulder as the last of his blue scrubs burnt away to nothing. He knew it wouldn't be long before Ronnie Macleod broke. What he didn't know, however, was how many more people he would need to kill first.

'What's that' Ron asked the nurse, but he received no reply.

'Do you think he might be able to speak soon?' Ronnie's eyes didn't move as he waited for an answer. 'Sorry, did you hear me?'

There was no response. The nurse just shook his head. Ronnie nudged his grandad, but Ron simply whispered to him, 'probably procedure.'

'Any results back?' Ronnie asked.

The nurse checked the sheet by the door and left, his old face wrinkling as he smiled behind the mouth guard.

'Why do you think Lewis did it, lad?'

Ronnie shrugged.

'Jim didn't have anything on him. He always told me if he did," Ron finished talking, yawned and then rubbed his eyes. 'There's no reason for Lewis to attack him. Two rapes are unforgivable. He wasn't a killer though.'

Ronnie found it odd that his grandad tried to quantify what sort of criminal he was. Twice he had been convicted of forcibly ruining a woman's life. Twice he had been found guilty of forcing himself upon someone else, and using them for power… the sex was an afterthought. Lewis liked to punish people, just like his mother taught him to.

'There was no reason for him to rape Seonaid, but he went and did it anyway.' Ron shook his head. Seonaid was the second girl on Lewis' criminal record. She was very close to Ronnie. Lewis had been convicted of sexually assaulting her, despite her inability to provide a solid testimony to the event.

'He's sick in the head. He was probably full of drugs, he was when I saw him.' Ronnie desperately tried to think of things to quantify the situation and prove to Ron that neither of them were to blame for the whole drama. 'Morag puts ideas in his head that Barge is out to ruin them. That'll be why he did it. No other reason. Remember, Morag is in there too for having a gun. She was the one to try and kill him first.'

The Truth Hurts

'What?' Ron asked confused.

Ronnie froze, he hadn't meant to tell him about that. He didn't need to know. He shook his head, bit his knuckle and sighed. 'Oh yeah, I didn't tell you about that.'

He then filled his grandad in on the day's events previous. The further he went; the greyer Ron's face went. He almost passed out at one point, and Ronnie was forced to hold him until he felt better. Towards the end, Ronnie cut some of the details short. He needed to know what happened, but not everything. He didn't need to know that Ronnie had decided to tell Lewis that his dad was not his dad.

Barge groaned.

The two jumped over, stretching over to see that he was okay.

He groaned again. His voice was masked by the oxygen flooding into his nose and mouth. Ronnie pushed his ear as close as he could, but it was no good. He was just too quiet.

'Jesus, Ronnie, take off the mask! He could be telling us something.' Ron tried desperately to stand, but his legs gave way each time.

Ronnie looked outside, but there were no nurses around. It was dark, and there were no prying eyes watching the room. Ronnie jumped over and ripped the mask from Barge's face. His eyes flicked, he took one breath, the largest that he could take and then he hissed.

His eyes shut, and he went back to sleep. Ronnie placed the oxygen back over his face, and looked to his grandad like he had no idea what it was that he had just said.

'What was that?' Ron asked.

'I couldn't make it out. I was hoping you did.' Ronnie replied.

'From here?' Ron spat. 'You must be kidding.'

'No,' replied Ronnie sheepishly. 'I'm sorry.'

However, Ronnie did know. 'Charles.' The same man was again interrupting Ronnie's life. What link this had, Ronnie wasn't sure. Did Barge know about Ronnie's true whereabouts the day the ship was wrecked? Or was he just aware that Charles was not missing, presumed dead?

'Gentlemen, it's time for you to leave, if you wouldn't mind.'

Ronnie and Ron weren't out the door, before the nurse – who had allowed them in originally – sprinted back into Barge with several her colleagues, including a doctor. Every alarm in the room sounded. Ron was too weak to move. Ronnie took one step forward, and seen blood cover the room. It looked as though Barge had suddenly haemorrhaged everywhere.

'Is he alright, son?' Ron asked.

'I think so, grandad. Let's go. We're just taking up room, here.' Ronnie continued to lie to his grandad until he was home. He was sure it was for the best. His grandad would be paranoid that lifting the oxygen mask had killed him. If it had, he didn't want his grandad telling anyone. He could see the headlines the next day; Ronnie the murderer. After all, Barge knew about Charles. So he also had to know the truth. He had to know that Ronnie was involved in all of this.

Despite his tragic passing, the papers would not report it. Nobody would care that he was murdered. For all the work he put into enforcing the law, to be killed by a notorious local criminal, it was as though he had never existed. It was sad, really. James Barge died that night, and nobody gave a fuck.

Nobody, except Charles. His plan was going slightly better than expected. He sat with a glass of red, and watched the fire before him smoulder as the last of his blue scrubs burnt away to nothing. He knew it wouldn't be long before Ronnie Macleod broke. What he didn't know, however, was how many more people he would need to kill first.

NINE

The sky was overcast and the sun was missing, making the morning darker than it should have. Jim's funeral, for Ronnie at least, was plagued by his grandad's anger. He was furious that Ronnie lied. He was certain there was something the two of them could have done. So, Ron told his grandson he would go on his own to his best friend's funeral.

Ronnie stood beside the crematorium doors. He still hadn't decided if it was a wise idea to go in. Would his Grandad say anything?

A number of Police Officers, Jim's colleagues, walked into the building as they waved towards Ronnie. Some stopped to say hello. There was no sight of his grandad, though. He had been waiting for over an hour now. He began to worry if something had happened. His grandad didn't have a mobile, and he had already left his home – he was sure of this. He'd checked twice.

He looked up to the sky as the rain started. A wind of sadness came over Ronnie. Jim was dead. Not just that, his brother was the one who murdered him. Barge had spent so much of his life trying to keep his family at bay, and it was this piece of work – which was all it was – that killed him. Ronnie was deeply embarrassed.

The hearse pulled up outside. The car was flowerless. A black coffin sat inside. The driver stepped out from the front seat and Jim was alone again. Ronnie wasn't sure if this was Barge's wishes, or if nobody had been there to plan his funeral. A second later, however, a black car pulled up inches behind. Ron climbed out.

'You'll leave me alone,' he shouted to his carer, slapping away the offer of help. 'I'm doing this on my own. For Barge. Do you think he had someone to help him up when that bloody boy stabbed him?'

The carer didn't know what to say. He didn't know where to go. He stood with his mouth open. Ronnie took a few steps forward to try and interject, but Ron's eyes opened wider in fury the moment he realised his grandson had shown up.

'You've some cheek being here, Ronnie Macleod.'

'Grandad-'

'Don't. There's nothing you can say to me.'

'I-'

'We could have saved him, if you'd bloody said something sooner.' Ron turned to point at the coffin, but he stumbled. His back hit the hearse, but he grabbed hold of the handle to pull himself up. 'There's no need for him to be in there. There's no need for my only friend to be dead. This is all on you. Don't you forget it.'

'What could we have done? He was bleeding out.' Ronnie wanted to shout at him, to put sense into his grandad. It was not the time or place. 'You can fall out with me over this if you want, but I'm not going to leave you alone. I'll still look after you, I'll pay for whatever you need. You don't need to fall out with me over this, we only have each other.'

'We do now Barge is dead.'

Ron walked off, leaving Ronnie by the door. The coffin went in, and Ronnie bowed to it. Maybe Jim's death was all his fault. He did, after all, provoke the murder. Lewis would not have reacted so badly if Ronnie hadn't told him the news about his dad. Yes, it was his fault. He couldn't face paying any final respects to a death that he personally caused. He turned to walk away, but someone from behind him tapped his shoulder.

'Mr Macleod?'

If it was Charles, Ronnie would headbutt him. Thankfully, it wasn't. A man, dressed in a black suit, stood with his hand outstretched. Ronnie shook it, and the man pulled a leather folder from behind his back. He was clean shaven. A bit too immacu-

The Truth Hurts

late, if you asked Ronnie.

'Mr Macleod, my name is Steven Taylor. I am a solicitor from the local firm here, Slater and Barnes. I understand this must be a tough time for you, however I have been assigned as the executor of the will of the late Mr James Barge.'

'You could wait until he's cremated, at least?' Ronnie asked, disgusted. 'The man is lying there waiting to be burnt and you're stood here selling me your services?'

'I really do apologise for this, you see, it wouldn't normally be my normal procedure for this… however, things are highly restricted by time.' He pulled a piece of paper from the leather folder and turned it to face Ronnie. 'This is Jim's will. You'll be aware that Jim had no family, nobody related to him by blood, alive at least, to sort out his affairs.'

'Yeah, I knew that. Have you come to rub it in that he was alone?' His grandad's biting comments in the last few days had been more than enough for Ronnie.

'Far from it, Mr Macleod,' his look was sincere. 'I quite liked Mr Barge, he was a gentleman. The reason I am here, and I'll be brief, is that James left everything in his possession to you. However, he did not own the house he lives in. He rents… rented it and the landlord is demanding that he has the property back today.'

'They can't do that, surely?' Ronnie looked confused. 'Surely we have time.'

'Unfortunately, Mr Macleod, under Scots Law the tenancy ends the day the tenant dies. He died over one week ago now, and the landlord does not wish to lose any more money. I realise that you would prefer to go to the funeral, but I cannot stop him. He has given us until three o'clock today, and then he will bin everything in the house.' Mr Taylor gave Ronnie a second to digest the information. 'I wish I could stop this, but I can't.'

'Can't you pay him?' Ronnie asked. 'Use the money Barge left?'

'Jim was in a lot of debt. He was already in arrears. Didn't he tell you any of this?'

'Why would he?'

'You're his next of kin.'

Ronnie suddenly remembered that Jim had noted Ronnie as his next of kin with the Police. Now this. All those years ago, Ronnie had promised to look after him when he moved. He hadn't, and now this had happened. The very person who told Jim he would care for him, ignored his calls as he was stabbed and then left him in the hospital to die alone. Now he was the beneficiary of all his belongings.

'I'll go see the house just now.' Ronnie peered into the crematorium, the service was well underway. He thought about telling his grandad, but he would only be angrier. Angry that Ronnie had left him to die, and then pocketed all his possessions.

He slid into his car and drove to Barge's home. He lived in a very nice area. Subconsciously, Ronnie was disappointed he didn't own his home – he would have loved to live in the street, in his home. It was a large, white, modern property. Two large bay windows looked out from the living room to look over the road and over into the hills behind the town. It was a majestic view. There was no grass, it looked very much like a concrete jungle.

'Fuck me, at last!'

Behind Ronnie's car, a man walked passed with an umbrella. He was thin and short, and looked at least twice the age he ought to. His scowl added many wrinkles into his prune shaped face.

'The bloody money I have lost waiting on this place being cleared. It's a joke. I hope you're going to be paying me?'

'For what?' Ronnie looked at him, and tried to stay calm. He took a couple of steps down the sloping drive towards the man. The landlord took a step back, nervously. 'You're hard, aren't you? The man who lived here was murdered last week.'

'Aye, well…' His voice broke, his forehead was damp. 'I'm still losing money. Money that I am owed!'

'Come and get it, pal.' Ronnie didn't blink. 'If you think you're the man to come and take that money from me, then you're welcome to try, pal.'

'Well, that's not… I mean, you can't be like that with me. I've lost a tenant.' The landlord now took several more steps backwards. The indicator lights of his car flashed as he pressed the button to unlock it. His eyes twitched slightly. He was very intimidated.

'It's a shame, isn't it? I'm stood here having lost a good friend, but that's meaningless. I mean, I'm never going to turn a profit on a friendship. I could sell the story of how he was murdered, or what I could do is phone my brother who killed my friend, and have him kill you too. How does that sound, you shit bag?' Ronnie's snarl was now inches from the landlord's sweating forehead. He thought that the landlord might cry.

'You've got until three o'clock. I'll be bringing sheriff officers, so, so you can tell them your concerns.' He rushed off to his car, not bothering to turn a glance back to Ronnie.

'I don't think they'll be interested in hearing that you're an arsehole, but I will tell them. Thanks!' Ronnie shouted into the car window as he drove off. He turned, walked to the door and thrust his hand into his pocket. The key opened the door, and Ronnie stepped inside. 'Hello?' he shouted foolishly. There was nobody home.

Outside, it was immaculate. Inside, it was dusty and stank of smoke. Ronnie wandered around the three-bedroom home very quickly, but realised there was little he wanted to keep. He didn't want to make money from anything. He would keep the car, it was far nicer than his. A Porsche, blue. It was about all he knew about cars. His car was a Renault. Fast, but rubbish.

Ronnie walked into the living room and sat down. This is where Jim spent his nights. He didn't even have satellite television. Ronnie thought to himself, how could a single man live on his own with Freeview? He flicked through the channels. Nothing was on. Point proven. He put the television off, and sat for a moment.

Given what his grandad had said, about Jim giving his life to have nothing, Ronnie didn't think it would be this bad. He had nothing to show for the debt he had, nothing to show for the work he had done. It appeared that he had spent his money on take away food and cigarettes, and then one day, Lewis killed him.

He stood up and wandered around again. In every room, the curtains were closed and it was pitch black. As Ronnie turned the light on, the bulb almost set fire to the dust. 'That's rotten,' Ronnie said accidentally as he took a full breath of burning filth. He had stumbled across Jim's office.

He fiddled through the papers, but he found nothing exciting. Most of them were blank, as though he had put them out to print on them and never bothered tidying them away. His printer sat up on a shelf, and many bits of paper sat in the tray. He reached up, and pulled them down to find various e-mails from Barge to different members within the Police. He knew he shouldn't look at them, but at the same time, he knew he couldn't not look at them. Worried that the bulb in the office might explode, he walked down to the living room where he could find at least a touch of natural light.

To: Penny, Sandra; Black, Terrance; Kerlin, Bob; McTurney, Sheila;
Cc: Barge, James;
Subject: Operation Leòdhas
Morning,
Thanks to Sandra for picking this up in my absence. Seems to have been some weekend! We'll debrief at the meeting later in the week, but if we could all collate the information we know about this by responding to this e-mail before the end of the working day today, I would appreciate it. Bob – this means you can leave early, like usual, if you get your work done for once!!
Jim

To: Penny, Sandra; Black, Terrance; Kerlin, Bob; McTurney, Sheila;
Cc: Barge, James;

The Truth Hurts

Subject: Re: Operation Leòdhas

We've picked up communication which would inform us that there is a plan to make an attempt on a police officer's life sometime in the next 72 hours. This is all the information I have on this, but the others will have far more detail.

Terry

To: Penny, Sandra; Black, Terrance; Kerlin, Bob; McTurney, Sheila;
Cc: Barge, James;
Subject: Re: Operation Leòdhas

The lead I am picking up today would suggest that Morag and Lewis Macleod are involved. Will provide more info as I have it.

To: Penny, Sandra; Black, Terrance; Kerlin, Bob; McTurney, Sheila;
Cc: Barge, James;
Subject: Re: Operation Leòdhas [IMPORTANT]

If the Macleods are involved, then we must not inform Ron or his grandson. Please keep all information relating to this strictly between this team. Thanks.

Jim

To: Penny, Sandra; Black, Terrance; Kerlin, Bob; McTurney, Sheila;
Cc: Barge, James;
Subject: Re: Operation Leòdhas

You're the one pals with them, Jim. Plus, my wife wants a night in. I won't be seeing anyone until I'm back in with this shower. Bob.

To: Penny, Sandra; Black, Terrance; Kerlin, Bob; McTurney, Sheila;
Cc: Barge, James;
Subject: Re: Operation Leòdhas

Charming Bob. Sheila.

To: Penny, Sandra; Black, Terrance; Kerlin, Bob; McTurney,

Sheila;
Cc: Barge, James;
Subject: Re: Operation Leòdhas
Hi Jim,
I have been digging into this all day and something just isn't adding up. I have a lead, but I am not sure it's correct. Can I run something past you?
Sandra

To: Penny, Sandra; Black, Terrance; Kerlin, Bob; McTurney, Sheila;
Cc: Barge, James;
Subject: Re: Operation Leòdhas
I'm in meetings all day – can you e-mail? Jim

To: Penny, Sandra; Black, Terrance; Kerlin, Bob; McTurney, Sheila;
Cc: Barge, James;
Subject: Re: Operation Leòdhas
Hi Jim,
Sorry – should have checked your calendar. I can confirm the lead for Morag and Lewis is solid. There's a third man involved potentially. He's been contacting Morag, anyway, using burner phones. The only thing is, when I check out system, he's been dead for years.
Sandra

To: Penny, Sandra;
Subject: Re: Operation Leòdhas
It's common for people to use deceased identities – happens all the time, harder to track. Who's he using?

To: Barge, James
Subject: Re: Operation Leòdhas
Charles [redacted]
Sandra

To: Penny, Sandra;

Subject: Re: Operation Leòdhas [PRIVATE]
Fuck. Keep this between us Sandra. Please? Jim

To: Barge, James;
Subject: Re: Operation Leòdhas
Ok. Want me to follow it up?

To: Penny, Sandra;
Subject: Re: Operation Leòdhas [PRIVATE]
No, I'll do it. Thanks. You follow up Morag, keep a close eye on her. Ta.

It was now quarter to three. He bundled the papers into his pocket, and walked out of the house. He didn't bother locking the door. Nothing in there mattered. As he walked down the drive, he seen the landlord hiding across the street. Ronnie laughed, and waved. He didn't wave back, so Ronnie stood and stared at him. The man peered back. Ronnie walked towards the car, but the window zipped up and all four doors to the Land Rover clicked as they were locked from the inside.

'I'll call the police,' said the man inside the car.

'You can't,' said Ronnie bitterly. 'He was murdered last week.'

Ronnie jumped back into his car, started his engine and his phone rang. It was his grandad. He winced and answered it.

'Ronnie, don't hang up. I'm so sorry, son. Please listen.' He was inconsolable. In between the pangs of absolute heartbreak, he sniffed and spat words out. 'I didn't want you to miss the funeral. I was just angry. Upset. Please forgive me. I can't fathom why I was angry at you. I just… Jim… my best friend…'

'I forgive you,' Ronnie said softly. He was careful not to make this any worse.

'You do? Oh thank you Lord.' The old man took a deep breath and blew it straight into the microphone of the phone.

'We need to go see Lewis,' Ronnie almost didn't want to say it. 'I don't want to, but if we don't, then who will?'

His grandad didn't reply.

'I can go alone, it's fine.'

'No, it's not that. I've known for a few days that we would have to face him. I'm just scared that I am going to hear the answers I expect from him.'

'I'll come get you, see you soon.'

They were at the prison in no time, and both men were signed into the visitor's room waiting on Lewis. Unlike Ronnie's last visit, the room was bare. They were the only visitors so far. The visiting system had been revised many times since that fateful day Ronnie last walked inside its doors.

'Listen, son… I don't want you to think that I'm not here for you, but… I don't think I can face him just yet. He did kill my friend.'

Ronnie put his arm around his grandad and hugged him tightly. 'It's fine. I'm surprised you came at all. I think I need to face him alone. He'll be different with me.'

'Why?' Ron asked, concerned.

'He hates me more than you.' Ronnie lied.

Ron stumbled out of the visitor room, back to the car, and Ronnie now sat alone waiting for Lewis to enter in to confront him. The last time Ronnie had sat in the room alone, his brother had just caused one hell of a brawl. He had sat, almost in the exact same position, with the prison officer waiting on Barge to come in. This time, Barge would not be coming.

He heard banging from behind the door down the hall to the rear. There was only one person who would be making so much noise. Lewis, with two officers, burst into the room. He was swearing, telling them to let him go. They almost dragged him back inside until he realised he had no option but to calm down.

Ronnie sniggered. He imagined that Lewis had fit quite nicely back into the prison. After all, he had spent a lot of his life in there. It would be like a homecoming, he suspected.

'Lewis,' Ronnie nodded.

'I'm saying nothing.'

'Lovely to see you, then.' Ronnie whispered. 'Why are saying nothing?'

'My representative told me. Say nothing, to nobody.' Lewis

didn't even look Ronnie in the eye, as though it took him that much effort to keep his mouth shut.

'I'm your brother,' Ronnie said with an incredibly light heart. 'You can talk to me, surely?'

'Nothing,' Lewis said loudly, craning his neck towards Ronnie. 'Nothing to nobody.'

'Who's your representative?' Ronnie asked.

'Does it matter? You won't know him. He's not a solicitor, but he's a good man and he's doing a fucking excellent job so far. He's had me do a few jobs, and he's helping me out in return.'

Ronnie sat and looked at him, puzzled. 'So, a man gave you a few jobs, and in return for helping him do those jobs, he's helping you fight a charge of murder? You can't be serious.'

Lewis stared at him, and didn't move his lips. He was deadly serious.

'Who is he?' Ronnie asked.

'You don't know him,' said Lewis, snapping bac

'I didn't ask if I knew him, ya fanny.' Ronnie didn't have patience with his brother. 'How long have you known him?'

'Long enough.'

'Smashing,' Ronnie said as he looked over his shoulder to see the time.

'He'll be here soon.'

'How is it?' Ronnie asked.

'In prison? Really?' Lewis scowled. 'It's fucking terrible. The bloke on my bunk keeps asking to suck my cock. Do I look like a fag?'

'Bit offensive,' Ronnie quipped and he wiped his nose with the end of his sleeve.

The door behind Ronnie creaked open, and a smile was bred up upon Lewis' face. Ronnie didn't dare move his head around his shoulders. He knew, despite his best hope, who was standing behind him. It was too obvious. Even, you, reading this now, must know who it was who walked through the door. You must have even half an idea why Ronnie went to see Lewis. It wasn't because he tried to kill Barge – he was never smart enough to do that on his own. It was to see who forced his hand.

'It's about fucking time,' Lewis spat loudly. 'I've been sat with this wanker asking me all sorts of questions, and he won't leave me alone.'

The steps behind Ronnie grew louder and louder and then, a hand was placed upon his shoulder. It was cold through his shirt. It felt deathly.

'I thank you for your time today, Mr Macleod, but there is no longer a need for you to ask any information of my client.' The forced fanciful intonation of his voice made Ronnie angry without even turning his head.

'Ronnie, meet my representative. Charles.'

By the time Lewis has finished talking, Ronnie's entire focus was on Charles. The two men said nothing to each other, but not even Lewis was stupid enough to confuse the nuclear tension.

'I have asked you this a number of times in your life, Lewis, but this time I really mean it.' Ronnie's pupils darted widely towards his brother. 'Are you stupid? Do you have any idea who this man is?'

'He's a good friend,' said Lewis.

'A good friend?' Ronnie asked, laughing. 'He's a bloody maniac.'

'Lewis…' Charles spoke softly, but he was cut off.

Ronnie stood up and walked off down the hall. He was sure he could manage staying in the same room as Charles, but he couldn't. The frustration inside him, that grew by the day, took over and he kicked his chair onto its back. 'I'm done with this,' he seemed to say as he walked down the hall. Lewis and Charles looked to each other, Lewis was confused. Charles just pretended to be confused.

'… do not speak to Ronnie anymore. He's only going to want to ensure your guilt.' Charles placed a hand on Lewis' shoulder, but the guard at the end of the room grunted to have it removed. 'You only talk to me, remember that. From now, though, you say absolutely nothing to anyone. If they ask, you do not answer. Do not even grunt. Look them in the eye to ensure that they remain scared of you. Fight if you must. However, from now until I next see you, you must be silent. Do you understand?'

'Yes, Charles. GUARD!'

Charles frowned at him. 'Nobody, Lewis. Nobody,' he stood and waved to the guard. 'I think we are finished, sir. Thank you for your time today.'

The guard looked at the two men, wondering why they had bothered at all for such a short meeting. If that was all he wanted to say, couldn't they have just phoned one another? Lewis walked back with the guard, until the two men heard Charles cough from the other end of the room. His expression was not one he had shown to Lewis before. It was conniving, thinking, deadly, dangerous.

'I don't mean to add to your work today, officer, but when we were talking just there... Lewis said to me, and I don't mean this as a literal quote, that he was thinking about stabbing you too. I don't want to scare you, sir. By no means, no…. it's just, he told me he'd love nothing more than, excuse my language, to rip your throat out. Whilst I must represent my colleague in his best interests, given that he has shown me the blade he intends to harm you with, I cannot, in good faith, allow him to carry out such a heinous act. It's in his left pocket.'

That was all he needed. Lewis kicked off, and the guard blinded him with pepper spray. Charles was out of the room before Lewis could even scream. More guards flooded in, and they too heard of Lewis' alleged remarks.

Ronnie, who was stood outside, would never learn that his brother was placed into solitary confinement for nothing more than a lie. Somehow, letters would be found – alleged to be from Lewis – describing how he killed Barge and loved every second. Then more appeared, describing how he would torture the next guard to anger him. His punishment was fitting then. He would never prove otherwise. His behaviour would prevent it. Ronnie would never dream of speaking to him, or his mother, again. The Macleod clan was finally in tatters.

Ronnie was still too angry to return to his grandad, who sat patiently in the car. Probably asleep. Ronnie couldn't believe what it had all come to. What started out as an odd kidnap, had torn everything up. Friends, family, memories, were all taken in and eaten by the storm of Charles. He looked to the car, and wondered at what point the single person he cared about would be dragged into the ordeal.

'Terrible news, isn't it? James was a kind man.'

Ronnie turned to see Charles leaning against the prison wall, around the corner from where Ron could see him in the car mirror.

'Get to fuck, Charles.' Ronnie faced him square. 'I know what you did.'

'No, you don't.' Charles was smug. He was smiling.

'Don't I?' Ronnie asked. 'Morag wouldn't be able to afford a gun in her wildest dreams. She's not even smart enough to find one. She walks outside with it, and she's immediately caught because she doesn't understand why doing what she did was wrong. You're telling me you had nothing to do with what she did?'

'Don't put words into my mouth, Mr Macleod.' Charles lit a cigarette and inhaled it sharply. 'I imagine you've drawn your own conclusion. You're very smart. You're most of the way there. However, you'll never figure it all ou-'

'It was you,' interrupted Ronnie. 'You gave Jim that injection. Lewis isn't the one who killed him. You are.' Ronnie took a step closer to Charles, to intimidate him. 'I'm smarter than you're giving me credit for, and I'm smarter than you'll ever be.'

Charles applauded and laughed. 'Yes, Ronnie. Yes!'

Ronnie stood and looked him, as he celebrated the murder of a close, family friend. He felt his fist clench tighter, as he tried to remain calm. Ronnie always found it hard to bite his tongue. 'Don't talk like that, not to me and not about Barge.'

'If you're so bothered,' Charles took another long drag of his cigarette, 'why don't you go to the police? Why don't you tell them that I am a murderer?'

The Truth Hurts

Ronnie didn't need to answer that.

'I need you, boy. You are a genius in disguise. Work with me. Help me, and I will show you the world. I'll make you the most powerful man in the world... after me.'

'Jesus Christ, Charles.' Ronnie gasped, laughed, and threw his hands up into the air in a total loss to desperation. 'I've said no. Nothing will make me change that.'

Ronnie hadn't admitted that he hadn't personally figured any of this out. Jim had. His e-mails were enough for Ronnie to bridge the gap between fact and suspicion. Then there was the night in the hospital. Barge wasn't whispering his name because he knew Ronnie's secret. He whispered his name because Charles was the nurse. Barge must have recognised him the second he walked into the room.

'Nothing?' Charles asked as he stubbed his cigarette out onto the wall leaving a black, stinging mark. Ronnie found it a suitable metaphor for the mark Charles left on his life. 'Are you sure?'

'Nothing. I've told you countless times.'

'I think I may have something to sway your decision.'

'I don't think you do, Charles. You've tried hard, but you've failed and I'm sorry. You won't be used to it, but this time, you're going to have to accept it. You won't break me.'

'Your grandfather, Ron... how is his health?'

'Fine,' Ronnie said threateningly. 'Don't you dare.'

Charles pulled a document, sealed with the stamp of Ronnie's local hospital, and placed it into Ronnie's hand. Ronnie took it, but did not open it. His eyes still did not break from Charles, and he gave Ronnie the same respect.

'What's this?'

'It's a report, from your grandad's last meeting at the hospital. I believe you were working that day, and you were short of cover so his carer had to take him. He never did tell you anything other than it was fine, like he always would. So why would you suspect anything?'

'If you've made this up, Charles, and I open this and find out it is false… I will punch you right in the throat. I don't care if we are outside a prison. I'd quite happily do time to hurt you.' Ronnie looked to the car, to make sure his grandad was still happily distracted. He did not want him to see this side of himself. This was not a version he could be proud of.

'Well,' Charles continued as though Ronnie had never spoken. 'He had previously had a check because, as you'll remember, he was struggling to swallow. It was rather sore for him, don't you remember? You will. I know you, Ronnie. Well, he told you that it came back all clear. He even told the carer to tell you the same thing. He didn't want to worry you, because, as he put it, you have enough on your plate with his other illnesses. One more won't kill him. Which is ironic, because this one will.'

Ronnie had seen his grandad get thinner and thinner in the months that had passed since his last check. He'd become a little greyer too. Ronnie had put that to old age. Neither man hid secrets from the other. At least, that is what both men thought.

'Cancer, Ronnie.' Charles had put himself off his next cigarette by the mere thought of it, and put it back into his jacket pocket. 'He doesn't have long at all. I'll be surprised if he makes Christmas. To be honest with you, the doctor gave him far less. Ron hopes he'll go in his sleep, so you'll think it's old age. The cancer would come out once he died, but then, what could you do? You'd only mourn the fact you wished you had known. Sure, you might beat yourself up for not finding out sooner, but what could you do? He would be dead. You can't kill him again.'

'Enough,' Ronnie barked.

'I know someone who can cure him, Ronnie.' Charles pulled out his phone and waved it in his face. 'The second you finish my job, I can bring my guy in and he can cure him. You'll have however many years Ron has left past his cancer. However, if you're still not interested, then you can have however many seconds left to watch him die… in absolute agony, of course.'

Ronnie opened the letter, and read it in its entirety. All signatures were legitimate. Ron did indeed have cancer in his oesophagus. It was ripping him apart dramatically. The doctor remarked that this was the most aggressive he had seen it. He was shocked by the effect it was having on Ron's body. He put it down to Ron's other illnesses having broken him. The cancer was just the end of a long, hard battle.

'Say yes, and I'll cure him when you're done. It won't take you long. You're a genius, Ronnie. There is nobody else who can solve this, I am certain of it. I would not drag you to this point if I was not so sure. I have spent my whole life looking for you – not you, but someone as good as you. There is nobody. I didn't want to have to break you. You made me do that.'

'You don't know me,' said Ronnie. 'How might you know I'm a genius? We've never met, not until you kidnapped me on that boat. You can't work anything out just from that. I might be the thickest clown you have ever met.'

'We both know that's not correct.'

'True,' sighed Ronnie. 'You've met my brother.'

'You're quite the comedian,' said Charles in a thinly veiled laugh. 'You don't have five As at Higher and another two As at Advanced Higher without learning to read a word or two.'

Ronnie ignored him. His grandad had cancer. He would die, if he didn't help him. Of everything that had happened to him, since Charles entered his life, this was the worst.

'If you agree, we leave this weekend. I reckon it will take you no more than a week. Enough time to save Ron. I will have my man on standby. I have money. He will take it. He will want what I pay him. You have my word, Mr Macleod.'

'If you kill him, I will kill you. There is absolutely no doubt in my mind about that,' Ronnie said, pointing to the car.

'Of that, Mr Macleod, I have absolutely no doubt.' He took a step back. 'Give me your word and we can begin.'

Ronnie scanned the report again and slid his hand into his pocket. He knew that Charles would do everything in his ability to have Ronnie agree to whatever it was he needed done. He put his phone to his ear, but he could hear a click. 'Give me your phone,' Ronnie asked.

Charles was anxious. 'Why?'

'If you want me to even consider this job, you'll give me your phone. I don't care what's on it, I just know that it'll be the only phone you won't have tampered with.' Ronnie outstretched his palm. 'Give me the phone, or I'll walk away.'

Charles gave him his iPhone. This one did not make the same clicking sound. He knew that he was safe. He made a call to the hospital close to his home, and a familiar voice answered. It was as honest as it was going to get.

'Hi there, this is Ronnie Macleod. Yes, I'm very well thanks. Listen, I think my grandad may be hiding something from me. Yes, he had an appointment with his carer. That's the one. He's been getting frailer, and I just worry he's told me a lie that he's okay. Really? Oh my word. No. Not your fault. Thanks for your help.'

Cancer. He was right. Charles looked almost smug about it.

'You can fuck off,' Ronnie said as he slapped the iPhone back into his hand. 'I want something else.'

'I doubt I will be able to help.'

'Then neither can I,' Ronnie replied boldly. 'I'll agree, when you agree.'

'It would depend what you want.' Charles wiped his brow with his handkerchief. ' I can't make a miracle.'

'You're not in a place to negotiate. My old man is almost dead anyway.' Ronnie choked a little on his words. 'You might cure him tomorrow and he'll be dead the next day. I want something to make this worth my while.'

There was a long silence, where Ronnie looked directly to Charles as he stared down at the ground trying to come to a decision in his mind. For a brief moment. Ronnie was certain that he would back down. It was certainly what he wanted.

'Fine,' Charles said. 'What do you want?'

'Why are you so interested in my family?' Ronnie's lips hadn't touched before he spoke again, interrupting Charles in his attempts to excuse himself from the question. 'I don't want a lie. I don't want a vague reason about the one time you met my grandad. This is a whole lot deeper than that. You don't take an interest in my brother or my mother because you worked with an old man. Tell me the truth.'

Charles sighed. He asked questions, he didn't answer them, but Ronnie was his last resort. He absolutely had to have him help. 'It's a long story, I'm not sure this is one for right now.'

'Tell me the abridged version then. I will walk away. There's a picture on my grandad's wall of the two of you shaking hands. You've ordered my own brother to kill a police officer and Morag seems to do everything you tell her as well. Now you're here, hassling me.' Ronnie stared at him, counting every one of the ten seconds that past. 'Come on, Charles.'

'Ron doesn't know the truth.'

'I don't care, I want to know. Right now.'

'Can't I just tell you another time?'

'No. You can't.'

Charles had never looked so nervous. He didn't want to say anything, he didn't want it coming out. But there was too much to lose. It was a tough choice to make. Yet, there was no choice in it. He just couldn't bring himself to make it. He either told him the truth, and risked ruining his name, or he left it and lost out on the prize he so desperately wanted.

'I'm going to leave now, Charles. You're wasting my time.'

'Fine,' sighed Charles. 'Lewis is my son.'

FLASHBACK IV

Ron inhaled deeply over his cup of fresh coffee. The bitter sting from the Latin American beans set his senses on fire. It had been a long evening, and this was exactly what he needed before an early rise the next day. School had finished early that Friday, as it always did, and Ronnie was more hyper than Ron had seen him, or expected.

'I can't wait, Grandad. It's going to be brilliant, isn't it?' Ronnie skipped from pavement slab to pavement slab, trying to swing a leg out onto the road before his grandad gripped his collar and dragged him beside the wall which ran along the houses.

'You can't go out onto the road, Ronnie. I've told you that countless times.' Ron scowled, and Ronnie calmed down. At least until he got home.

'I know, Grandad. I'm sorry. It's just, this is the most excited I've been for it. I don't even know if I will sleep tonight, my head is full of bees and my tummy is full of butterflies. I've never had a proper one before. Never in my life.'

That broke Ron's heart. To know that he was the first person giving young Ronnie something he absolutely deserved, it made him twinge with sadness. See, Ronnie had had six of them before but nobody around him, other than his grandad, had cared. In fact, Ron was sure he was the only one who remembered. Yet that didn't matter. What did matter, to them both, was that this would be the best birthday yet. Ronnie would turn seven with the biggest smile on his face.

It was probably his own fault for winding him up so much about it. After two hours of continuous sofa jumping – to escape the lava, Ronnie said – Ron had had enough and sent him to bed warning that no presents would come if he weren't asleep by the time Ron came to turn off his bedside light.

Ronnie was asleep in seconds. His grandad watched him sleep. In the first few weeks since moving in, Ronnie slept with a scowl on his face. Often, Ron found himself hugging Ronnie as he whimpered in his sleep. Morag had never cuddled the boy in his life, and he could tell that the bed terrors had not just appeared overnight. They were manifested in a childhood of abuse. These days, however, Ronnie slept smiling. Sometimes he would laugh out loud in his sleep. Ron hoped it was him. He hoped Ronnie remembered the laughs they would share. He wanted to be sure that everything he did now made the boy happy.

He had tried to stay up to watch Crystal Maze, but he fell asleep. He had gone through to his bed, and he was certain he had only just closed his eyes again when his heart jumped out of his pyjamas and the corner of his bed twanged with the springs.

'Jesus Christ,' he shouted as he opened his eyes, rubbing them. 'What the hell is going on?'

Ronnie, dressed in bright yellow pyjamas, was jumping up and down on the end of the bed. 'Happy birthday to me, happy birthday to me, happy birthday dear Ronnie…' He lifted his feet and jumped high, forcing himself forwards to his grandad. '…happy birthday to me!' Ronnie hugged his grandad tighter than he had in his entire life.

'Happy birthday, lad.' Though he was angry to be awoken, there was something innocent about it all. Ronnie was happy, and all he had to do was make sure he went to bed in the same mood. 'Did you sleep well?'

'No,' Ronnie said, bouncing as though the entire concept of sleep was completely unimportant to a, now, seven-year-old boy.

'What do you mean no?' Ron said, choking on a Rennie. His black coffee before bed had jabbed at his stomach all night and his throat was alive with stomach acid.

'I heard you coming into my room, so I pretended to be asleep. You were there for ages too, so I just sat with my eyes shut until you went to sleep and then I read my stories until the sun came back up and I thought to myself, I'm going to wake grandad up.' Ronnie spoke entirely innocently, reading the back of a Brut aftershave bottle as though it interested him. 'So, I did.'

Ron shook his head, and got out of bed.

'What's for breakfast?' Asked Ronnie.

'Whatever you like, lad.'

'I want…'

Ronnie ran out of the room without answering him. He was too excited to open his presents, and when he opened his eyes in the living room he almost fainted. The living room couch must have stretched out to at least eight feet in length, and it was full, from edge to edge with presents. Some big, some small. Some tall, some wide. There were one or two that Ronnie would struggle to lift on his own.

'Wow.' Ronnie took the biggest gasp of air. He wasn't sure he would be able to take anymore. He was in so much shock. 'Presents.'

Ron helped him to a seat before he fell over, and he allowed his small grandson to take it all in. He would look from the gifts to his grandad, as though he were certain none of this were true and he would wake up back in his nightmare that he escaped one year ago.

'Is this really all mine?'

Ron didn't need to tell him a third time. He ran into the pile and tore the paper off, throwing it all around the room leaving books, sweets, clothes and all sorts of video games for his PlayStation. There was one present left, and it was the biggest in the room. It was almost as tall as Ronnie.

'Read the tag,' said Ron, pointing to the label on the front of the box.

'Dear Ronnie,' he said as he flipped it over. 'Happy birthday, lots of love, mummy.'

There was a sort of bittersweet feeling to it all. He was sure she hated him, but here he was, stood in front of a box that was wider than him and almost as tall. He tore a small piece, and seen the brand. Raleigh. That was all he needed. He tore at it, pulling at larger pieces of wrapping paper and whipping at others so that the box fell over revealing a black and red Raleigh bike.

'No stabilisers,' Ron said with a smile. His grandson was over the moon.

There was a moment of calm. Where Ronnie didn't know how to react. He verged on an anxiety attack. His mind did not know how to translate the overloading senses into emotion. His breathing shallowed, and then it stopped. Ronnie went white.

'Can we ride it? Can we?' Ronnie had begun jumping from couch to couch again, and Ron had to jump up to grab him midair. He wasn't sure, no matter the cost of them, that the springs inside the leather couches would last much longer. 'Please grandad. My mum bought me a bike!'

'She did, she was hoping you would like it.'

'I love it! It's the best present I've ever had. Oh my God, I always wanted a bike.' Ronnie patted the box with his small hands, and then he hugged it.

'Mum's know best,' Ron said, smiling.

'Can I ride it?'

'No,' said Ron, almost breaking Ronnie's heart. 'Not this morning, anyway. We need to go and see someone special.'

'Lewis?' Ronnie asked, with a sigh. 'I don't want to see Lewis. He's not nice.'

'Not Lewis, lad. Santa.'

It would not be possible to fit any more excitement into a young boy. He had peaked, and if he died tomorrow, he would die happier than he would ever be the rest of his life. He ran and ran until he had to stop and sit down to stop himself being sick. 'Santa? Are you kidding me?'

Ronnie was born on the 21 December. His birthday was four days before Christmas. Ron's bank card knew this only too well. A truck full of gifts for each day had cost a pretty figure. He had not forgotten that he no longer worked, and that each payment dwindled his remaining balance. If Ronnie had many more birthdays like this, then Ron would be forced back to work. He would need to give Ronnie a traditional day next year – drink, drugs and the Police arriving to arrest him just before dinner.

Ronnie put on his new jeans and his favourite t-shirt, and he was stood by the door waiting for almost half an hour before his grandad came to the door. 'Ready?' his grandad would ask. Ronnie nodded, and he ran out to the car.

They drove for almost ninety minutes. There were plenty Santa's in between, not that Ronnie would know, but Ron wanted one that would be somewhere new. Somewhere that they wouldn't be recognised.

The Gyle Shopping Centre was full to the brim. One person would walk out, and five would walk in. Ron looked to the door and shuddered. He hated crowds. He hated the eternal, false apologies that people would give as they tried to barge their way through. *Oh, sorry I didn't see you.* Of course, you didn't. You were staring right at me, and our eyes met, but there was no way that you noticed a man one foot taller and wider.

Not only that, but the queue to meet Santa was a two hour wait. Ronnie had lost the will to live after a further ninety minutes. 'We're never going to see Santa, grandad.' He hugged his grandad's leg. He was a lot smaller than the other children around his age. Whilst the others ran around with each other, Ronnie stayed close to his grandad. He wasn't ready to trust a friend yet.

People were dragged either side of the queue like cattle. The people to Ron's left were coming in, and those to the right were leaving. It was a lot tighter to the right. There were twice as many people, and four times as many bags. Ron could hear the credit cards cry. They had taken a pounding.

'We're next!' Ronnie threw his hands into the air and fell to his knees. 'Santa, Santa, Santa! I am going to tell him what my mum bought me, would that be okay? Would she be okay if I told Santa what she bought me?'

'Of course,' said Ron, smiling. 'He'll want to know that your

The Truth Hurts

mum has been behaving, just like you.'

Ronnie froze for a moment, and looked to his grandad with his eyes opened wide. 'Have I been good?'

'Well…'

Ronnie's eyes began to well up. The fact that his grandad had not been able to answer immediately was enough. Ron had to kneel and hug him tightly, whispering into his ear. 'You've been perfect, lad. Santa will already know.'

'What a relief,' said Ronnie as he sniffed loud enough for the end of the queue to hear him. 'I thought… I thought he'd take my bike. My mum would be mad.'

The elf called Ronnie forward and he sprinted inside the Grotto to meet Santa Claus. Meanwhile, Ronnie scraped his wallet for eighteen pounds fifty. He could not believe the cost. If Ronnie just wanted to sit on an old man's knee and tell him what to buy for Christmas, then his grandad could offer him that for free, and for as long as he wanted.

'Look who the fuck it is,' a voice snarled from behind him. At first, Ron didn't notice that there was someone behind him. The large words, THANK YOU FOR YOUR PURCHASE, still ringing in his head. 'You come to these sorts of places to keep away from people like you.'

He turned, and his heart dropped. In all her yellowing glory, stood Morag. Ron could smell the mulled wine from her breath and her eyes wobbled from one side to the other. She had a plastic bag, but it was empty. It was a Safeway bag, with dribbles of red wine in the bottom.

'Did you heat that mulled wine up before you drank it?' Asked Ron.

'Does it fucking matter?' She said, snarling.

'Suppose not.'

Ron turned back to the grotto, before realising that he was giving too much away in doing that. He tried to turn back, but Morag had already caught on. He knew that. She was too bright for her own good.

'Is Ronnie in there?'

'Yes,' said Ron. 'You won't be seeing him.'

'How the fuck not?' Morag shouted louder this time, and people were noticing their conversation. Ron peered into the Grotto, but he couldn't see Ronnie. He hoped that Santa had an extensive list to write down. He didn't want him walking out to see his mother. Ron knew it was about to get bitter. 'You're always trying to hurt me, Ron.'

'There are children,' Ron said staring above her to the crowds behind. 'You cannot be talking like that when there are children around, Morag.'

She looked to the young boy behind him, who was no older than ten. Then she looked back to Ron. 'I'm sure he's heard the word cunt before, Ron. I want to see my son for Christmas. I'll get him a wee selection box out the 99p shop.'

'Just for Christmas?' Ron asked, his lips trembling. 'What about his birthday, Morag?'

Morag looked at him, clueless. She had absolutely no idea what he was talking about, but more importantly, she needed another drink. She was beginning to shake.

'I mean, you're the one who sat and gave birth for however many hours. You'd think, given the pain, that you'd remember it was today. Or are you just that bad a mother that you can't remember the date that everything happened.' Ron put both clenched fists into his pocket. 'This is exactly why you don't get to see Ronnie.'

'Everything?' Morag's eyes screwed up as she looked to Ron.

'Are you fu-' Ron had to stop himself abruptly. 'Are you kidding me?' Ron looked around him for a security guard. He needed her to leave him alone. 'Walk away from me right now.'

'I need to get my boy something for his birthday-'

'So, you can remind him again five minutes later about how much you hate him, and you wanted to kill him when he was a baby?' Ron hadn't been this angry in seven years. 'You honestly cannot comprehend how easy it is for you to ruin the last few pieces of respect I have for you. I look at you, and it disgusts me.'

'Excuse me sir,' the elf to his left tried to break the conversation apart, but Ron swung his hand in her way to stop her pushing him.

'You are not getting to see him, Morag. He got his present from you. A bicycle. I shouldn't have paid for it. I shouldn't have paid for any of it, from Lewis, from the two of you. He's gone in there thinking that you and his big brother have gone out of your way to make him happy for once. I'm hoping it might take the edge of the years of abuse. Now, you can sit here and tell me what you think about me and how much you hate me, but I am going to put my energy into what matters… making that little bloody lad happy on his birthday.' He took a breath, holding back his tears.

He hadn't even finished speaking as the guard came up from behind and scooped Morag into the crowds. She fell onto her knees, and as she was pulled, the strangers swallowed her up and she vanished. It was as though she had never been there at all.

'I'm really sorry, pet.' Ron turned back to the assistant. 'It's a long story, and it's full of hate. It's the only thing that gets me angry.'

'It's okay,' she replied awkwardly. 'I just wanted to ask, would you like your photo with Ronnie and Santa?'

TEN

Ronnie laughed the whole way home. Ron was asleep when Ronnie got back into the car, and he didn't wake the entire way home despite Ronnie's chortling. Of everything about how Charles displayed himself, as the intellectual gentlemen who appeared to be incredibly rich… he had an affair with Morag. The heroin loving, abusive, criminal, scum bag woman that everyone knew.

'His fucking dad!' Ronnie set himself off again. 'I can't believe it.'

Charles' attempt at an excuse was that he needed something and Morag was the only person willing to give him it. He didn't explain why this lead to them sleeping together, or how they came to have a child. It was all part of the end game, allegedly. Ronnie didn't believe any of it.

Only when his cheeks were aching and his sides split, did Ronnie stop laughing. He had suddenly remembered his grandad was dying. So it was then, that he agreed to help. He was sure to make the point that he was helping Ron, now Charles, however. The fact that he was enabling Charles to further his "business" was a coincidence, in his book.

'He will be in touch,' Charles said in his parting comments.

'Who?' Ronnie asked.

'My colleague, I just explained that.' Charles frowned. 'Don't you listen? He will tell you everything you need to know. Good luck.'

He waited until he was back at his grandad's home before waking him. They went inside, and he carried his grandad to bed. As he sat now, looking at him, he struggled to understand just why he had never quite realised how ill his grandad was. His skin was almost grey, and his eyes were more bloodshot than usual. He had spent many years with a wheeze, but this wheeze caught on the phlegm in his lungs. He spent more time coughing it up, than he did resting.

'Are you sure you're alright?' Ronnie asked.

Ron coughed, and then coughed again. Before he knew it, he had been coughing for well over a minute. He had clenched hold of the side of the bed, dragging breaths into his lung. He nodded, and lay down on his pillow once again. He was knackered.

'I'm not sure that you are,' said Ronnie. 'What's up?'

'A cold, I think...' Ron was still gasping. 'Nothing to worry about.'

'You look awful,' Ronnie said as he interrupted any pleas of protest with a firm, open hand.

Ron croaked at him, as he fluffed around to find his grandson's hand. His skin was cold and leathery. It gave Ronnie a fright when he first felt them. There was a definite moistness to them. He was clearly nervous of the truth. He didn't even look him in the eye, he just ignored him. Ronnie just wanted him to be honest. He already knew everything.

'I...'

'It's cancer, isn't it?' Ronnie blurted it out accidentally. A moment later, he realised what he'd done and just opened his mouth for no sound to come out. He began to sweat himself now, and he felt his grandad's hand tremble on the side of the mattress.

'I... Sorry...' Tears fell from his grandad's eyes. His old, wrinkly skin was a draining board for them and they fell straight down to his striped pyjama shirt and duvet. He had lost the ability to speak.

'It's fine,' whispered Ronnie. His grandad immediately gripped his hand tightly. 'Honest. You don't need to worry about what I'm thinking. All I'm worrying about is you.

'I don't want to leave you,' Ron spluttered through his tears.

'You were always going to leave me. That's how this works.

Otherwise it's a tragedy. Don't struggle with this battle on your own just because of that worry. It's hard enough to have cancer. Dad did that, and you know how you felt about that.'

Ron completely forgot he had told his grandson that. He didn't die of cancer, of that he was sure. These days, he couldn't remember what had happened. His mind was full and accurate, but he had long tried to forget about his son's passing. It hurt him too much. That was why he wouldn't mention it. He did not want to tear open an old wound. If he thought about it one more time, he knew that it would kill him.

Ronnie consoled his grandad for some time. It was almost as though the tension between the two vanished entirely. It was so obvious to Ronnie now, why he had been so angry. He was fighting cancer alone.

'I'm taking you on holiday,' Ronnie said, unannounced. He had planned to take his grandad with him, to care for him on this job that Charles was forcing him into.

'I'm not fit enough to be going anywhere, lad. I haven't been on a plane in years.'

'Are you mental?' Ronnie asked with a smile. 'I don't have the money to be going abroad, this place and your care drains me. I'm on beans and toast back home when I'm not in here with you. We're going somewhere local… sort of.'

They spoke for many minutes after, but it was meaningless nothings from the football fixtures at the weekend to what Ronnie had had for his lunch that day. Finally, Ron was calm enough again that his eyelids began to bounce slowly up and down as he ventured closer to sleep. 'Do you remember…' He spoke softly. 'When you were a lad…'

His eyes closed.

Ronnie's phone buzzed as he clicked the front door shut and rattled the handle to make sure it was locked. It was odd to do that, there were so many emergency keys, Ronnie was sure you could get inside anyway.

'You're taking the piss, Ronnie.' The voice on the end of the phone pranged into Ronnie's ear. *'I've been outside all fucking*

night waiting on you.'

'Love you too darling, I'll be there soon.' He was sure he'd told them to phone. Well, in all honesty, he wasn't. He had forgotten what he'd agreed to. To a point, he didn't care. It wasn't as much about what he was required to do, it was more that there was an end goal that he absolutely needed. He *had* to make his grandad better. That was it.

Once he was home, he opened his car at the same time as a door to a black Audi. A tall, pasty white man climbed out. He was completely bald, devoid of stubble or even eyebrows. He was almost leathery. His eyes were dark, and sunken into his head.

'You ill?' Ronnie asked, half smiling.

'Fuck off,' the man said. 'Any funny business, and I'll break you.'

Ronnie was not surprised to find tension between him and the man. He was sure Charles would have warned him that Ronnie could be *mildly* annoying.

'Ah, but you can't,' said Ronnie as he slid his key into the front door of his home. 'I'm the chosen one. Charles needs me. You can't hurt me when your boss has selected me of the billions and billions of other people who live on this here planet. He's even picked me over you, can you believe that?'

'Just let us in the house, will you.' His Glaswegian accent bit hard. He was getting impatient. He barged into Ronnie's house and almost took the front door off its hinges when he slammed it shut. This took Ronnie by surprise, and so he had to exaggerate just how shocked he was; gasping, and falling against the wall.

'My... you are so strong.'

The man gave no response. He stormed off down the hall into the kitchen, and Ronnie heard his case thud against his wooden table. He had spent two grand on that, and his new friend was trying to hammer his way through the varnish. Perhaps he should start being a bit nicer to him, he thought. Bugger that, he thought immediately after.

'You haven't even told me your name,' Ronnie said as he climbed from the floor.

'You don't need to know my name.'

'Can I make up a name for you?'

'Do whatever you want.'

'I'll call you Doreen.'

'My name is Brian.'

'See,' Ronnie patted him on the back and almost immediately regretted it. 'Brian is a lovely name. Are you named after anyone, Brian?'

He was ignored. He was too busy making himself a sandwich to notice. He piled it into his toastie machine, and struggled to close it due to the filling being over an inch thick. He ignored the cheese fall out either side as he turned back to Brian, who looked like he was about to walk out.

'I work for Charles. I'm not here to have you chat me up, Mr Macleod. I'm here to tell you what you need, and I'm fucking going. Do you understand?' Like most Glaswegians, bad language was more a grammatical pause than an offensive remark. Ronnie realised that, and took time to question if he had Glaswegian roots. He *loved* to swear. 'Do you know what Charles' business is?'

'He likes to know everything, about everyone.' Ronnie sipped his tea, and choked. He reminded himself of Charles' paternal relationship to his brother and sniggered. 'His fucking dad.'

'What?'

'He likes to know everything,' repeated Ronnie as he stifled a laughter.

'No, who's fucking their dad?' Brian asked.

'You're a creepy man,' said Ronnie he peered at Brian, chewing a large piece of his overcooked toastie. 'Most people around here, if you must know... Fife is an odd place.'

Brian ignored Ronnie – he had quickly realised not to question anything that he said. 'Charles is a very powerful man, and like you said, he likes to learn. He controls men, because

The Truth Hurts

he knows things about their lives that would ruin them. He controls towns, because he knows exactly what makes up the people who run them. He runs countries, because he knows their deepest, darkest secrets. For all of those reasons, Charles makes a lot of money for us and himself and he is very, very rich. Mr Macleod, people often make allegations about the existence of the illuminati. Charles debunked that quite early on. However, if the illuminati were to exist, Charles would be the closest thing to it.'

'Question,' said Ronnie. 'I know you don't like them, but hear me out… how does me knowing what wee Charles does for a living help me do this fucking mission? Are you guys just taking the piss or what?'

'I think you're taking the piss out of us, Mr Macleod.' Brian opened his case once again and dragged out more documents. He threw them carelessly onto the table, and slammed the lid of his case down over the other files inside. Ronnie really wasn't taking the piss, though. Brian really had lost him.

'I don't have all fucking night, Mr Macleod. Charles believes there is something in this country that he wants, and he wants it very quickly. He believes the answer lies in Lewis.'

'In my brother?' Ronnie flinched. 'Listen here, I am not going inside my brother. I asked him about that sort of thing in prison and he got really angry.'

'The Isle of Lewis, you unfunny arsehole.' Brian slid a map over, which had the island circled in red pen. 'Do you know much about the family from which you descend?'

Ronnie opened his mouth to answer, but Brian quickly realised how widely he had left his question open to a total sarcastic bastard. *Your ancestry*, he snarled. To that, Ronnie had no idea.

'The Macleod clan ruled the island until their power was forfeited to the Scottish Crown. The history book will tell you who they were, and more importantly how they lost their powerful role on the island. Charles believes this to be a lie, to hide what he is looking for. Your family were defending something, Mr

Macleod. Someone found that out and they slaughtered the lot of you.' Brian passed Ronnie an old children's book.

'I've read it,' said Ronnie, serious for the first time.

'You can't have,' snapped Brian, sliding it back along the table.

'You can't be serious. It's hardly a secret text.' Ronnie sniggered, but very quickly realised Brian was very serious indeed. 'Can you?'

'Leod, son of Olaf the Black, was the original keeper of the secret. His son, Torquil, and his brother, Tormod, were the keepers after that. Again, history tells us that Old Rory slaughtered the family and the Mackenzie clan would rise to power. Charles believes that family wanted what the Macleod Clan had. They did not decide to overthrow the Clan Macleod just because. Blood was not shed just because. They wanted something, and it was very clearly lost that day. Charles believes this is the final piece to his puzzle of world domination.'

'You sound like Pinkie and the Brain. *What shall we do ton-*'

Ronnie wasn't sure what happened, but he never got to finish his sentence. His eyesight went, first. Light spun into his head and then everything vanished into a soup of black. Then a sharp pain crossed the right line of his jaw immediately followed by a cracking thud upon the rear of his skull. By the time he had come to, he realised he was on the floor. He was left lying, unconsciously nursing the pain that now thumped inside the back of his head.

He threw one hand onto the drawer in front of him and hoisted himself up. Brian was shaking his fist, like he had just washed his hands. Ronnie was fully unimpressed. He held his mouth, but kept his other injuries secret.

'What are you doing?' Ronnie asked. 'Don't hit me, not in my own house.'

Brian reached into his inside jacket pocket, and laid a small handgun down onto the table that they both sat at. 'I'll shoot you in it next time you decide to be smart, Mr Macleod.'

'What does Charles believe is on the island?' Ronnie tried,

The Truth Hurts

albeit light heartedly, to get Brian back on side.

'He doesn't know,' said Brian. 'That's why we need you to go and figure it out.'

'Wait, how can you know that clan wasn't wiped out?'

'We don't. You're around though, so there's a chance they haven't been.'

'You don't know what I've to return to, though.'

Brian shook his head, and took out a photograph. He turned it, and slide it across the table. In front of Ronnie sat a coloured image of stones, set out in the form of a cross, sat upon a hill. Ronnie looked to it, and Brian, several times. 'I don't get it.'

'*Clachan Chalanais*,' said Brian. 'The Callanish Stones, we believe, hold the secret.'

'Smashing, sounds like you've solved it yourself.' Ronnie immediately winced. His humour reminded him that he was an inch away from a broken jaw.

Brian had almost changed his opinion of the sarcastic bastard across from him. He snatched back the photograph and attempted to calm himself back down into the zen he was in seconds earlier. Then his hand snapped out and caught Ronnie's chin again. Ronnie fell back and hit his head even harder against the drawer which had bounced open when he caught it the first time.

'I've told you plenty times tonight, Mr Macleod.' Brian looked over the counter. Ronnie was holding his nose which was bleeding. 'Don't fucking mess with me.

'The stones were erected in the late Neolithic era, used for rituals in the Bronze age, Mr Macleod. That is as much as we care to know about them in their earliest use. We make guesses, sure. These only push us from the true reason why these exist. We believe, but cannot confirm, that Leod's ancestors made these stones, for whatever purpose. Their true purpose is sure to show us where this object, or objects that Leod held, are hidden.'

Ronnie was punch drunk by the time he got to his feet and slumped onto his breakfast bar stool. He wiped the small dribble of blood from his nose, and he looked at Brian, his eyesight completely fuzzy. 'If these things have existed for so long, how come nobody has gotten even close to solving their true purpose?' Ronnie twitched, his head rumbling. He was too scared to argue with Brian over what he had just done.

'They have, or else the Macleod Clan would never have vanished. The Mackenzies knew what they were after, and they clearly failed.'

'How very odd,' Ronnie said, reading the file.

'And that… is all I can tell you, Mr Macleod.' Brian began to pack his things. 'It's all we know. You leave tomorrow morning, there is a bag by the door, you seen it when you came in. It is filled with all the money, information and tools to get you started. There is also a telephone, you must use this, and only this to contact Charles. You do not discuss this with anyone else.'

'I'm bringing my grandad,' Ronnie said, almost cutting him short.

'You can't.'

'I bloody can,' Ronnie retorted aggressively. 'He's coming with me. I'll protect him.'

'I'm going to have to tell Charles.'

'Fucking tell him then.' Ronnie bent over, his brain cramped. 'I don't care.'

Brian would not respond. Instead, he would pack everything into his suitcase and leave for the door. Ronnie rushed behind him, to the front door, where he stood and stared at Brian as he walked away. He was still in pain from the punch, and that angered him. He did not like to be embarrassed, by anyone.

'Brian!' Ronnie shouted as loud as he could, and Brian turned to look at him in the same motion as he opened the door to his car.

'I'm going to hit you twice as fucking hard the next time I see you. I promise.' Ronnie flipped his middle finger and slammed the door shut. Of course, not without double locking it and staring through the peephole to make sure that Brian drove off into the night, leaving him alone.

FLASHBACK V

Things had not gone well. Ron wasn't sure how much time had passed since he came in and slammed the front door, leaving his keys in the lock. It was surely a day or more. Darkness had come and gone twice from the window overlooking the fields to the rear of his house, but he did not look out to them. Instead, he cried. He cried harder and longer than he ever had in his entire life. This was the memory that Ron Macleod forced himself to forget.

He had had the happiest moment in his life on the same day as the darkest. In that single second of his life, the feeling of invincibility was ruined. He no longer felt like the luckiest person in the world. He felt dead. He didn't care about everything outside of his mind. None of that mattered anymore. There was nothing that could possibly change how he felt.

Four hours earlier, he was on top of the world. Ron had just come back from Dubai. The Investment Bank, of which he had worked since his days as a boy, had sent him there to close one of the most important deals they had ever tried to make. There was nowhere to hide. If he came back having blown the deal, his entire career would be wasted.

'Ladies and gentlemen, we will shortly be arriving in Edinburgh where the temperature is a cool six degrees. For those of you on your first visit to Scotland, jumpers are available from the main terminal.' The pilot's Stockbridge accent and abhorrent posh Edinburgh chortle was unmistakeable. 'Just to prevent any complaints, jumpers are not available from the main terminal.'

The locals on the plane chittered and laughed. Ron heard

them from behind the curtain dividing first class from the rest of the world. He would never have paid for it himself, but given that millions had just flooded into the business, his boss felt it necessary to treat him. He had just finished the smoothest, richest crème brûlée that he could have dreamt of. He barely wanted to lick the remaining morsels from his mouth, just so that he would never be able to forget its incredible taste.

'How was that for you, sir?' A tanned, Liverpudlian took the tray from the shelf in front of him. 'Would you like anything else before we land?'

'I'm fit to bursting,' said Ron, patting his stomach. In these days, it did not hang over his belt. 'I'll be too fat to leave the plane the way I'm eating.'

He looked out of his window and smiled as the mountains and hills came into view. Scotland made his heart beat like nothing else, and a smile appeared gently on the edges of his lips. He tapped the tune to Highland Cathedral on his knee with his hand. There was no greater a patriot than Ron Macleod. He knew everything there was to know about Scotland, and even more about his ancestry. He had taken jobs, voluntarily without pay, just to learn more just so he could teach more.

The aircraft would splash down upon the tarmac at Edinburgh International Airport and screech to a halt mere feet away from the fields in front. Ron would be let off the plane first, sitting in the first seat of first class, and he would run off to collect his bags. He had someone very important to meet. Someone that he was very excited to meet, but someone that also made him very nervous. He wasn't sure if that person would like him, though he hoped greatly that he would.

'Some weather, isn't it?' An elderly man stood beside Ron, as they waited for their bags, and smiled. 'I can't believe we decided to come home.'

Ron smiled. 'Aye, I would have stayed longer… but I'm meeting someone.'

'Anyone exciting?' Asked the man. Old people were always nosey, thought Ron. He tried to make a mental note never to be like that.

'Well,' He paused. He wondered if he should tell anyone. He had kept it a secret for so long, that it felt wrong to finally let it out in the open, especially with someone he had never laid eyes upon until this very second by the carousel. However, his mouth was quicker than his brain. It was out before he thought about it. 'My little grandson was born today.'

The old man smiled, and nudged his wife to tell her the good news too. She appeared from behind him, and she mouthed the word congratulations. Her husband shook his hand, and reached into his pocket, fumbling for a five pound note that he thrust into Ron's hand. 'From us, to him. May the lad have the greatest luck in the world.'

Ron rushed to his car, and by the time he had thrown himself into the driver's seat, he had broken sweat. His grandson was born at 11:40am, and it was now 11:45pm. He was over twelve hours old. He wondered if the little boy would have any idea who he was and if he knew that a man existed who had raised his dad… or was he just hungry, and desperate to latch on to a nipple one more time.

He held his handset to his ear with his shoulder as he reached out onto the A8, driving far faster than he should have been. The phone rang, and a few moments later an elated voice came on the phone.

'Well hello grandad,' said his son. A baby screamed in the background. 'Good job you're rich enough to afford a phone in your car. The wee one is excited to meet you, where are you?'

'The flight was delayed,' said Ron, pausing to hear the gargles and moans from his newest, greatest love. 'He sounds lively.'

'Hasn't shut up since he was born. I think he's going to be a talker.'

'Can't imagine where he gets that, Fin.' Ronnie laughed with his son. 'Listen, I am just driving down the road now. I'll be there soon, but here, listen… Morag… has she been…'

'Don't, Dad.' Fin sighed. 'I'm here for Ronnie.'

'Ronnie?' Ron almost shouted down the phone loud enough

to deafen someone. 'Is that his name?'

'Oh shit,' Fin spat. 'It was supposed to be a surprise. He's another Ronnie Macleod, named after his grandad. He suits it. He's a right old shit as well.'

Again, the two men laughed. They hadn't talked much in the past few weeks. Ron had been working, and he felt guilty. Fin had, stupidly, put himself in a position he could never get out of. At school, Morag had been a gentle, kind soul. Now, she was bitter and ruined. Fin, blinded by an earlier love for her, thought he could change her. That was, of course, before she was pregnant. He had really fucked up, but he was not about to leave his son.

'Lewis,' Fin shouted. 'Put down that bottle. Ronnie needs that.' There was a fumble on the phone speaker as he placed the phone down to grab him. 'Honestly, he's a wee shit and he's at the age where he should know better.'

'Don't fucking swear at him, Fin.' Morag shouted at him in the background.

'I'll see you when you get here dad, ok?' Fin's voice moved from the microphone to the other side of the room, and he could be heard bickering senselessly with Morag.

Ron could sense the stress in his voice, so he let him go. He couldn't believe that his son would let pride get in the way. As time passed, Fin realised that Morag was different. She was not the young girl who smiled her way through life. She was bitter. She was angry. She hated everything and everyone but her little Lewis.

Ron walked into the hospital ward with a balloon that he had paid over the odds for. The nurse at the front desk smiled, and directed him to room nine. There were plenty wards, but only a few rooms. Fin was unlucky enough to be trapped alone in a room with a woman he didn't want to be with. They had long separated, though it had never been said verbally. Fin didn't want to leave his boys, and she wanted to use him for as long as she could.

'Dad,' he exclaimed as Ron walked in the door. They both hugged tighter than they had done in a very long time. 'It's so good to see you, come meet Ronnie.'

Morag barely even looked at Ron as he laid down the balloon and smiled at her.

'Hi Morag,' Ron said, smiling. 'How are you, pet?'

'Whatever.'

Ron looked to her, and then to Fin. Fin wasn't looking back. He was scowling at the mother of his child. 'You could be a bit nicer to my dad, Morag. He's come all the way from Dubai to see us.'

'Did I ask him to come, Fin? No. I didn't.' She had a good point.

Ron walked to the small cot beside him, peered over the edge and felt his heart gush and break all at the same time. He looked to his son and couldn't help but feel uncomfortable about the look in his eye. There was something... different.

Ronnie Macleod was fourteen hours old. He was barely fifty centimetres in length. He was only a fraction of that from one elbow to the other. However, he was the single most beautiful thing that Ron had ever laid his eyes on. His jet-black hair was oversized on his tiny head, and every few seconds his small blue pupils would peer out to see who was out there.

'He's gorgeous, lad.' He shook his son's hand. 'Congratulations.'

'Aye, he is.' The two men stood over the cot for some time in silence, admiring a young man whose innocence was white, perfect and pure. Neither man would admit how close they were to crying, but both knew that this was the most perfect day of their lives.

'He looks just like you,' said Ron to his son.

'He doesn't look like fucking anything,' said Morag from behind them. She was hugging Lewis who had settled now to watch television. 'Not unless anyone in your family is a potato.'

'Aunty Marjorie,' the two men said together.

'Can I have a word with you dad?' Fin looked back to his wife. His green eyes almost scowled as he tried to hide his hatred to his wife. 'Outside.'

'Don't come back if you do,' said Morag, glaring. Fin sighed in return.

The two men walked out of the ward, and through the front door of the hospital into the night sky. It was bitterly cold. Winter had long set in. The car park was empty, so both men took few steps outside before they stopped to face each other.

'I don't know what I was thinking, Dad. I love him more than anything in the world, but why did I have him with her? What went wrong for her to turn like that?' Fin bowed his head. 'I can't live with her. I'm sure she's on something.'

Ron noticed for the first time that Fin looked tired and dejected. He was always so positive and full of promise. There was nothing that could get him down, but as he stood before his father, he looked as though he had had enough.

'You alright?' He asked.

'No,' whispered Fin. He began to walk down the path, away from the hospital towards the main road. Ron followed him, walking just a few inches behind him. 'What do I do? Seriously? I walked away from her and Lewis when I found out about the affair, and I was stupid enough to come back. I can't leave Ronnie, but I don't want to stay with her. There's nothing I can do.'

Though they had never proven it, Fin was certain that Morag was sleeping with someone else. It was just a feeling, more than anything. She never wanted to be close with him. She never wanted to let him lay a hand upon here, far less anything more romantic. So, it was, that Fin deduced that there was someone else. Ron resisted to agree.

'Why did you go back, then?' Ron asked, standing still in the hope Fin would too.

'I wish you'd asked me that then. I might have changed my mind.' Fin kept walking.

The two men walked in silence as they walked away from the car park, and turned right onto the main path to the busy A7 carriageway. Traffic flew past left and right, and both men could hear the whizz of the vehicles as they raced to and from the city centre.

'It's been getting me down, all of this. I can't imagine a world

The Truth Hurts

where I leave my boy with her and that demon child. I know he's mine too, but he's a little bastard. I've been around less than a year and I hate the two of them more than I could hate anyone. Only Ronnie's kept me here.'

'Now lad,' said Ron. 'That's sounding a bit too much like crazy talk.'

'You've never thought about it?' Asked Fin.

'About what?' Asked Ron in reply.

'How she can exist like that. She hasn't said a good word to me since we found out she was pregnant. How did I not realise she just wanted the money? She finds out I'm a banker just like my dad, and all she saw were pound signs. I can't believe I've done this to myself. I'm going to have her chasing me for money until I die now.'

Ron didn't know what to say. He looked inside himself for any word that might console his son, but there were none. For every part of him that wanted to make everything better, there was equal part which knew that things would never get better. She was too insidious. There was no escaping her.

'I'm fed up,' said Fin. 'I am out of options.'

They stood by the main road. The road had a speed limit of thirty miles per hour, but cars and buses alike had barely gone under fifty. Ron had only just realised how biting the backdraft of the passing vehicles were. His coat was pulled each and every way as vehicles of various sizes passed by.

'You're just tired.' Ron reached out to grab Fin's hand. He held it tightly, but not tightly enough that Fin was able to pull away. 'Come back to the hospital with me.'

'You're right,' said Fin.

'I am?' Ron said with surprise. 'I mean yes, I am. You're tired.'

'Yeah,' replied Fin. 'Tired of fucking living.'

The X95 service from Edinburgh to Carlisle had raced past the hospital eight minutes late. The bus driver had put his foot down to catch up, aware of the consequences if he turned up to the Hawick bus stop as late as he had the previous week. What he had not accounted for, were the consequences of driving past a depressed man, in the middle of the night, at fifty-eight miles per hour.

Ron's heart stopped the second Fin reached out. He heard the clatter of bone and skin and metal and glass as Fin's body connected with the front of the bus, killing him instantly. He heard the rubber tires crunch bone as Fin fell under the bus and the front tyre rolled over him. His skull would pop, and Ron would see the streak of blood and mush laid out before him.

He could not take his eyes from it, but he no longer wanted to see his son like that. His corpse lay strewn under the bus, with this left arm laid in front of the rear tyre and his left leg behind it. There were people screaming on the bus. Ron was crying. The driver just sat and stared. He pressed open the door.

'I didn't,' the driver couldn't say anything else before he burst into tears by the wheel of the bus. 'I'm so sorry. Jesus Christ.'

'I know.' Ron tapped the side of the bus and walked away from Fin and the bus. He would tell a cleaner what happened, and walk straight past. He didn't see the panic he raised in the hospital. He just walked through to Morag in the maternity ward.

Fin Macleod could not see himself leave his son, but neither could he see himself live with Morag for an eternity. He was not a religious man, and he believed that after death, he would never be aware of his misgivings on Earth. So, he killed himself knowing that he would be none the wiser of what he would leave behind. The minute he stopped breathing, thought Fin, was the minute he stopped being conscious.

'Your wish came true,' said Ron as he burst the door to Morag's room wide open.

A small nurse, no more than five-foot-tall, sprinted into the room a moment later. 'Mr Macleod, are you alright?'

'Just a moment, pet.' Ron walked up to Morag so that he stood merely inches from her face. 'I don't know why, and I don't care how, but whatever you did to my son... I will never forgive you. Ever.'

'Mr Macleod,' the nurse spoke again, but Ron turned to give her a blank stare which told her he wasn't finished.

'What's your problem?' Morag asked.

'What's *my* problem? My problem is my son just took me outside to tell me that he couldn't see a world where he coexisted with you. He decided to throw himself under a bus. He's just broken my heart, and what's worse, that lad there you've just given birth to will never meet his father. Do you think that's appropriate?'

There was a long silence between the two.

'Fin just killed himself, does that mean nothing to you?' Ron's voice creaked as he held back the tears.

'Not really,' Morag said with her attention somewhere else. 'You can go now, if he's dead.'

The nurse, with the help of her larger colleague, dragged Ron from the room and took him out of the ward. By the time he had calmed down, he had forgotten what it was he had done in the seconds after she said that. He held a glass of water, and a pill that the nurse said would help him. He didn't know what it was.

Ron would always remember that he didn't do enough for his son. He never made enough effort to stop Fin dying that night. He never pulled hard enough on his hand to pull him back from running out onto the road. A father should always do enough to save their child. Of that, Ron had no doubt.

In his old age, he had forced himself to forget how his son stopped existing. He would stop remembering that he was there, for the simple reason that he could not live with that knowledge that he had failed someone so close to him, yet helped people who only used him for profit at the bank.

He would not allow himself to be traumatised repeatedly, closing his eyes to see his son stare at him as he felt the weight and power of a bus plough through his soul. He would, however, realise that he could never make the same mistake with little Ronnie. He could never allow him to make the same mistake as his father. So, it was then, that he would never tell Ronnie that his dad took his own life. Ron would silently, and selflessly, give his life to his grandson.

He would wait for Morag to fail, and he would seek the right to raise Ronnie himself through the court. He would make sure that he never felt alone, or sad, or disappointed, or in danger.

Did he succeed?

ELEVEN

'This road is crazy,' groaned Ron. He held onto the door handle and frowned at his grandson, who was speeding round corners and up hills. 'Where are we?'

'You know where we are. You used to drive me this way all the time.' Ronnie three a glance back.

'True, lad.' Ron inhaled sharply. 'At least I went slow enough for you to enjoy the view.' He gripped tighter as the car went faster. His grandson had not appreciated the sarcasm. 'So why the holiday, son?'

Ronnie's – well, Jim's – Porsche roared up the A9. It was still dark, and the mountains were hidden from view. The road snaked through the wilderness, with only average speed cameras to remind the two of them that civilisation existed nearby. It was black with no other cars around them. Only two LED beams of light from the car illuminated the tar in front of them.

'Just a break, is all. I haven't been off for a while and I thought, given what's happened recently, we should just go somewhere else.' Ronnie turned up the heating in the hope that it would make his grandad drowsy so he would stop asking questions that Ronnie did not want to answer. 'Away from the family, the issues, the stress and the drama.'

'It's a good idea son, I've been stressing so much. Mostly the cancer, but I can't help but wonder the toll this all plays on you. You work so hard for me, and I just can't shake the idea out my head that nothing has gone right for you.'

'Tell me about it,' said Ronnie as he turned down the heating again. He was melting, and his grandad's eyes were wide open. 'Listen, I'm used to things going wrong. I've spent my whole life surrounded by everything going wrong. For me, that's normal. I tend to gauge things on how wrong they're going. If someone hasn't died, or been arrested, or hit me, then that's a good day. Anything above that is a bonus.'

'It shouldn't be like that.'

Ronnie gripped the steering wheel tightly and shut his eyes. His brain burnt the inside of his head, and he gripped his tongue with his teeth so hard that he almost bit through it. His grandad did not notice, but Ronnie breathed heavier as the pain subsided.

'There's something I need to tell you,' said Ron. 'I've tried not to tell you, but I'm dying and this cancer is ripping me apart. I don't want to die and know that I haven't been completely honest with you, lad.'

'What?' They were on the dual carriageway to Inverness. Ronnie took the opportunity to race past several lorries. He had hoped the speed cameras wouldn't tag him for speeding. He was too impatient to care.

'It sounds crazy though... I don't... Please don't think I've been hit by the dementia train.'

'Just tell me, Jesus.' Ronnie sighed. 'It can't be any worse than some of the tales you've told me in the past.'

'The other week, when Jim was in and you'd came around to see me... you asked me who a man was in a picture. Do you remember? Charles. We told you that, as far as we knew, he was dead. Do you remember?' Ron sat up, pushing upon his stick. 'I stuck to the story that Jim has always told. I didn't tell you the truth. I didn't want to lie to you. I just couldn't tell Jim.'

A familiar feeling rose in Ronnie's stomach. Again, Charles' seedy hands had dug deeper into Ronnie's life, and Ronnie's family. How the hell could one man, who he had never heard of before his trip, be so embedded in who he was, and what he came from? 'I was just asking, grandad. You don't need to...'

'I do,' interrupted Ron. 'I need to tell you this. You have to know.'

'What would it change?'

'Everything,' said Ron tensely. 'Everything.'

They entered Inverness, but Ronnie was going at such a speed they barely stopped to look at the view. Ronnie looked over at the stadium. He was surprised that more footballs didn't end up past the gap between the two stands and out into the loch. Then he remembered, the quality of football was terrible. Not offensively terrible. Just… terrible.

'If you feel like you'd feel better, then I'm happy to hear it.'

'Charles, well, he never died,' Ron sighed. Ronnie looked at him, surprised that Ron had chosen to be this open. 'He never went missing. I knew where he was. He went missing just after that picture. Not for any other reason than… well… I screwed him over. He pushed me too far, and I ruined him.'

'You ruined him?'

'You have to understand, Ronnie, he was… he is an awful man. He would… will do whatever he can to get his way, and he did that with me. Only, I had nothing else to lose so I didn't care what he did. If he killed me, I wouldn't know about it. You weren't born yet, yes Lewis was, but he was a demon from the moment he was born. I don't want to speak ill of a child, but he's only grown to prove I was right. Charles was a demon too. The more I think about it, they were very alike.'

Ronnie smirked.

'What?' Ron asked.

'Nothing,' said Ronnie. 'I'm just listening, sorry.'

'You're alright, lad.' Ron smiled. 'Charles wanted me to look into something. I'd just been promoted, took some time off… and I enjoyed studying, so I said okay. He was fascinated that something lay out in the Outer Hebrides. Treasure, I think. He was right that the history of it all didn't add up, so I wrote him a file on all the inaccuracies of it all.'

Ronnie's eyes glazed over as he flashed back to the report that was in his bag. Was this the same one that his grandad was talking about? There was no mention of his name, though admittedly Ronnie still hadn't read it. In fact, he hadn't planned to read it and he was more than halfway to the port.

'He wanted more from me, and he got really quite aggressive. I didn't want trouble, so I studied it a bit more and before I knew it I was over there asking people questions... people who did not like being asked those kinds of questions.'

'What sort of questions?' Ronnie interrupted.

'There are people on the island who have hidden secrets from us mainlanders for centuries. You walk over there, asking questions about what's hidden, and they'll come for you. You see, I found out that perhaps the Clan Macleod – the family we descend from – were killed for this treasure. The second I was there, the second they realised that a Macleod was sniffing about once again, people became very suspicious. Angry people came looking. Naturally, I wasn't hanging about. I left. I came home and told Charles, this is where I ended it. He wasn't having that.'

Ron took a break to drink water, and a bite of an apple. He spat it straight back out. How could he forget he hated that taste of apples. It was too bitter.

'I came home, and he came to my door more upset than he had been the entire time since we started this research. People were looking for him, and he didn't know what he had done to upset them. Thing was, he hadn't. I had. I'd used his address, his contact number. The people who wanted to kill me to get rid of our bloodline decided to go for him. That was when Charles Mackenzie went missing, presumed dead.'

Ronnie slammed the brakes on the car. 'Charles Mackenzie?' He spat. His mind was rushing. 'He's a Mackenzie?'

'Yeah,' Ron said calmly. 'I told you that. I'm sure I did. He went by a different name but it's what I always called him.'

'I wouldn't say you ruined him,' said Ronnie. 'That's a bit too tame.'

'You wouldn't?' Ron was surprised.

'You haven't heard from him since?'

'No,' said Ron looking out the window to the sunrise over the dam miles ahead, setting out the road to Ullapool. 'But you have.'

Ronnie's heart stopped. He almost swerved the car off into

a fencepost, but caught himself just before. 'I don't know what you're on about.'

Ron laughed out loud. 'I didn't either, until now. I just always wondered why you asked me about him. He's nothing, unless you know his story. My story. The photo is there as a constant reminder, just to me, that he almost ruined my life.'

'He's Lewis' dad,' Ronnie said, trying to distract his grandad. There was no point denying what was true. Ron had the exact same reaction as his grandson did when he first found out. In fact, he laughed most of the distance between then and Ullapool. Just when he had calmed down, become used to it, he would laugh even harder.

'Well, I didn't expect that.' Ron wiped the tears from his eyes.

'Does he have his own family? Ronnie asked.

'Why did he get in touch with you?' His grandad avoided the question entirely.

'I... have no idea, I brushed him off.'

'Did you?' Ron asked, his eyes a little wider.

'Yeah, told him I wasn't interested and he should leave me alone.' Ronnie had to turn the corner quicker than he thought. Well, the truth was he was so distracted with the conversation, that he forgot to concentrate on the road and almost crashed again. This was not, however, what he convinced himself.

'Yet we are on our way to Lewis, on a random holiday... that you haven't told me anything about, or shared any sort of plan.' Ron looked out the window. 'I am your bloody grandad, Ronnie. My body might be giving up on me but my bloody mind isn't. Why did you agree to this? You bloody fool.'

Ronnie, up until Jim's funeral, had never faced his grandad's anger. Now he had pissed him off twice in the space of a month. This time though, he wasn't upset. His fury was fixed on Ronnie. It meant more to him this time.

'He can help you,' Ronnie said, clenching his teeth.

'No,' said Ron. 'He bloody can't help me. He might tell you that, but he can't. No. That's wrong. He might be able to, but he won't. He'll find a way to ruin you, son. Jesus, Ronnie. You're an idiot. You've given yourself to him. He's never going to let you go.' Ron was almost spitting chips in anger to his grandson. He could barely look him in the eye.

'I've spent my whole life handcuffed to someone wanting to use me,' replied Ronnie. 'Charles is nothing new. I told you, I live my life to help you and make sure you're okay. If he can cure you, whatever I must do, I'll do it.'

'I would rather the cancer killed me.'

A long period of silence followed.

Ronnie didn't want to hear those words from his grandad, and now he had, he was desperate to know that he didn't really mean them. He would have done anything else to cure him if he could. He had continually turned him down until he nothing else. Charles' had his grandad's life in the balance and this was something, foolishly perhaps, he was not prepared to gamble with.

'I'm sorry for saying that, of course I don't want to die.' Ron took a deep breath and sighed involuntarily. 'Well, he's got you now. We need to start planning ahead of him.' He took another deep breath, and closed his eyes. 'The bastard,' Ron shouted.

He gave Ronnie a fright, so much so, he almost hit the 'WELCOME TO ULLAPOOL' sign. Neither said another word until Ronnie had parked in the queue for the Stornoway ferry. They were far too early, but not early enough to be first. An old couple, far older than Ron, fell out of their campervan.

'The old fellow can barely get in and out of that thing. Look at them,' said Ron sarcastically. 'If you can't get in and out, surely you shouldn't be allowed out. Put them down. Except me. I'm alright, amn't I lad?'

'Eh,' Ronnie paused. 'You mean ok as in…'

'Charming,' said Ron. 'Look lad, you have to be honest with me now. I know you want to hide things from me, and not tell me the truth, but if I am getting on that boat with you then you and I are in this together. Does he know I'm here?'

'Yes.'

'Shit.'

Ron quickly became distracted by a sight in the distance. He squinted, raised his glasses, making his eyesight worse, and then put his glasses back over his eyes to squint again.

'I bet you've seen that bloke down there before, haven't you lad?'

Ronnie looked down to the entrance to the runway. A man, clad in a dirty, lime green jacket and wild and whacky beard stood scowling over to the blue Porsche.

'He's not looking at you like that for nothing, my boy. Charles' orders.'

'I don't think that's why *he* is looking at me like that.' Ronnie sniggered. 'The last time I was up, I gave him a bit of hassle... purely for being a jobsworth. That and, well, he was annoying me so I just whispered sweet nothings in his ear.'

The man, Ronnie had nicknamed Scruff, began to walk towards his car. He tapped the front, and Ronnie felt offended. Seconds later, he signalled for Ronnie to put down the window. Ronnie looked to his grandad, who's eyes implored him not to continue with his battles with the man.

Ronnie opened the window by a crack of an inch.

'You can't park here,' said Scruff.

'Not this shit again,' Ronnie said. 'Why not, is your granny parking here?'

'I'll pretend I did not hear that, sir.' His professional manner waned only seconds into the conversation. 'This lane is for our larger cars, you need to park in the next lane.'

'Your colleague there told me to park here.'

'He's new,' said Scruff. 'I am asking you kindly if you would move your vehicle, sir.'

Ronnie looked to his grandad, and then back to Scruff. He was tapping the wheel of the car vigorously. Ronnie wanted to tell him to fuck off, but his grandad was beside him. He lived as a nice man, because grandad thought that he was nice. That was all.

'Can you believe this guy?' Ronnie said to his grandad.

'It's Charles, I'm telling you.'

Scruff was still stood by the Porsche, refusing to move. The more Ronnie ignored him, the more impatient he got. By the time the next minute had passed, Scruff had chosen to tap the window repeatedly. Ronnie tried to keep calm, but his veins were pumping harder and he could feel his face get redder. He opened the door, and attempted to step out.

'Listen pal,' Ronnie said, putting one leg out. 'I'm not putting up with-'

A gun stared back at him.

'Brian was right about you,' Scruff said. 'You are a wanker.'

Ronnie looked to his grandad. Neither knew what to do.

'Get back in your fucking car,' Scruff spoke again. 'Move into the second fucking lane. Charles asked me to be polite. I've lost my fucking patience to be completely honest with you.'

'Certainly sir,' Ronnie said sarcastically. 'Could I please have the contact details of your manager? I wish to compliment him on his wonderful staff.'

'Eat my shit, Macleod.' Scruff began to walk off. 'Oh, and don't fucking move from the car. I don't want this gun accidentally going off.'

Scruff vanished, and both men sighed a breath of relief.

'You won't be getting that roll and sausage then, grandad.' He looked to his grandad, laughing, but there was nothing coming back but fear. 'You alright?'

'Aye.' Ron was frozen stiff. 'Having a great holiday, lad. Where are the mojitos?'

'I don't think they have anything but given the reception we have had so far I'm sure he'll be more than welcome to let you drink his piss, if you asked.'

The two men laughed.

'If you could be any soup,' said Ronnie. 'What soup would you be?'

'What?'

'What soup would you be?'

Ron put his fingers to his chin and thought about it seriously. 'Probably French Onion.'

'Manky bugger. Who eats French Onion?'

'Old people with no teeth.'

In time, the queue began to build up and the ship had arrived in the port. Scruff, looking very official now with his cap on, walked over to Ronnie's car. Ronnie glared at him, but of course Scruff could not do anything in the eyes of the public. Instead, he directed Ronnie to be the first to load onto the ship. Ronnie noticed that Scruff had stood in front of the next car, stopping the rest.

'Fuck,' said Ronnie.

'What?' Asked Ron.

'Sorry.'

'What is it, lad?'

'Nobody else is coming onto this ship. You know what that means.'

The Porsche rolled over the lip of the ship ramp and Ronnie revved it up the ramp onto the second floor. The car echoed in its new surroundings. At the very end, stood a man. One that both men knew extremely well. He walked round to Ronnie's window, and Ronnie rolled it down.

'Good afternoon gentlemen, and welcome aboard this sailing to Stornoway. I am led to believe that it will be a calm sailing today. It's so much of a relief, given how bad our seas are, isn't it? It has been an awful, awful week for weather up these parts but you two gentlemen seem to have brought the Southern weather with you, haven't you?'

'Fuck off Charles, it was raining.'

'Ronnie!' His grandad hit him. 'Sorry, Charles.'

Charles ignored Ron's very existence.

'Before we allow the others onto the vessel, there are safety issues that I need to… raise with you both. Namely, I cannot have you crossing onto this island with something which may danger you, or the task at hand. Please step out of the vehicle.'

'Is this one real?' Asked Ronnie, his back to Charles as he shut the car door.

'Excuse me?' Charles asked.

'Is this sailing real, or have you paid for some mug to sail me into the middle of nowhere again?'

'What?' Ron asked.

'Nothing,' the two men said.

'Lionel here is looking for anything which you might have brought unnecessarily.' Charles reverted back to business. 'It shouldn't take more than a few moments. How was the drive?'

'You don't care,' said Ronnie.

'How very rude,' said Charles.

Lionel, more affectionately known as Scruff, did indeed take no more than a few minutes, and the rest of the cars began to load on. He handed Charles a box, which was now cabled tied shut. He whispered into Charles' ear and left.

'I will hold onto your phone and your iPad, Mr Macleod.'

'Will you fuck,' interrupted Ronnie. 'They're mine.'

Charles gave the box to another man, and it was taken from the ship.

'I would love to leave you with them. I wouldn't love to bore you with the reasons why. We are very much behind schedule with this short stop, so I need to ask you to go to the observation desk and enjoy the sailing over to Stornoway. I've left a spare burner phone in your car. You can use this to contact me if you lose the one Brian gave you.'

Ronnie was pushed up into the stair by the second man, his grandad quickly followed.

'Good luck, Mr Macleod.' Charles had left, and the door was shut on Ronnie. He turned to his grandad in the tiny corridor, and shook his head. 'What was all of that about? Why can't I get my phone?'

'I told you, he's an odd man. He controls us now.'

'Me, you mean.'

'No, us. I'm here too.'

Ronnie helped his grandad up the stairs, carrying him most of the way. There were several flights up to the observation desk, and by the time Ronnie lay his grandad into a chair, he was shattered. He almost fell asleep, until the roll of the ship woke him up.

The ship began to roar, and the two men were launched forward with the other guests aboard. It was a full sailing, and there was barely an inch to move. Ronnie and his grandad were sat at the front of the ship, looking out to the sea as it roared out of the island.

'Hold tight,' said Ron with a dirty smile. 'We don't want it happening again.'

'Oh great,' said Ronnie, angry. 'Now all I can think about is dying.' His throbbing headache clamped itself around his brain.

TWELVE

'I don't get it.' Ron winced as he squirmed in his chair, trying to ease the pain in his back and neck. 'Why did we not just go to the Police?'

'Lewis murdered the police,' Ronnie replied, careful not to slip up on the truth.

The ship's observation deck was bustling. Seats were scattered in every nook and cranny and each one, except Ronnie's, cradled a sleeping pensioner. Even Ron, as hard as he tried, dropped off to sleep every now and again before jolting away in his chair as the ship rocked over a wave.

'We should have still reported this to the Police instead of getting on the ship.'

'You'd have gone behind my back if it was the right thing to do.'

'What are you talking about?' Ron looked perplexed. 'I don't have a phone.'

'I should have done a lot of things differently,' sighed Ronnie, conscious that he needed to change subjects. 'My whole life has been filled with regrets.'

'You can't think that way lad,' Ron fumbled at a packet of cheese & onion crisps. 'Give me a hand, will you?'

Ronnie opened them, but not before he had stolen two for his effort. His grandad was furious. *'You're just like your mother,'* he joked before demolishing the packet. He wasn't giving Ronnie a second to reconsider committing the crime again.

A tannoy mumbled in the background. Ronnie turned, but he could see nothing but a sea of balding grey heads. There was one thing, he had never felt younger. It put him in a good mood. 'Do you want anything to drink?'

'I'd love a tea,' said Ron.

Ronnie stood up, and smirked. "Now,' he spoke far louder than usual. 'You know you're not allowed to go anywhere without me, so make sure you don't move. I'll be back for you, don't worry.' He looked to the person mind him, smiling. 'Sometimes he wanders off. Would you mind watching him?'

Ron's eyes shot a look which told Ronnie exactly what he was thinking. He was not a man to use bad language to express his dissatisfaction, but there was nothing closer to telling someone to fuck off.

The boat moved slowly in the water, yet inside it felt as though it were climbing up and down skyscrapers. Ronnie's nerves were put on edge. In reality, the ship was sailing one of its calmest journeys in weeks. He felt as though he was seconds from death. His knuckles turned white as he gripped the steel handrail down the stairs to the first floor.

'Café?' Asked Ronnie, barking to one of the members of staff wiping the table. She pointed down to the back of the boat. 'Thanks.'

He walked past many people and their dogs, locked into the middle of the boat, holding tightly onto one another. There were lots of green faces who had been to either end of the boat and been unable to keep their stomach down. They resigned to the middle of the boat in hope of comfort, they were left choking on the stink of wet dogs.

The staff member behind the café was a young girl, no more than twenty years old. Her curly blond hair fell down the sides of her temples and her raisin brown eyes clashed with the sharp red of her lipstick.

'Good evening sir,' she said in a coarse islander accent.

'It's half eleven in the morning. How hard are they working you?'

'Oh yes,' she said blushing. 'How can I help?'

Ronnie ordered a tea, a coffee and a sandwich. Unlike his outburst in the garage, he managed to hide his contempt for the extortionate money for a sandwich. 'I could almost buy four loaves of bread for that on the mainland,' he said.

'What?'

'Just milk in the coffee,' Ronnie realised his humour was missing.

'What's your business in Lewis, then?' She asked as the coffee groaned into the paper cup.

'We... we're over to have a look around. Local tourists, maybe.'

'It's a place and a half to visit. Steeped in history and mystery. That's why I love going home. Never gets boring.' She spilt the coffee across the floor, and turned to look sheepishly at Ronnie. 'I won't charge you for that.'

You better bloody not, thought Ronnie.

'You know much about the island?'

'No,' said Ronnie reflecting. He knew nothing, for all he'd read about it.

'I'll tell you my favourite, sir. It's the standing stones in Callanish. To most people, they're just big lumps in the grass that people put there to look up to their Gods. Other people came, and changed it for their God. You know what I believe?'

'I haven't cracked mind reading yet,' he said as he pocketed some free shortbread. There was a price in the box, but he quickly realised she was paying no attention to it.

'They're giants, protecting the land for the Gods above.' She stopped making the tea, and smiled with her eyes closed. 'They've been there too long now, sir. The people back then didn't have the means to bring those rocks there. They had to have come themselves.'

'Do you find that everyone has their own story for Lewis?' Ronnie asked.

'Almost certainly, but they're all beautiful tales to be told. Some are terrifying, but they're just stories.'

'Do you know the terrifying ones?' Asked Ronnie, cautiously.

'Only one,' she smiled.

Ronnie looked to the lady.

The Truth Hurts

The lady looked back and smiled.

'Do I need to pay you to tell it?' Ronnie asked, perplexed that the conversation died a death there.

'Oh,' she giggled. 'I didn't think you were interested.'

'How hard *do* they work you?' Ronnie's brows involuntarily spasmed into a look of concern.

'There are rumours that people are going missing on the island. Nobody knows who they are, they're not well-known. They go in the night. Yet people talk, and they all have one thing in common.' Her voice was lowered now. 'They all have the same surname.'

'That's less of a myth and more of a story that should be on Crimewatch,' Ronnie paused. 'Why do you think they're targeting the same surname?'

'We don't know. Isn't it bizarre, though?'

'Yeah, a bit. Are the Police bothered?'

'Tormod? Not really. They're not giving him what he needs to be able to help.'

'Tormod?' Ronnie asked, copying her tone. 'There's only one Police Officer?'

'Well this isn't Glasgow, sir. We don't have much crime. Didn't have. Tormod wants to help, but he needs the resources.'

'There are people going missing. There are surely resources.'

'Allegedly.'

Ronnie was getting frustrated by the young lady now. None of what she was saying made any sense. 'What is the name of the family that is going missing?' He asked sternly, less appreciative of her time now.

'It's... I hear that they all have the surname MacLeod.'

It was all about confirming his suspicions. He wanted another confirmation. A local source telling him the same information as the mainland was vital to ensure that he was not wasting his time, and he was not stupid with their safety.

Would you like anything else?'

'No,' said Ronnie, and he burnt his lip on his coffee. He had reached the door of the café, back to the bowel of the ship when he had a sudden thought. 'Excuse me?'

The girl turned and smiled to him. 'Yes, how can I help?'

'The Police Officer... Tormod. If I wanted to speak to him, where would I find him?'

'He's not often around, he manages the Western Hebridean Islands you see. If you go to the Stornoway Police Station and ask for Inspector Mackenzie, they'll find a way for you to speak to him if its urgent.'

Ronnie turned his back and smiled. He would not be going to see a man named Mackenzie, no matter what it was worth.

It took forever to get back to his chair, swaying between the waves and bouncing around the other passengers. By the time he sat down, half his coffee had scalded his hand. He had made it to the stairs, when the lid fell off. He was too worried about falling, he carried on. It was a ridiculous idea in the end.

'This must be an everyday occurrence for you, grandad.' Ronnie tried for a sip of his tea but the look was enough. 'Surrounded by this lot.'

'It'll come to you too, son. Don't you forget it.'

'Hopefully I'll be too spaced out to know it,' Ronnie was sure the lady next to him had wet herself. That, or the stench of the sea was coming through the thick glass window in front of him. 'What do you think is over there, Grandad?'

'Maybe nothing. You can't build your hopes up. There's every chance we won't find anything. There's too much willing to chance.' Ron gripped his hand. 'One step at a time, Ronnie. That's how we do this. Don't think too far ahead.'

Ronnie needed to think ahead. He needed a backup plan. Something that would give him security. Something that, if he needed it, Ronnie could use as a bargaining chip.

He tried to turn his head, but his neck snapped and the back of his head caught fire. Again, he closed his eyes, and again every muscle in his body tensed as he tried to ignore the overloading pain.

'Grandad,' Ronnie started talking until he noticed Ron was fast asleep. If he was going to move, this was the time.

The Truth Hurts

The pain died down, and Ronnie turned his head. There were too many old heads bobbing up and down to sneak a look at the wide-open sea of nothing. They were in the bloody way, he moaned as he stood up and walked to the back of the room.

Suddenly, a leathery hand grabbed him. Ronnie jumped. An old man stared. 'I know you.'

'I've had a one-night stand or two, but I can't remember you. Sorry.' Ronnie wrenched his hand from his grip and continued down the back of the ship. The old man continued to look at him, peering over his half-moon spectacles.

'You're Lewis,' he said. At least, that's what Ronnie thought he heard him say.

'No, I'm bloody not,' said Ronnie. It was still too raw. 'That's my brother, you cheeky bastard.'

Ronnie moved his feet quicker, taking larger steps. He was sure that what he needed wasn't far away. The feeling came from his gut, and if he had learnt nothing more important, it was to always trust his gut. The water swelled from one side to the other, and Ronnie struggled to keep his balance as the buzzing in his head grew momentarily. He closed his eyes, listening for voices.

'Why can't you do that from home?'

'Tell me about it. He wants it that way.'

'Sometimes he's ridiculous.'

'I spent the night with him. I couldn't stop myself leathering him. I would kill him in a heartbeat.'

The elevator doors closed just as Ronnie turned the corner and the elevator began counting down to the basement floor where the vehicles were kept. Ronnie, without a moment's thought, jumped down the stairs and fell face first into the linoleum. He ignored the guard asking him to take his time. He was desperate to reach the car floor.

Down the bottom of the stairs, the door was locked. There was no way in. Ronnie punched it in anger. How did he not know this would be the case? It was locked right in front of him less than an hour before.

He climbed up the stairs and stopped. The same emergency door from below opened. 'See you later.'

Suddenly he was nervous. It seemed almost too easy, but he was a realist and he knew he was unprepared. Yet, he didn't have time to worry about that. It had to happen now. Right now. Ronnie's heart pumped blood faster. He would do it. Three. Two. One.

Upstairs, Ron had woken up to find that Ronnie had disappeared. He had no idea how long ago he had vanished. He had had a cracking nap, though. It was the best sleep he had had in a while. His eyes opened, and they began to nip. They stung with the stench of urine. It was almost bitter. He turned to the old lady two chairs away from him and shook his head. 'Some people just can't hold it in these days.'

'I'm soaking,' the old lady said slowly.

Ron could have been sick there and then. He felt his cheese & onion crisps gurgling in the back of his throat as he struggled to his feet, holding on to the silver bar in front of him to stop him falling over. He took a few steps, and finally found his balance. He moved away from the old lady as far as he could go. He wasn't bothered about someone taking his seat, nobody would go near enough for the smell that layered around the woman.

From just behind him, he heard a voice. 'Here, you're not supposed to be moving away from your seat.'

Ron turned to the old man and shook his head. 'He was joking, you old tit,' he barked.

By the time, he had made it to the staircase, he knew that he had made a terrible decision. 'I can't climb stairs,' Ron whispered to himself. 'I can't climb bloody stairs.'

'Don't go down them then,' a voice said from behind him. Ronnie had just walked out from the elevator, his nose packed tightly with tissue paper and blood. He sniffed, and winced. 'I walked into something when the boat lurched.'

'I don't remember the boat lurching' said his grandad. 'What did you do?'

Ronnie looked either side of him, and then down the stairs.

The Truth Hurts

He looked up to the corner of the room and seen a camera staring dead on him. 'Nothing,' he said, staring deadeye into the camera.

'I need help back to my seat... but that old woman has pissed herself,' Ron choked on his words as the ship rolled to the right, rocking him backwards. Ronnie grabbed his shoulder to keep him up. He only needed one hand. Ron was light now. 'If I ever get like that, you kill me. Alright?'

'You mean I can't enjoy it?'

'Absolutely not.'

Ron was angry. Ronnie kept laughing, much to his grandad's dismay. By the time, they were back in the chairs, the smell was even worse. Ronnie could barely breathe for the smell. The old lady even knew this was bad. She sat, looking down, sad.

'How did she even get here, if she's on her own?' Ron asked.

'Don't.' Ronnie replied.

'Aye, lad. I'm the one in the wrong.' Ron's sarcasm almost nipped his grandson.

It seemed to take forever before she finally decided to stand up and walk away. In all that time, enough people had left the observation deck to leave Ronnie and his grandad alone for several feet in either direction.

'So where do we start, when we get over there?'

'That's a question,' said Ron. 'Where do we start? I say we go there with the exact reason you told me we were going.'

'What?' Ronnie was confused.

'A holiday. You told me we were coming here on holiday. Let's be *tourists*.'

The tannoy rang a moment later, ordering the drivers back to their cars.

Ronnie stood up just as the Isle of Lewis rose up from the sea. Its lowland grass was a fluffy complement to Harris' rocky surface that sat to the south. Mist rolled along the length of the island, as if to hide its secrets from interested viewers.

Ron, rather than struggle on his own, looked to his grandson for help. Instead of waiting, Ronnie picked him up and carried him down to the car bay.

   'Look at that lad,' Ron said as they jumped from the final step into the basement. 'Blood.'

   'It's not mine,' said Ronnie. His nose made him wince again.

   'I know,' said Ron. 'That makes me wonder who got it worse.'

FLASHBACK VI

'Your mum is a whore.'

Ronnie was fourteen when he first felt it. His ears crackled a little at first. Then he felt as though something was trying to burst out from underneath his veins. His cheeks blushed a little, but his irises stayed put. Tunnel vision focused him on his target. He was losing his temper.

Yet, it would never come to light. Why? Everyone knew his grandad, and they knew he was his boy. He was a good kid, just by name. The idea that he might do something bad was simply preposterous.

'She's a dirty fucking bitch,' said the boy in front of him. Ronnie looked up from the bench where he sat alone and gave no response. The boy was tall, but only marginally taller than Ronnie. He was much fatter. His black jumper, emblazoned with the school logo, was tight. There were concerns that he might break through the seams by some of the staff members… voiced only in the staff room, amongst friends. It was strange then that everyone else knew it too.

Ronnie never had any friends. He avoided relationships of any kind. He was too ashamed of the house he had been brought up in, and the people who brought him up. Part of making friends would be disclosing part of himself, and he couldn't think of anything worse. Unfortunately for him, his family was infamous. Everyone knew everything regardless, so he was lonely for no reason.

'Leave me alone,' Ronnie whispered. He tried to read his book again.

'Would she fuck me?' Asked the boy. 'Would she fuck me if I

asked, Maclcod?'

Ronnie didn't bother replying. He wasn't even sure the boy knew what he was actually asking. If he had wanted to, he would say no. Given who his mother was though, it likely wouldn't be true. By this point, Morag was fully addicted to the wonder and glory of heroin. He would visit only to find her eyes rolling in the back of her head. She was in ecstasy. She had never been so happy. This was not an exaggeration.

Each time Ronnie went to see her, he was left disappointed. He visited in the hope that his mum would change, but she never fucking would. His grandad had told him repeatedly never to visit his mother. He told him that until she tried to change, it would only make him feel worse. In retrospect, he was right. At the time, he could *never* be more wrong. Ronnie wouldn't believe it. His mother could be nice if she tried.

'She would suck my cock, I bet.' The boy pushed Ronnie's shoulder, causing him to look up again. Ronnie put down his book, and stopped pretending that he was ignoring him. The boy took this as a sign for a fight. He rolled up his sleeves. 'Fucking bring it, you little shit.'

'I'm not going to fight you,' said Ronnie. 'Leave me alone. I don't come to you for bother. I don't even talk to you. I just want to get on my life, okay?' He never once considered defending his mother.

'Nah, mate.' The boy cracked his knuckles, and punched his left fist into his right palm to show his toughness. 'I'm going to fight you. You bitch.'

Ronnie was many things, but he was not a bitch. Given everything he had been through, this was something that could not be possible. He had stood inches from his mother as she wished him dead, her opiate-flooded phlegm splashing against his face. Her three remaining teeth would shake in her gums with the violence and verbosity of her scream. Her beloved son, Lewis, would call Ronnie from prison just to blame him for his mother being upset. This fat child was nothing in comparison.

'I don't want trouble,' said Ronnie. He stood up, but he was pushed back onto his bench. He looked around, but they were alone. Whatever motivation the boy opposite him had to fight Ronnie, it was not to show off. 'Don't touch me.'

The boy grabbed Ronnie by the collar, trying to intimidate him. Ronnie just looked back at him, standing upon his toes. 'Put me down.'

'Make me, bitch.'

Ronnie tried to swat away his clenched fist, but he was pushed harder against the wall. The boy's grip now sat an inch from his throat, with the pressure increasing by the second.

For all he wanted to be different, Ronnie was just the same as his mother and brother. His grandad had helped him, sure. Helped him to hide it. Ronnie only wanted to hide it from his grandad. Nobody else matters. He couldn't allow his grandad to know that he, Ronnie Macleod, was as much scum as the rest of his detested little bastard family.

'Don't ignore me,' said the boy.

'Put me down,' Ronnie growled. His anger becoming him. 'Right now, or else.'

Ronnie still can't be sure what exactly happened. The boy said something, it was fuzzy, which suggested Ronnie should give him a reason to walk away. So, it was, that Ronnie clenched both fists and hit him with one hard punch. The boy collapsed to the ground, screeching through his rasping throat. Ronnie only remembered his own final words to the boy.

'I'll punch you in the throat, that's what.'

Ronnie would never be punished for the punch, because they'd never prove it was him. According to the school register, he had never turned up to school. How could an absent boy knock a bully unconscious? Well, you'd have to prove where he was alleged to be to rule him out... we'll get to that. No matter what the boy would say, or the detail he would give in his statement, the police would not take further action. This was Ron's boy, he would never act out. All the teacher and the officers knew that.

Meanwhile, the boy would be admitted to hospital. He would

never fully recover. As an adult, his breathing was laboured, and he couldn't walk far without support. Even as teenagers, he would scowl at Ronnie. It didn't matter to the boy that he provoked Ronnie to do something in revenge. He just didn't need to debilitate him. He could have hit him anywhere but his throat. Only a disgusting creature would think to do such an act.

So where did Ronnie go after school?

He wasn't stupid. He needed somewhere that, if people came looking, he would look innocent. You can't just walk out of school. Not unless you are found somewhere you shouldn't be. Somewhere that, legally, you can't be.

'Well, look who decided to fucking turn up.'

Morag opened the door, her words slurring into one another. She had a belt strapped to her arm. Ronnie knew what that meant.

'Hi, are you alright?' Ronnie asked as he walked in and she slammed the door shut. The house stank of damp, and it was littered with trash. The condition of the property had worsened considerably in the time since Ronnie had gone to live with his grandad.

'Lewis is fucking gone,' she whimpered. 'He's fucking gone.'

'He's in jail, mum. He'll be out again. How are you?'

'It doesn't matter to you how I fucking am. Don't come round here and act like you give a fuck about your own mum.' She scowled and Ronnie and turned, but she lost her balance and she face planted into the hall wall. As she stood up, she punched it and her knuckles crackled through the plaster. 'It never matters how I am anymore.

'I'm just asking,' said Ronnie with a smile. He hoped she would return one. She wouldn't.

'Don't ask then. I need another,' She walked through to the kitchen and Ronnie went to the living room. He had come with the intention, and the hope, that his mother would make amends with him… that she would finally see past all the hate she held for him.

'Lewis,' she screamed from the kitchen. It sounded as though she had just ripped a kitchen door open. 'He did not fucking rape her.' Ronnie heard her slump onto the kitchen lino, crying. He seen her kick an open cupboard door so hard that it flew from its hinges and thudded against the PVC door out to the overgrown garden. A breeze rushed back inside to fill the space it left.

Morag had not taken Lewis' imprisonment well. She didn't blame herself – oh no. The problem was though, she didn't blame Lewis either. She thought that the girl deserved to be raped. She had once said to Ronnie that, 'if your pussy flaps are hanging out, you're asking for it, aren't you?' Ronnie did not agree. Naturally, the very statement itself made him sad that a people, a woman, would think that way. He couldn't understand what had happened to her to hold such a crass opinion of consent.

His mother walked into the living room, her eyes bright red from crying. 'I'm out of smack. I'm going to murder some cunt if I don't get it soon.'

She fell over her bag, on her way to her phone. She picked up the handset, still lying on cigarette ends strewn across the floor, and thud her finger into the keys as she dialled a number.

'Aye, it's me.' She barked phlegm down the microphone. 'Don't fucking hang up. I don't care if you're *busy*. I need more, you prick. I need it right fucking know.' She paused. Her eyes incensed now. 'I'll tell them what you did to me. They'd love to know. Aye, you will be right over. I'm giving you two minutes.'

Ronnie sat on the edge of the couch. It was fabric, and wet. He was sure his mother had emptied herself upon it again. He just wasn't sure if it was urine, or something worse. If she was on as much heroin as he thought, there was no way there would be any bowel movement. She'd be as constipated as she was angry. Maybe that's why she was angry.

'Tell me...' Morag asked, as she threw the handset across the room to Ronnie. 'Why do you hate me?'

'I don't hate you,' said Ronnie. His face screwed up. 'I wouldn't have come today if I hated you.'

'Well I fucking hate you.' She looked Ronnie dead in the eye.

'You make me sick. You little rat. Don't think I don't remember you grassed your brother to the Police. I know it was you. That stupid Barge bastard told me.'

'I didn't,' Ronnie stopped himself. What would he gain from arguing with his mother? He was here to make amends. 'What's been happening?'

Morag didn't say anything. She just snarled at her son. His fists began to clench, and he shuffled them under his thighs to control it.

It felt like minutes of silence before an older gentleman walked into the door, without ringing the bell. He was suited and booted. Ronnie was sure he was some sort of authority. Nobody so polite, and clean, would be coming to visit his mother out of courtesy of kindness.

'Really, Morag, I can't keep doing this for you.' The old man stepped into the living room. 'I appreciate the troubles you are facing, but there is only so much of this that I can source to help you out. Surely you realise this?'

'You got me hooked to this.' She ripped the bag from his hand and opened it to sniff deeply inside. Ronnie didn't think it smelt of anything, but Morag almost passed out then and there at the thought of what she would soon be doing to herself. 'Maybe you could apologise.'

Ronnie wouldn't realise until many years later that it was Charles who fed Morag the heroin. He didn't even know, even then, his life was manipulated and ruined by the man who was now sending him to the Isle of Lewis on a wild goose chase. He would never understand how deep rooted he was in everything.

Charles had indeed hooked Morag onto heroin, teasing her slowly to make sure she didn't back out. He didn't have to push for long before she demanded it by the kilogram. Her only thought and concern, whilst Lewis was in prison, was for her golden-brown painkiller. She got it, because she had a secret. A fifty-five-thousand-pound-per-year secret that Charles did not want anyone to know.

Morag, then, had a reason for Charles to provide her with as much heroin as she needed, at no charge to herself. It was the only time in his life where Charles was the one being blackmailed. Not out with his control, I should add. It was a means to a gain. An expensive gain.

'Morag, I implore you to ease off how much you are taking. What am I to do if you die?'

'Bite my cunt.' She knew he was being sarcastic. 'I won't die, because I'm here to ruin your life, just like mine was ruined.'

By now, Morag had melted it down and cut in the baking soda. The spoon she used was black now, and her hand shook as she tried to lie the needle in the heaven that awaited her. The needle inhaled the syrup, but she didn't wait to appreciate it. She was too hungry for it.

She slapped the inside of her right arm, and then her left. She snarled, as her veins stayed hidden in her arm. Her own body refused to have anymore. That didn't stop Morag. She struggled to her feet, fell into the kitchen, and came back with the kettle. Steam was floating from the spout. She looked to Ronnie, smiled, and then poured the scalding water straight onto her hand. She screamed, howling at the pain. Her skin was red, touched with violet streaks. She plunged the needle deep into one and forced the needle so hard, it almost broke.

A second later, and the needle was in her wrist as the drug plunged deep inside. She was passing in and out of utter grandeur. Everything in life was ignored. She could fail to be happy right now. She had the golden-brown goodness flowing round her, helping her forget her pain. She lay her head back and all the saliva in her mouth drooled out either corner of her mouth and mixed with her greasy hair.

The old man walked out, having never thought to look in the corner of the room where Ronnie sat silently. He was now alone with her, as she wheezed heavily. She wet herself, and Ronnie could smell the acidity in her bladder.

It made him angry that someone would treat his mother like that. It made him angry that she needed to have the drug to cope. It made him angry that everything she lived for came in the form of a needle. It made him angry that she still resented him, even when she was high. He could tell as much. The frustration inside was now violent. He could quite easily let go.

'Ronnie...'

He looked up.

'Ronnie....'

She was struggling to her feet, smiling.

'I got a secret.'

She shook from side to side, almost falling over.

'You want to hear it?'

Ronnie shrugged.

'I wish you were dead.'

He stood and shook his head. 'You don't mean it.'

'I fucking do.'

'I shouldn't have-' Ronnie stood up to leave, but she cut him off.

'I spent my whole life waking up, wishing you were dead. Every morning, I would hope you'd be gone in your sleep. Every day, I would look at you, even as a baby, and just consider shaking you until you stopped. It didn't fucking matter how... I just... I just wanted you dead. I didn't want you to exist. You ruined my life. Do you know how many children die from SIDS each year?'

'No, why... '

'One less than there should have been,' she interrupted. 'Fuck you, Ronnie. Fuck you.'

Ronnie's lip quivered. He was just a kid at the end of it. He didn't need to hear what he was hearing. He became angrier and more focused on his anger too.

'I'm going to do it.'

Ronnie saw his mum pick up her needle before she stood up. She must have known he would, but she hadn't considered it a problem. She probably thought she would strike before it was too late. The problem was, she'd lost three stone in a year and weighed as much as a bag of air.

She ran at him, and Ronnie did it again without thinking. It was almost identical. It was odd that nobody drew any conclusion. Why would they? Ronnie would tell them what happened. Barge, trusting of Ronnie, would always believe him.

'So, Ronnie,' he said, holding his hand as he sat on the couch more than an hour after Morag had been taken in the hospital. 'What happened?'

'I told you,' Ronnie barked at him. He gave him a stare which showed no respect. He was stressed and manic. He did not want trouble for what he had chosen to do.

'I know you did,' Barge responded with more kindness. 'I need to make sure I understand everything, though.'

'This guy came in, he gave her drugs, he asked her for the money and she said she didn't have the money to pay it. He watched her inject herself, and he tried to find the money... she wasn't having it. Neither was he. He punched her in the throat. She collapsed.'

'These are the types of reasons that you should never come here alone, Ronnie.' His grandad was by the door. 'She does these kinds of things, and this is why you can't stay with her. Aren't you content living with me, lad?'

'I am,' replied Ronnie. 'I wanted to see if she had forgiven me yet. If she had stopped hating me.'

'She doesn't hate you.'

'She...' He almost let his story slip. He stopped. He wouldn't say anything else.

Everyone, in his adulthood, thought that his mother hated him just because. They thought she wished him dead, just because. They would never know the real reason. Ronnie had only thought about it for a second before he punched her repeatedly, delivering one final blow to her throat. He screamed at her, reminding her never to say anything bad again. Then he punched her again. Five more times. He kicked her. He wanted her to feel how much he hurt.

That is why she was angry. She was angry that she would never get any justice. She would never be able to tell her side of the story to anyone and be sure that they believed her. Why would they? Ronnie was a good guy. She was vermin.

THIRTEEN

An elderly gentleman, who Ronnie was sure was just being pleasant, spoke to the two of them in an accent which threw him completely off guard. He stood and stared at him, but the old man just walked on when he realised he was never getting a reply.

'Probably foreign,' the man said to another pensioner several feet down, pointing back towards him.

'What did he just say?' Ronnie asked his grandad.

'Something about… something.'

'This is going to be harder than I think it is, isn't it?' Ronnie's head dropped, and he shut his eyes. For the first time, he was regretting his decision. 'Maybe we should just give up and go back home… I'm kidding.'

The two men walked away from the harbour and wandered into town. Stornoway was almost like a large town back home. It was quieter, though. They walked until Ron found himself struggling up the path beside Macleod & Macleod.

'Fancy that,' said Ron, pointing to the sign.

'Yeah, smashing… glad we came all the way to see that.' Ronnie pointed to the café across the single lane road. 'Let's go in here, for cake.'

Ron ordered himself a piece of carrot cake that was the size of his head. Ronnie ate a small slice of millionaire's shortbread in three bites and downed a white chocolate milkshake in as many gulps.

The café was small, but quaint. Art hung around the walls, paintings and photos from local authors who charged well above what their art would ever be worth on the mainland.

'See that painting,' Ronnie said to the woman who carried over his grandad's cappuccino. 'There's no way someone would pay four hundred for that, surely?'

'I couldn't comment,' said the young girl with a smile. 'I've been here two years though, and it's never moved from that spot.'

There was a chortle, but Ron was left admiring the work. He had seen it somewhere once before, but he couldn't think where it was. 'The Blackhouse,' he exclaimed suddenly.

'The what?' Asked Ronnie, confused.

'That picture is of the Blackhouse on the west. Isn't it, lass?'

She nodded.

'What the hell is a blackhouse?' Ronnie asked again.

'Well, you see sir, these days you'll find that most people on the island live in whitehouses. That's what we call modern dwellings on the island. They're traditionally small, but they're comfortable. These days, most families have added bits on to make their houses a bit homelier. Back in the day though, you'd live in one of them. A blackhouse. Made of peat and straw. Your whole family would live in there, hidden amongst the smoke before it bellowed out the wee hole in the top. It's meant to be warm and lovely but… I wouldn't fancy it.'

'The last family left theirs less than ninety years ago, lad.' Ron chipped in like he was just as knowledgeable as the Gaelic local.

'The Macleods?' Asked Ronnie.

'Goodness no,' said the girl with a giggle. 'The Macleods would have torn them down more likely than lived in one. They were in the castles and the brochs.'

'Brochs?'

'Defences, more or less.' Ron smiled. Ronnie just stared.

'This island is the weirdest place.' Ronnie looked to the two, and they just smiled.

'Anyway, I'd better go before the dishwasher overflows and my manager over there gets angry with me. It was nice chatting.'

The girl walked off, in the eyesight of a young man who stared at her from his laptop. He had been looking at her the entire time but hadn't bothered to get up and personally serve the two couples waiting by the till.

'No bloody point going to see a blackhouse then, is there?' Ronnie asked.

They settled the bill, after arguing who would pay it. Ronnie and his grandad then walked down to the river and they both leant against the wall.

'I'm bloody shattered,' his grandad said as he swayed to one side. Ronnie grabbed him and held him still. 'I'll be alright. Thanks.'

'We are in this place to figure out something that we haven't heard of, have never seen and don't know the first thing about. I wish I'd never bothered. It's a fucking nightmare.'

'Language, Ronnie.'

Ronnie looked up to the castle on the hill across from him. It sat across the river from the rest of Stornoway. The Castle of Lews was now a museum, and a venue for functions, but its grandness and stature in the surrounding environment was a cut above the rest. Its perfect, leafy grounds reflected as a contrast to the concrete jungle where the rest of the Stornoway citizens lived and worked.

They were sat across from an IT company. Its black vinyl a contrast to the white rendering on top of the brick. Ronnie wondered how an IT company in the Isle of Lewis could afford four vans. How many people used a computer on Lewis?

'You'd think they'd give us a clue,' said Ronnie.

'Who, Charles?'

'No, these ancestors of ours. I mean their secret is our secret. Are you hiding something from me?' Ronnie stared at his grandad.

'No, why would I?'

'Yeah, exactly. Why would you?'

'You tell me,' Ron laughed. 'Don't look up there. I've looked. There's nothing. Absolutely nothing. They're turning it into a hotel now.'

'How can you not know if the world around you is changing, but you know about a hotel hundreds of miles away?'

'It was on the telly, lad. Britain's best refurbishments.'

'That was the name of the show?' Asked Ronnie, with one eyebrow high on his head.

'I don't remember.'

Ronnie had given it one more thought before deciding they would start tomorrow. Lunchtime was long past and he wasn't keen on staying out late with his grandad, especially if there were people looking for their namesakes. So, it was, that he made the fifty-minute journey to Aird Uig.

They would head out to the grassy peats of Lewis and admire its beauty as the sun reached out and touched the greens and blues of the grass and the lochs. The road would reach up to look down over the land, and for a moment the two men forgot that they were ever there to worry. The road fell into a single track, and its surroundings became more natural, and virgin. Animals spread across the road, in between the many miles which separated neighbours.

They were minutes from Aird Uig now, but their journey came to a stop. Ronnie looked to his grandad, with no idea in his mind how they were about to overcome what was in front of them.

'There's a bloody highland cow on the road,' said Ronnie, hitting his head gently off the steering wheel.'

'Drive round it,' said Ron.

'I can't, there's deep verges.'

'Oh aye,' he seemed to say, like he already knew.

'Why did you suggest it then?'

'Toot the horn.'

'I'm not tooting the horn.'

'Och, one blast will be fine.'

'No.'

Ronnie looked around the car for anything he could use. The cow was inches from the bumper now, looking into the window to see who was inside. He was worried that the cow would decide to have them for its dinner and spear the car with its horns. So, it was helpful then, when Ron reached over and gave the horn a blast.

The cow jumped in fright and stared at the car with more vigour now. A moment later, the cow moved off the road and Ronnie put his foot down to make the Porsche race past the cows, down the tightly twisting lane into Aird Uig.

'God, Ronnie,' his grandad gasped. 'It's a shithole.'

'Language,' retorted Ronnie. 'It didn't look like this on the internet.'

Aird Uig sat in front of an old RAF base. It had now been taken over by the community, in the hopes it would revive its usefulness as a piece of land. Currently, though, it was home to hundreds of sheep who did not take kindly to being disturbed.

The bed and breakfast looked old, and more like a house than an inn. It sat on a slope, and beneath it sat a ginormous drop. The view around it was rocky and beautiful. The sun peered in from a gap in the hills, but it did not touch the mossy garden or the rotten brickwork of the B&B.

'Make sure that handbrake is ok, lad.' Ron gave it a light tug, and Ronnie was left to stare at him.

'Aye, that's the car secure now… no danger.' Ronnie shook his head, smirking.

The two men climbed out of the car and looked concerningly down to the slope below. Ron looked to his grandson and scowled. 'I don't think I like the thought of that slope being so close to the side of the road.'

'I think we have bigger problems,' Ronnie said, nudging his grandad to face the other way.

The front door had opened, and a big, bruising woman walked down the path to where they were parked.

'You can't park there,' she barked.

Ronnie felt a heavy amount of déjà vu. He wondered if he should tear off her mask to find someone who worked for Charles. *You can't park there.* Fuck off, he thought. Fuck right off.

'Please move your car to the other side of the drive way, our guest Jeff has asked specifically for this space.'

'Why?' Ronnie asked.

'He is a regular. He dislikes having to move his car in the morning when the other guests wish to leave after breakfast.' She put a hand on either hip and stared at the two men.

'That's fortunate, that's exactly what I was looking for in booking with you. In fact, if I wasn't stuck in behind a couple of cars I would probably take a point or two off my Trip Advisor review.' He shook his head and slammed the car door shut.

Ronnie could tell that she did not appreciate his humour. She walked to the boot, where Ronnie quickly took a step to stand in front of her.

'Let me get your bags,' she barked. Ronnie noticed she spoke very sharply and loudly. Her sunken eyes, in her greasy skin, made her look very ill. He wondered how close she was to her heart giving up.

'I'll get the bags, thanks. We will see you inside.'

She turned and waddled back into the house. Ron looked at him and gave him a sigh of relief. He then walked to the boot, but again, Ronnie stopped him.

'The bags are in the back seat,' said Ronnie.

'Didn't we pack them in the boot?'

'No,' Ronnie said abruptly. 'The boot is... tiny. Nothing would fit in it.'

Ron was no genius, but he was sure that there was plenty of room for the small amount of clothes the two men had brought with them. He was also sure that he had thrown a bag into the boot before they left. However, as Ronnie said, his bag was in the back. How odd.

They entered the B&B, and Ronnie held his nose. The smell of fish was revolting from the hallway. It had been cooked, and then cooked again. It filled every crevice in the room.

'How many nights?' She boomed.

Ronnie shit himself. He was caught completely unaware, too busy contemplating what sort of human would coat every surface of their home, and business, in laminate wood.

The Truth Hurts

'My name's Shelagh, by the way.'

'You've even laminated the roof,' whispered Ronnie.

'What?'

'Three nights,' Ronnie said confidently. 'Just the three, I hope.'

Shelagh picked up their bags and threw them into the room. The thin door almost crumbled as her fat forearm crushed into the centre of it. She thumbed a key into Ronnie's hand, and mumbled something about the front door always being open.

'Breakfast,' she shouted. Ronnie and his grandad looked to one another. It was barely four o'clock in the evening. 'What do you want?'

'For breakfast? Tomorrow?' Ronnie could tell Shelagh was holding her breath, trying not to kick off. He began to wonder how many of the 1,500 five-star ratings were honest and true, rather than a coerced statement in a trade for her guest's release.

'Porridge please, love.' Ron smiled.

'Don't chat me up, old timer. My husband is in the kitchen.'

Ron looked to Ronnie, pleading with his eyes that he would just make up any sort of order to allow her to leave them alone. He had never felt so close to being beaten, even with Morag in the room.

'You're having porridge too. Good night.' Shelagh walked out of the hall, leaving the two men standing outside of their ground floor room.

Ronnie opened the door and sighed, there was a double bed inside.

'I am not telling her,' Ron said before Ronnie had had the chance to turn around. 'If you want to tell her and get knocked out, you go ahead lad. Otherwise, we'll be topping and tailing.'

'I am not sleeping in the same bed as you, grandad.' Ronnie kicked his bag into the room. He could sense Shelagh's anger from the kitchen. She had just screamed something about her husband being a useless bastard, before a plate smashed. 'You could be right.'

Ronnie laid his grandad into bed alone and squeezed together the two chairs in the hope he could fit between them to find some sort of comfort. He considered giving up and diving into bed, but he couldn't. The last person he had ever lay beside was Seonaid. There was something that didn't lie right with him knowing what happened to her. So, he sat up with the lights out and watched his grandad sniff away in his sleep.

The closed curtains still let light in from the wide windows which were open at the top. Ronnie could hear everything, from the sea brushing in and out on the coast to a sheep bleat sadly in the distance. He had one hand on the curtain, to peek out, when he heard feet crush the broken stones outside of his window.

'Yes?' Shelagh barked. 'He's here. I'd have called you if he didn't turn up, don't you trust me?'

She was on the phone. Everything about her tone told Ronnie she was speaking with Charles. He shut his eyes, imagining how she was standing. A fag in one hand, a knife in the other ready to stab anyone who came within earshot of her. Bloodshot eyes, as she did when they met her. A greasy complexion.

'No, I haven't heard from him. I called him twice and it went to voicemail each time. I can't help if he's gone off the radar, what do you want me to do? Go bloody find him?' She took a long draw on her cigarette. 'Listen here, you've come to me with a job and I'm doing. Don't think you can treat me like you've treated the others. I don't put up with nonsense. I don't have five stars on TripAdvisor for nothing.'

The front door opened, and a timid voice peeped from behind it. 'Still no word from Brian. Should I phone the Police?' Ronnie couldn't make out her reply, but he felt her temper soar from behind the glass. 'I'm sorry, I'm just worried,' a man replied.

'I'll ask him in the morning, Charles.' Shelagh was back on the phone. 'It's going to seem pretty odd if I break into his room in the middle of the night to ask if he's seen someone who punched his lights out. He's hardly going to want to help, is he?'

Ronnie heard a second pair of footsteps enter onto the gravel, and before he knew it there was a slender, male shadow stood facing the curtain to which Ronnie was facing. Ronnie's breath shallowed. Shelagh's phone beeped to end the call and he heard her slap the device into the man's hand. The shadow flickered as the man grimaced at the veracity of Shelagh's hand.

'Does he know?' Asked the man.

'What?'

'What Charles wants him to look for?'

'Nobody knows, Andrew.' Shelagh spluttered for several minutes, and for one moment, Ronnie was convinced she would never stop until she fell unconscious. 'He… He's convinced that if he sends enough people with the same surname, that one of them will figure this out.'

'It doesn't make sense to think that they'll figure it out.'

'The Macleod family owned this land,' Shelagh spoke timidly for the first time. 'They ran things until one day, they were shipped off this island. The secret history is that the family guarded someone…. someone that went into hiding when they died.'

'Who shipped them off?'

'The Mackenzie family.'

'Your family?'

'Yes,' she sighed.

Ronnie's stomach became extremely unsettled. Yes, Charles was the basis for all the problems in his life at that moment, but it appeared the crisis, in the absence of a better word, was more ingrained into history than just one man. The Mackenzie family had come up several times. Each time, there was an issue. Ronnie began to wonder if this feud, between his family and theirs held the secret. What if the Macleods were hiding something from the Mackenzies?

Splatter.

The sound did not come from outside, or Shelagh. This was inside. Inside the very room where Ronnie sat. He didn't notice at first.

Splatter.

It was not the noise that drew his attention, but the smell. A

piercing, acidic blood stunk out every inch. He almost vomited.
Splatter.

He turned to his grandad and through the dark he could see the wet patches of blood. His grandad, in his sleep, was vomiting. He would lie still. His body would then lurch. Blood and stomach acid would splash from his throat hitting the faux wood laminate floor.

Ron wretched again. Ronnie swept across the bed to lie above him. He could smell the acid. He could feel it. It burnt his nose.

He said nothing. He listened for a breath. *Rasp. Rasp. Rasp.* He was alive. His throat was surely burning. Ronnie's heart was racing. He picked him up with one arm, he weighed no more than a small child these days. He threw him onto his shoulder and left the room open with his clothes lying in a heap next to his bag. He picked up as much as he could with his free hand and forced his way outside.

Shelagh and her husband were there. They looked at Ronnie. Her husband, a thin, pail, frail man looked aghast.

'Is he alright?' He stuttered.

'Aye, he's smashing,' said Ronnie, barely stopping to look at them. 'Do you want a photo with him?'

She wanted to react, but it was her husband's best nature and pleading glint in his eye that stopped her. She smiled, and opened the gate allowing Ronnie out of the garden. Her husband followed too, trying to grasp the bags from Ronnie's hand. 'Let me help,' he said sternly.

Ronnie hadn't thought about the offer until Andrew's hand was touching the boot. He heaved his shoulder up, letting his grandad thud onto the backseat of the car and screamed outwards telling him to back off.

'Oh my God,' Andrew shouted. 'Shelagh! Jesus Christ.'

Ronnie smashed his head against the roof of the car as he lurched out the car. His hands hit the rubble several seconds after his face, and the numbing thunder in the back of his head took over his vision so that he saw pinpricks of light in either eye. He kicked the rear door of the car shut and stood too his feet.

'Why do you have a bloody body in your boot?' Shelagh bellowed. 'We will have to phone the Police. I took money, but I am not having this nonsense in my village.'

It was too late. With his blood boiling round his body, Ronnie picked up a boulder the size of his fist and threw it with all his might towards Shelagh. It made a dull thud as it bounced from her head. She was unconscious before she even sunk to the ground.

Andrew had barely said the word please, never mind 'don't', before Ronnie had punched him in his chin to break his jaw. He had aimed for his throat, as only Ronnie did, but he missed for once. Ronnie watched, as he fell to one side, as Andrew's momentum also dragged the body out of the boot. It flipped around and mumbled something. Ronnie didn't know what. He had taped his mouth.

Ronnie stood between the man and the moon, shutting out all possible light. The two unconscious hoteliers sat behind them on the dirt track. He admired his work tonight. It wasn't easy to overcome one fighter, never mind two. The fact they hadn't laid a finger on him was testament to his aggressive prowess; nothing to do with the fact they weren't looking to fight in the first place.

He smirked at the body beneath him. Endorphins were rushing through his veins. Then the back of his skull cramped, and his eyes shut out all light again. He fell to one knee and drove his fingers into the stones and the dirt. The pain was getting worse. He needed to keep going. He stood back up, looking back down to the ground.

'You got a problem?' Ronnie asked.

The man laid there. His hands were taped. He just scowled.

'I can't hear you. You will need to talk louder.' Ronnie enjoyed tempting the man, knowing he was utterly incapable of doing anything to quench it. He took his big Timberland boot and thrust his foot into the man's stomach and brought it down a second time upon his head. The man ceased to move.

'Fuck you, Brian.'

Angry Ronnie stepped into the car and slammed the door shut, hitting the steering wheel and resting his head upon it with his eyes shut. That was not the plan. Shelagh and her stupid husband ruined everything. He turned to the back seat, where his grandad lay peacefully and sighed. It was about him. It always had to be about him.

Calm Ronnie pushed the car into first gear and set off through the night. This Ronnie felt guilty for what he had done. Yes, Brian was his bargaining chip and that was ruthlessly necessary. They were down in the ship's basement when Brian politely told Ronnie that he wasn't to be down with the cars until the ship was in the port.

He was playing his part. Ronnie didn't.

He fought a brave fight, but he was being overpowered by years of experience in brawling. At one point, he was on the floor with an elbow in his throat. Brian wanted to kill Ronnie, yes, but he wasn't allowed. There were orders.

Brian turned to leave, and in an instant, he was unconscious. Ronnie had grabbed the nearest fire extinguisher. The metal pinged off Brian's skull. After that, it was just a matter of taping his limbs together and heaving him into the boot of the car.

However, he didn't need to harm Shelagh or her husband. They were both involved. They would have likely understood why he was arming himself against Charles. There was clear tension between the two of them too.

Ronnie was beginning to feel different. He felt a pressure inside of his head to be who he was always expected to be. He was feeling the real Ronnie bleed away as an angrier, less respectful man took over. Someone who enjoyed violence. Someone who took revenge seriously. He was an evil fucker. He knew that. The blood in his family was toxic. Lewis was a criminal. Morag was too. It would hardly be surprising for their youngest to follow suit.

So why did others not see that version of him? Were they just taking Ron's word for it?

The road opened into two lanes and the Porsche's growl grew louder. A cow, trapped in its headlights, narrowly kept its life as it stumbled into a ditch by the side of the tarmac. Ronnie's foot edged closer to the floor.

Darkness was approaching, but Ronnie had to save his grandad first.

FOURTEEN

Stornoway sits to the East of the island. Many roads wind round the island like veins, breaking off to single farmhouses every few miles. One artery bleeds towards the single town on the island. As you drive in, it is hidden from view. A single corner brings it all into view. There is emptiness, then civilisation. It does not blend. There is no soft border.

A dead fox lay beside the 'Welcome to Stornoway' sign. Ronnie raced past the irony without a second thought. He ignored the moonlit lochs and looked over them to the beauty of the night sky on the island. Stars looked down upon him, clearly disappointed in the choices he had made. They did not twinkle. They sat in the sky, dull and unassuming.

His grandad was sleeping softly now. His wheeze disappeared. Ronnie had pulled over an increasing number of times, the quieter he became, to check he was still alive. If he died now, before they'd done anything, it would all be a waste. Especially now Ronnie had lost his backup plan.

Just then, the mobile found a signal. It sprung into life, illumination the car brightly in white and emitting a hideous, monophonic ringtone. The radio interface flickered suddenly, and the speaker barked, *'unknown caller'*. Ronnie's finger held slightly above it. He held it like a trigger, before sighing and pressing it.

'Hello?'
'Good evening, Ronnie.'
'Sorry, who is this?'
'You know who it is.'
'Hello?'

Ronnie knew what he was doing.

'I can't get in touch with Brian, and I have been trying to contact him for a number of hours now.' Charles knew what Ronnie was doing too, but he was not in the mood to play his games.

'Isn't he the one who's supposed to be following me?'

'I've given no such command.'

'I believe you,' muttered Ronnie.

'Have you seen him?' Charles asked, unaware.

'Ok, now I don't believe you.'

'I asked you a question.'

'Why would I have seen a man who was not instructed to follow me, Charles?' Ronnie sniggered, but not before muffling his mouth to hide it. He could not work out Charles was playing a game, or worse, if Charles had worked out that he was. He did not need the answer to enjoy himself.

'I am not having a good day, Mr Macleod. I have a lot on the line, including the matter you are so kindly helping me with. You will understand then, I am quite stressed. I just want to know where my associate is, yet you choose to annoy me as you have done to all of us in our time together. Please, don't annoy me further. Have you seen Brian?'

Ronnie hung up. He almost drove onto the grass verge as he took out the battery and the SIM card. He decided there was no further need to talk to Charles until he found whatever he was supposed to give him.

Anyway, they were at the hospital now. He left the car by the front door, blocking access for any emergency vehicles. How many people on the island would be rushed to hospital after midnight anyway? They'd surely die on the way; the roads were treacherous. Ronnie almost crashed, and he was a very safe, experienced driver. Only three write-offs to his name.

He burst into Accident & Emergency. He expected to be stood holding his grandad, but it was dead. Back on the mainland, it would be full to the brim. There would be large LED words flashing across the wall telling visitors of the minimum four hour wait. A woman would be stood by the double doors into the ward handing out single paracetamol like a medicinal buffet.

A nurse stopped, surprised that there was someone in the reception for once and said something that neither man could understand. They looked at each other, eyebrows raised. 'You'll be from the mainland then, how can I help?'

'My grandad is very ill,' Ronnie shouted, albeit by accident. 'He's throwing up blood and he has cancer, treatable but serious. Can you help?'

'Aye, of course,' said the nurse in an overly positive tone. 'We wouldn't be a hospital if we couldn't. This way, boys.'

They followed her through several double doors, past empty rooms with flickering lights before they came to the end of a long, brightly lit hallway. She pointed into a room and smiled. 'I will be with you shortly.'

'If all those rooms are empty, why did we need to walk to the very back of the ward?' Ronnie asked, his grandad nodding off in his wheelchair.

'The bulbs aren't working,' she said plainly, as though that was an entirely acceptable reason why an entire fucking hospital was sitting empty and unused. She left, and a few seconds letter she was back. 'So,' she said as she sat down. 'What's wrong again?'

'He's vomiting blood, and he has cancer.' Ronnie's forehead bulged with the large vein running down the middle. His head was hurting again. 'He needs urgent help.'

'I know, I know.' She stared at her screen as though she crashed alongside her computer. The desktop wheezed, and she blinked again before standing up and walking out of the room.

'You're fucking kidding me,' whispered Ronnie.

Four minutes passed before she swanned back into the room, looking for a pen for her newly found clipboard. 'Sorry about that, the computer crashed so I need to complete this form by hand. It's a lot quicker using the computer, and it'll only mean I'll need to type this up later but... what can we do?'

'Gutted for you,' retorted Ronnie.

The Truth Hurts

'Sorry?'

'Nothing, can you help my Grandad?'

'What's your name, sir?' The nurse interrupted Ronnie. He couldn't tell if it was on purpose.

'Mine?'

'Yes.'

'Ronnie.'

'And your grandad?'

'Ronnie.'

'No, your grandad.'

'Yes, Ronnie. We have the same name. Ronnie Macleod.'

The nurse stared at both men. Her wrinkled forehead crinkled up as her eyebrows raised. 'Sorry, I didn't catch that. Surname?'

'You heard me,' Ronnie said. 'It's Macleod. M-A-C-L-E-O-D.'

The pen rolled from the clipboard and hit the floor, bouncing and clattering several times. Nobody spoke. Ronnie's eyes moved from the pen to the nurse's eyes. She was staring at him again. 'Okay, I... have all the information I need.' She stood to walk out of the door, and she hadn't moved far from the room before Ronnie's gut was telling him something was wrong.

'Excuse me,' he shouted.

She didn't come back.

'I'm okay,' whispered Ron. 'You're worried. What's wrong?'

'Just worried about you, grandad.' Ronnie was lying.

Ronnie thought back to the reason they came to the island. To cure him. If he did die, then there was nothing left for Ronnie here or back on the mainland. What would become of him if the only thing he cared about was lost? He wasn't going to die, Ronnie knew that. Macabre thoughts were always poignant in his head though. He needed to think it through, to consider death to the point his body was taken by anxiety. All of this... to move past his fear, just to ignore it and pretend he never thought about it. Until the next time.

'Good evening.'

A friendly smile appeared at the door. It was the doctor,

dressed in a white lab coat and a tartan dress with white collar. She walked in, sat down, and her green eyes tried to reassure the two men that they were finally in capable hands. She was beautiful. Ronnie was certain of that.

'My name is Doctor Ainslie Dìon, the on-call doctor this evening. You'll have to forgive me as my colleague did not make me aware you were here, it was only the light in the rear of the hallway that made me realise there was a patient.'

Ronnie looked to his grandad, and then realised he would not be thinking the same thing. Why would the odd nurse not tell the doctor they were there? Something inside of him, mainly the thought of his surname, was making him anxious.

'Can I… just confirm both your names?'

For Christ Sake, thought Ronnie. 'Listen, the form is right. We both have the same name. Ronnie Macleod. My grandad was throwing up earlier. He might look fine now… it was probably the paracetamol to be honest.' He spoke sarcastically. 'All we want is to get some medicine and be on our way. Surely that's not too much to ask? We do need to leave very quickly.'

'Yes,' she replied almost instantly. 'I think you might need to. How long has it been since my colleague left?'

'I don't know, ten minutes?'

'Shit.'

'Is… is he going to be alright?'

'Your grandad?' She asked, distracted by the gap in the window blind. 'Yes. It's nothing more than a bug. I doubt he's eaten which has led to him retching the stomach acid and then the lining which lead to the awful smell. It's unrelated to his cancer, I would almost guarantee it. But right now, I need to come with me.' She stumbled to the door in a panic and turned back to Ronnie. 'Please, now. Pick him up if he is unable to walk with us.'

Ron was thrown over his grandson's shoulder and he felt his head bump against the doorframe as they quickly rushed out into the corridor. Ronnie meanwhile was focused on following the doctor. He wasn't sure why he trusted her, but given how bizarre everything had been and the nurse's reaction in particular, it felt the safest option to keep the two of them alive.

They had walked for many metres before she opened a door and ushered them in. When the door slammed shut, she locked it and closed the blind. There was a dim glow from the lamps outside, but they were otherwise in complete darkness.

'I don't mean to sound crazy, but you are both in terrible danger.' The doctor paused to catch her wheezing breath. 'Why did you come here? You must know what is going on here.'

'Quite a funny story really, we came for medical he-'

'To Lewis!'

'Holiday,' said Ronnie. His grandad nodded in agreement.

'You need to leave the island.'

'Why?' Ron asked, squirming.

'It's not safe right now, for either of you.'

Ronnie already knew why. He knew that sooner or later she would mention a name, or names, which would lead him right back to why his life was a complete mess in the first place. 'That doesn't answer his question,' said Ronnie. 'You better just tell him.'

'They're looking for you,' replied the Doctor, as she scattered the room, checking the blind. 'For all of you.' Ainslie looked incredibly frustrated as she pulled out her telephone. She hurriedly tapped on it, before turning the screen. Ron read the headline.

'A man went missing.' Ron was paraphrasing. 'We are men, yes.'

She scrolled through her phone further. She showed him another headline, and then a third and a fourth. She almost hit Ron's face with the force she flipped the phone round.

'It's the surname thing again,' interrupted Ronnie. 'All the people missing from those articles have our surname. People are thinking its linked. They can't be sure, but there are so many alleged cases that its hard to rule it out.'

Ron stared at his grandson, not even bothering to blink. 'I told you no secrets.'

'You've not exactly been in the condition to discuss these

sorts of things, have you?'

'You think I can't think because I have cancer?'

'No,' said Ronnie firmly. 'You were throwing up all over the place and you've been out cold for the last two hours whilst your body tries to stop you tearing your stomach apart. Now, can we focus on surviving?'

Ainslie looked through the blinds again whilst the two men bickered. Suddenly, she opened the door and flicked a finger to Ronnie who picked his grandad up by surprise. They rushed through several more doors as the colder, darker side of the hospital beckoned them.

'Where did you park?' She asked.

'I probably shouldn't tell you that,' mumbled Ronnie.

'Another bloody idiot who's blocked the emergency entrances then.' She stopped to roll her eyes specifically towards Ronnie. 'This is the rear of the entrance. You will need to find your own way, but it won't be easy… they'll be round there.'

'Who?'

'Whoever the nurse has told!' As she shouted, she edged Ronnie out into the cold night air. 'Do not going back to anywhere you have been, they'll already know where you're staying. I've taken your number from this form. I'll call when it's safe.'

'How do I know I can trust you?' Ronnie asked.

Ainslie looked down to her feet. 'It's hard to know who you can trust on the island these days, Mr Macleod. We have friends disappearing by the day and a Police Officer who couldn't bother his arse to come to the island for a cup of tea far less a crime. Yet, here I am letting you go free instead of handing you over. I think you can trust me, Ronnie.'

She shut the door. Ronnie was left holding his grandad, as the silence surrounding them mixed with the anxiety in his head began to make his ears ring. His feet felt a lot heavier as he dragged both himself and his grandad around to the front of the building.

Just as he passed the second corner, round towards the front. He stopped, and peered round. There were men, all over the car park, looking for something. Someone. Two men. Macleods.

'Anything?' One bellowed.

'Nothing,' the other shouted.

'How the fuck can they have just vanished?'

'They've not gone far, the car's still here.'

Ronnie's heart was racing. He didn't expect for any of this to happen at the hospital. There was nothing he felt he could do to win here. He'd even left his phone in the car, which was surrounded by people desperate to accost him and his grandad. Even in his moment of need, Ronnie had no way of contacting Charles. It was the first time ever that he was gutted not to be able to speak with him.

'Can I help you boys?' A Glaswegian accent blared over from the other side of the carpark. Ronnie couldn't see who it was. 'That's my car you've got your hand on, pal.'

'You're going to have to stop there, friend.' The second voice was much closer, and more local. 'Please identify yourself by confirming your name for me.'

The man ignored the request. He kept coming closer, and the other men became more frantic – as though they had not encountered someone brave enough to challenge them before. They all took steps to close the circle in. There must have been at least six of them.

'For the security of the people inside this hospital, sir, can you please confirm your full name for me.'

'My name?' The man shouted.

'Yes sir.'

The man flexed one arm and then the other. He raised his hood, so that his face was completely blackened in the night sky. Meanwhile, the other men dropped the items in their hand that were no use and rolled up their sleeves.

'My name is Ronnie.'

'Your surname?'

'Macleod. My name is Ronnie Macleod.'

Ron, who was now stood beside Ronnie, leaning against the wall, mouthed to his grandson that this wasn't possible. Ronnie couldn't look at him. There was no way there could be another one of them.

'Can you confirm that again, please?'

'I'm not telling you again, pal. I need to get into that hospital to see my grandad. Are you going to let me past, or what?'

'There's a warrant out for you, Mr Macleod.'

'There isn't.'

'I have nothing to gain by lying.'

'I said...' The Glaswegian turned angry and his attitude suddenly became familiar to Ronnie. 'There fucking isn't.'

'I think he's getting aggressive with us.'

The whole situation lasted three minutes if the other men were lucky. He took two out at once with a stiff kick and a loud uppercut which slapped into the man's open jaw. The rest were slightly trickier; they tried to attack him at once, but they fell too. In no time, he was left dragging them into a single pile. Ronnie was in no doubt who was standing in front of him.

'You're safe now, you coward.' Brian looked from one side of the car park to the other. 'You better go hide before they find you. Or worse, before I do.'

Brian walked away.

Ronnie threw his grandad back onto his shoulder. His grandad would protest that he could walk back on his own, but Ronnie would tell him they didn't have enough time. He would throw him into the car, this time without his belt, and drive off without even putting his own belt on. They were out of Stornoway in a flash.

'I can't believe what just happened,' said Ron.

The phone began to vibrate, interrupting Ron. It was an unknown number. Ronnie had only just hit the answer button.

'Ronnie, this is Ainslie. Do not hang up.'

'How is Charles?'

'Who?'

'Charles.'

'I don't know who that is.'

'Very funny. Your friend, Charles. The one that told you all about us.'

'I have never met a Charles in my life.'

Ronnie looked to his grandad, but he shrugged and mouthed the words, *I don't know*.

'What is it?'

'Why are you here?' She asked again with more sincerity behind her.

'Sightseeing.'

'Tell me the truth.'

'Hol-'

'Ronnie, no.' His grandad interrupted. 'We are here to investigate something. For a friend.'

'You stupid bastards,' said Ainslie.

'Excuse me, hen,' said Ronnie. Annoyed. 'He might be a stupid bastard, but I'll tell you right now... I'm above average.'

'You cannot have come over here, looking to investigate something, and think that this was a good idea... can you? Really?' Ainslie wasn't waiting for a response. 'I know what you are looking for, and I am telling you right now. It's not here. You'll never find it.'

'I don't think you do know what I am looking for, with the greatest of respect,' said Ronnie.

'We don't even know ourselves,' added Ron. Ronnie scowled at him.

'Do you think I would be helping you if I didn't have a clue why you were here, Mr Macleod?'

'So, you do know Charles.'

'I do not know Charles, no.'

'Then you don't know why we are here.'

'Mr Macleod, I understand that you may be quick to judge... but you must be clever enough to have noticed that I am currently wearing a wedding ring.'

'That's alright, I wasn't chatting you up.' Ronnie thought about ending the call, purely out of boredom.

'My title doesn't give a lot away since graduating from university with my doctorate. If I hadn't worked so hard, you'd find my name is Mrs Ainslie Dion. My-'

'Hen, I love stories as much as the next man, but if you are right, me and the old man have a group of clowns chasing after us to kidnap us and sell us on for all kinds of acts... given how handsome I am, I can only imagine their sexual nat-'

Ronnie did not understand what she interrupted him to say. It was Gaelic, but she sounded very mad. He could tell that much.

'My maiden name is Ainslie Macleod.'

There was a second of clarity, as though both men finally understood the air of fate that surrounded them meeting Ainslie tonight. Almost immediately, that clarity vanished as more questions flooded into their mind.

'You are not going to find what it is you are looking for, gentlemen. Why are you looking for it?'

It felt as though Ronnie was already placing too much trust upon this woman he had spent such little time with. As such, he did not respond.

'Someone has promised you something, haven't they Mr Macleod.'

Ronnie did not reply. Seconds of silence passed by. Each more awkward than the last. He thought about hanging up again. Oddly though, he wanted her to speak again. He wanted to more in the slim hope that she knew more than all the other voices that had pretended to know the truth about the island.

'Mr Macleod?'

'Yes?'

'Has someone offered you... please take me off loudspeaker.'

Ronnie looked to his grandad, and he was encouraged to do so. He took the phone, as they burrowed through the countryside, heading north to avoid detection, and placed it to his ear.

'Ok,' he said.

'Has someone offered to cure your grandfather in exchange for what you are on this island looking for?'

'Maybe.' He gave nothing away to Ron.

'I don't want to be... I... I... Ronnie, I need to be really honest with you.' He could sense a sadness in her voice that he had not heard before.

'Go on.'

'Not by phone. Not here. Meet me at Tur Chlamain. It's as south as you can go. In Harris. Make sure you aren't followed.'

'We're heading North, through Lewis.'

'We need to talk, Mr Macleod. This cannot wait.'

'Why not?'

She told him.

Time ticks by, but not when you can't see it. You can feel it, when you're not frozen by fear. It's a fine balance. In moments of anxiety, you can feel time fly by. It almost speeds up until you fall off the cliff edge. At that point, time ceases to exist. It is no longer a concept. Nothing else matters.

Ronnie felt that. He felt it more than he had felt it in his entire life. His breaths became shorter. His forehead was cold, dripping with warm sweat. His hands gripped the steering wheel so tightly that the pain in his head and chest meant nothing.

His grandfather would ask him repeatedly what it was that caused them to turn around and head the other way. Hadn't they chosen this direction so that they wouldn't be caught? Why were they now driving the other way then?

Ronnie would not respond. He would not utter another word to his grandad. Instead, his full concentration would be put to the road in front. The car had long past one hundred and ten miles per hour. As had Ronnie's heart rate.

Ronnie Macleod Snr. The man that this whole trip had happened for. The man that Ronnie Macleod Jnr. had given so much of his life to support. The man who had quit his job to raise his grandson in exchange for a fulfilling career. The man who had put his body on his line to prevent a boy from being abused every single day. The man who didn't need to put up with any of the shit he did, but he did it out of love. The man who had cancer. The man who had been told by Charles, that he would be saved if his grandson helped.

That man? He could not be cured.

FIFTEEN

'If I ever find out that you lied to me about this, I will go out of my way to ruin everything that you hold dear to you.' Ronnie stood in the graveyard, focused on Ainslie. 'He means everything to me. I won't lose him because you're playing a game with me.'

'I live in Eoropaidh, which is the other side of the island.' Ainslie was gentle in her speech, she could see Ronnie was visibly angry. 'I'd rather not be here if I'm honest with you. If I wanted to do anything, I'd have let you come to my hometown and did it there. Why would I try anything all alone?'

They were stood in the grounds of *Tur Chlamain*. This was Saint Clements Church in Rodel, and it was as south as one could go on the island of Lewis and Harris. Ronnie had only agreed because of what Ainslie had told him by telephone – Ron's cancer could not be cleared by modern medicine.

The bitter wind fell in over the rocky hills around them. It seemed to find its away over the ancient walls around them and swirl around the valley where it would never escape. The rain, which always seemed to dash around the island, fell here for eternity.

'You're absolutely sure that he cannot be cured?'

'I'm not going to upset you with the why,' Ainslie said. 'I am only telling you so that whoever you are helping can't cheat you when you're done. Your grandfather won't recover. The only medicine that will help him now are the ones offering respite from the pain.'

'I was told there is a doctor, the only one in the world, who knows how to cure this specific illness.' Ronnie stopped talking, to look at her and see if he guessed her reaction. 'There is no such thing, is there?'

'I am the sole researcher of Cancer treatments on this island, Mr Macleod. That's about as lonely as you get. Even I must talk to all the other specialists to progress our understanding. I wish I could tell you otherwise, but if there was a way to cure your grandad, I would have been told about it. Don't you find it odd that there is one man, hidden from society, who can cure cancer?'

Tears rolled down his cheek. He tried to hide them. He sniffed, to put her off, but in the end, he cried. When he finally realised that his grandad would die, and he would have to watch helplessly, the bigger tears and the louder screams came from within him.

'I am so sorry.'

'So am I.'

He dropped to his knees and looked to the ground.

'He can't know,' said Ronnie. 'He can't know that he can't be cured.'

'I'm not sure that's your decision?'

'Well, it is. I look after him. I am the one who makes sure he's okay every single day. I'm the one who makes decisions about his life, not him. Never him.' He looked to her, his eyes raw. 'He will never know that he can't be cured.'

Ainslie did not know how to respond, so instead she stood with him until he collected himself and he was back on his feet. The two seemed to think nothing of it, until Ronnie broke the silence.

'I'm sorry,' he said. 'It's been a long time since all of this started.'

'Want to talk about it?' She asked.

'No.' Ronnie said, lying. 'Do you?'

'I want to help, so if it would help... yes.'

Nobody could ever hope to understand the mess that Ronnie had got himself into. There were still too many secrets, and by that, too many risks to himself if it all came out. Charles was only the beginning of a web of lies. There were other secrets tied up in other people's lives that Ronnie didn't want anyone to work out.

'I still don't trust you.'

'It's hard to trust anyone these days, isn't it?'

'What's that supposed to mean?' Ronnie asked.

'I'm a woman, with a certain surname, who agreed to meet a complete stranger away from anyone. Who is more at risk right now?'

He looked down the hill to his car. His grandad was inside, sleeping. He was much better now. For whatever reason, he had picked up back to his usual self. He was still going to fucking die, though.

'There is a man, who told us he could cure my grandfather in exchange for whatever is on this island,' he sounded so stupid now that he was saying this to someone for the first time. 'He kidnapped me and forced me into a corner. So here I am, stood before you, trying to find whatever, or whoever this family kept secret.'

'There's nothing,' Ainslie quickly replied. 'Well, that's not true. There's something. It's lost. Nobody knows what it is, or where it is.'

'Something?' Asked Ronnie. 'It's not someone?'

'It's something, for sure.'

Ronnie sighed. 'So, you're telling me that not even the people on this island, of this family, know anything about it?'

'Oh, people did,' said Ainslie. 'They were sworn to secrecy, and, as I said to you... they've been kidnapped. Killed.'

'Jesus.'

'It's nothing new,' she sighed. 'It's happened for years. The whole fake news is nothing compared to what happens here. Since the seventies, the heat for this has only picked up. The people behind this have never been investigated. To me, that just shows the corruption on this island. Everyone believes it's something huge. Everyone.'

'The Police?'

'Yep.'

'Wow.'

'My father was killed,' Ainslie said quietly.

'I'm... sorry.'

'Me too.'

Ronnie stumbled over his words. 'Why was he killed?'

'Officially?' She asked. 'Suicide. He knew about what they were looking for. When he wouldn't talk, they killed him.'

'Who did?'

'I don't remember. A man.'

For a moment, he almost skipped over the almost insignificant detail of the man's age. He was too angry about the pointless murder of a man he had never met. As the seconds passed by and he cared less and less, he realised his obvious mistake.

'What was the name of the man?'

'I told you. I don't know.'

'You have to remember something. Jesus Christ, he killed your dad.'

The two stared at each other, scared to speak. Neither was sure the other believed what they were saying. Neither knew the other could be trusted.

'You're lying,' they both said together.

'No, I'm not,' they both said immediately after.

'I find it hard to believe that someone killed your dad, and you haven't done anything about it,' said Ronnie.

'I'm doing something about it right now,' replied Ainslie. She pointed to Ronnie. 'You're the answer.'

Ronnie almost looked behind him. 'Me?'

'You.'

She began walking to the church, and he followed. It stood quietly amongst its surroundings. It was small by nature. Its spire was the only part which peered above the wall which encased the dead Macleods.

'This place was built in the fifteenth century. It was built to celebrate our family but named after Pope Clement I in the hope it would keep prying eyes away.'

'Did it?' Ronnie asked, interrupting.

'No. Rodel has been raped and pillaged of its fortune for centuries. Everyone knew there was more to this place. Why else would you name something in the Hebrides after the Pope?'

'Whatever they took, is it the same thing I'm looking for?' Ronnie opened the church door and let Ainslie walk in. It was dark, so the two turned on the flashlight of their phones and entered.

'No. The only thing that hid here was power. That was all people were interested in back then.'

'And now,' said Ronnie. He thought about the American elections. The fervour of the entire world, desperate for neither despotic candidates to win the polls. It was the first time in his lifetime that people had voted wanting neither person to win. This was like now. He didn't want Charles to win, but he didn't want anyone else but himself to win. The only thing was, he could never win anything out of what was happening. Not now.

They walked to the far end of the hall and stood by a grave. Ronnie read the notice. Historic Scotland had since taken over the building's upkeep and thankfully, for Ronnie, they had erected informative screens everywhere. This was the first time he had taken such an interest in his history. It intrigued him.

'Those signs are wrong,' whispered Ainslie, pointing up at another one across the main hall of the church. 'You'll find a lot of people have differing views on what happened on this island and what the Macleods were really doing here. Some families are split by it.'

'It's Historic Scotland, hen.' Ronnie looked at her with disbelief. 'That can't be wrong.'

'The greatest Macleod, the reason we all exist,' said Ainslie, walking back to the first grave Ronnie had stood by. 'That's who has this secret you're looking for. That's where my dad thought the secret was being hidden.'

Ronnie looked around. 'That's great, where is he?'

'Right in front of us sits the 8th Chief.' She ignored him. 'Further down the wall there sits the 9th Chief. Neither of them was

The Truth Hurts

great, though. Our family's power was draining long before they came to power.' Ainslie sighed. 'History doesn't tell us the truth, not all of it.

'See, these people who lie here aren't true Macleods. They can't be. They were never born here. They came from Skye. Dunvegan Castle.'

She walked away from Ronnie. Soon, she disappeared through door and up some stairs. He quickly followed her and almost fell into a claustrophobic coma at the size of the hall. He barely fit. He climbed through, despite being slightly concerned about Ainslie. She was now very melancholic.

'Listen, Doctor,' Ronnie shouted up the stairs. 'I'm sorry for what happened to your dad, but I don't think you're up for this.'

'You wouldn't know.' She snapped bitterly at Ronnie for the first time. 'Nobody you care about has died, clearly.'

'Yet,' said Ronnie, hoepfully forgetting Jim ever existed.

'We are in the attic now.' Ainslie pointed to the opening which made for a window across the landscape. 'We own that land. We will never realise that though. We will never rule again. The ancestor, the one that this church was never built in memory of, existed to serve better than the scum who lived here.

'The last to be buried here, who really mattered to these bastards, was Mary. A poet. A bloody poet. Can you believe that? She died aged 105, and she was laid here. But not a real Macleod. She wasn't even born with the blood of one, for Christ sake. She was born as one by friendship alone. Do you know what was wrong with her, Ronnie?'

'No,' he said, holding back considerably now.

'Nothing. She seen the Macleods for who they were. Liars. Frauds. She asked to be buried face down, shamed to be with these people. Shamed to have ever written down praise for them. She knew, Ronnie. She knew.

'She was banished because she knew. She buried herself face down because she knew that these people were not of the pure blood that Leodhas himself was.'

'The greatest ancestor,' Ronnie whispered. 'You see him as the greatest.'

Ainslie glanced him, and then she stared as she began pacing the room. She cackled. As she pulled at the bow holding her ponytail, she moaned at the obvious pain she was enduring. 'I don't see him being the greatest, you moron. He *is* the greatest.'

There was an obvious change in her, and Ronnie was unable to work out why, or when it happened. He wondered if he should just walk away, but as time past by it was clear she needed help. Even if he wasn't the person to help. He felt the pains in his head come and go, and he was worried that he would be crippled with pain one more time. He was worried he would be angry again, too.

'This is all valuable information, Ainslie. It really is. I do need to get going.'

'You don't see it yet,' said Ainslie. 'Perhaps I was wrong.'

'Wrong?' Ronnie asked.

'I have to be wrong. There can't be another explanation.' She was talking to herself, away from Ronnie. 'There is no other answer. I am wrong. Yes. Wrong.'

Around eighteen months prior to this, Ronnie had been involved in a conversation where people were saying only the poor and disadvantaged could be resigned to poor mental health. He had always advocated that it could affect anyone. He began to see before him that he was surely right. He considered phoning those people to say that he was right, but then he realised it probably wasn't the time to be thinking of that conversation.

'Ronnie, only the true heir to Leòdhas knows where his secret lies.' She turned slowly and stopped. Ronnie realised she was blocking the exit. 'It is written that way. Hidden from view. That's why people have been going missing. They've been trying to find the true heir. Kidnapping, not finding, killing.'

'Okay,' said Ronnie 'Clearly that means that's not me.'

'Not possible,' said Ainslie. 'Those people who came after you at the hospital, they were one of the families looking for you... everyone knows you are here.'

'You just said yourself, that only the true heir knows where the secret is.' He took a step towards her, but she did not move. 'I think it's well established now that I don't have a clue.'

Ainslie rummaged around her pocket and pulled a crumpled piece of paper. Her hands were shaking. Her eyes were now bloodshot. She was no longer pristine and beautiful. Ronnie began to regret that the thought had ever crossed his mind.

'Here,' she shouted. 'Look at this. This is the well-known and most-accepted image of our saviour Leòdhas. This is him.'

She thrust it in Ronnie's face, and his first thought was exactly what she was trying to portray. This picture, of Leòdhas, could easily have been a picture of him. It was scarily similar. The crinkle in his left eyelid. The awkwardly dissimilar eyebrows.

'You could just have a photo of me,' snapped Ronnie sarcastically. 'I'm not going to pretend that isn't the most likely, and scariest option here.'

'You are the heir of the true Macleod clan.' Ainslie now ignored Ronnie completely. Her eyes were rolling. 'You are the one that was chosen to come back home. You are the one who will bring the Macleod secret back to life.' She sounded almost demonic in her chant. 'You are the one who finds the secret. You are the one who finds the truth. Set us free.'

She dropped the paper now it had had its use. Her eyes did not flicker. She did not blink. They were fixed on Ronnie. It chilled him, but it did not scare him. He supposed she was trying to threaten him by this point, to make him angry.

'Do you know what that means, Ronnie?'

'No,' said Ronnie. 'I don't. I think you're going to tell me, though.'

'I've known it for a while. I didn't at first, because I was too blinded by rage. You see, they killed my father. Why would they do that? Only because he's not the true heir, and he can't help them. He knows too much. They must get rid of him.

'He was my dad. I am his kin. If he's not the true heir, then I'm certainly not the true heir.'

She went still, and silent. Her skin went blue. 'Where's the secret hidden, Leòdhas?'

'Okay, I'm not Leòdhas,' said Ronnie as he put his hands forward to try and calm her. 'I am Ronnie, and I do not know where this treasure is. If I were to know, then my grandad would have known. He has studied this thing for years and he's never worked it out. That means just like you, I can't be the true ancestor... that was it, right?'

'Liar.'

She put her hands into her pocket, scrunched whatever was inside and bit her lip. She bit it so hard that blood began to run down her chin. It all happened very slowly. Ronnie felt like the last few minutes were longer than the entire time they had been there.

'Are you...' Ronnie's eyes closed themselves shut and Ronnie's hearing vanished. He tried ripping his eyelids open, but the colour had drained. The world was black and white. 'Help me, doctor.' He sobbed and begged. The pain was unbearable.

'Your eyes were dilating in the hospital. Sometimes one, sometimes both.' She was towering over him. 'Sounds serious, but we're not here for that.'

Ronnie pulled himself up with the bricks in the wall behind him. 'You're crazy,' he said through gasping breaths. 'Come with me, we'll find help.' He held out his hand and bent both his brows sympathetically.

'Tell me,' said Ainslie. 'Right now.'

'I don't know what you are asking me about, Doctor. I really don't. I can't see. I can't feel anything. I need you to help me, and in turn, I will help you.' He reached out aimlessly to grab hold of her. 'Please, Doctor.'

She seemed to break out into a daydream. Her arms fell lifelessly to her sides, and her eyes glazed over. Suddenly, a cloud passed above her. Her hand lifted from her pocket, and a blade flashed. She would run at Ronnie, eyes set upon his chest, screaming, *mharbhadh fior oighre*! That meant, *kill the true heir!*

The Truth Hurts

She raised the blade. It shone in the moonlight bursting through the windows. She would strike down, looking at Ronnie. Her ankle would wobble, as she rose into the air and came down faster. Just then, Ronnie thrust a hand towards her. His head crackled. His brain bubbled. His eyes twitched. His fist drove into her throat.

She fell to the ground with a thud as her skull splintered one of the floorboards beneath her. Blood would edge out from behind her head. She would hold her throat, her mouth trying desperately to take in air, only to be prevented by her swollen windpipe to protect her from the hit. It would be her own body that would slowly kill her. Ronnie knew, as the blue tinge grew from her lips to her ears, that she was not making it out of the church alive.

'They'll... find... you...'

She took her final breath, and her limbs slumped on either side. Her eyes lay staring at Ronnie, as he shook his hand in pain. Her last effort in this life would leave a haunting scar in his already aching brain. He had done it again. This time, though, he didn't choose to. Unfortunate circumstances had brought him here and a bit of bad luck had made him a murderer.

This had been the most promising lead. He had fallen upon the information without doing any work at all... and now he'd killed her. In hindsight, he wondered how much she said could be trusted. It didn't match the information on the boards around the church. She said it herself, everyone had a different story. Was her version the truth? If it wasn't, was his grandad incurable? It had left him with more questions than before he arrived.

Ronnie climbed down the ladder from the top floor of the church building. He looked up, relieved to find that Ainslie's body was not visible. A moment later, he smashed up the ladder and picked up the pieces. Given the condition of the church, he doubted any staff from Historic Scotland visited often.

By the time he made it back to the car, with bits of wood, his grandad was awake and sipping on a bottle of water which had sat in the car for a couple of days. It tasted bitter, but it was all that was there.

'Did she help?' Ron asked.

'I guess,' Ronnie replied, sliding into the car.

'You look worried, lad. What's wrong?'

'You've some cheek to be asking that,' Ronnie said, deflecting. 'You've been throwing up all night, and I've rushed you to the hospital... yet you still want to ask me what's wrong?'

'Just looking after you, lad.' Ron looked up to the church. 'Where is she?'

'She...' He paused. 'She likes to sit there at night, so she is going to stay back for a bit. Being there helps her gather her thoughts, she said.'

'How odd,' said Ron.

'Yeah,' said Ronnie.

He tried to talk again, but his phone began to ring. It was another anonymous number.

'Hello?' said Ronnie.

'My good associate Brian told me a very disappointing story this evening, and he's keen that I take steps to rectify this.' It was Charles. 'I'd really rather not have to waste my time, but he's very upset about what's happened this evening.'

'I-'

'There's a lighthouse on the Butt of Lewis at the opposite end of the island,' he sounded infuriated. 'Be there tonight. No later than sunrise. I just... I can't fathom a man like you. Here is a brave fighter, who you beat senseless *twice* and he still came to bloody save you. I have given him strict instructions not to endanger your further Mr Macleod, but given what you are doing to him... I am hard pressed to ensure he keeps to his word.'

'You don't even know where I am,' said Ronnie.

'Don't test me, Mr Macleod.'

'I-'

'It's a long drive from St. Clements, Mr Macleod. I would suggest you hurry to meet my associate before he gets any... angrier.'

FLASHBACK VII

Ronnie sometimes made bad choices.

'You little cunt.'

Voices were thrown loudly at each other. Ronnie and Lewis were barricaded in a room. If Lewis tried to leave, Ronnie would wrestle him back. If Ronnie tried to leave, Lewis would hit him on the back of the head and drag him inside.

'Fuck you, Lewis.'

Seonaid was Ronnie's girlfriend in his life. She was amazing. She was the most perfect woman a man could meet. She was nice, and polite. She was not romantic, but she did everything she could to please her man. She would cook the most wonderful dishes and she would make sure their small, intolerable flat was a palace.

It wasn't just Ronnie who thought he was punching above his weight. His friends, from school, would often ask him how he managed it. She didn't see that though. She was with a loving man, who cared for her dearly. It was the least she could do to ensure that his life was as comfortable as possible. They were opinions that existed in the dark ages, but they were her opinions. She was never brought up to think differently.

Then she broke up with him.

Ronnie wasn't sure what he did wrong. She had been raped, and in her eyes, men were abhorrent and the worst sort of people. Ronnie would never go on to talk about her again the day she walked out. He would mark it down as one of the darker moments of his life. He could never come to terms that he hadn't been able to protect her. His grandad, Jim Barge, everyone knew not to bring it up with Ronnie.

Of course, the rape was unforgivable. Ronnie deeply regretted that it had happened to her. It had to be something he had done, or not done. He had let her down and led her down a path which put her into such an unforgivable fate. It made him sick to think that she was used in such a way. He had tried to help her, but she didn't want his help. He couldn't help. He felt useless and affected by it too. He understood, that he could never relate. He was still heartbroken by it, though. He still hurt that he couldn't help her solve it.

'You fucking didn't.'

'I fucking did.'

He was never supposed to be caught. There was never supposed to be anyone else around when he did it. The crime was too easy to commit, and even easier to get away with just if nobody caught him. He didn't even know why he did it. He was committing the crime before he had even thought a second time about it.

Next door to Morag Macleod lived an elderly lady. She looked ninety on a good day, but her birth certificate marked her down to be only seventy-five.

She was unbanked. She did not believe in a banking system, and as a result her entire assets remained inside her council house. She would never benefit from the joys of an ISA, or the crumbled interest rates that a bank would offer her to save with them. Why save for 0.05% when you can save for nothing?

She also had dementia.

All he needed to do was walk in, tell her he was going to help, and walk out with enough money to buy whatever it was he wanted. A car? Sure. You could have a car with that sort of money. You could have anything you wanted, and he wanted something. He just hadn't decided what it was.

He walked in, he put the money in his bag and he walked out the back door like he had never been in the property at all. Nobody was supposed to see him... Those who worked would be out, and the rest would still be asleep. He had timed it all so perfectly for a spur of the moment theft. He closed the door, lifted the handle and smiled.

He'd gotten away with it.

Until Lewis caught him, as he stood beside the fence smoking a cigarette.

'I'm not fucking with you, Ronnie. You know what is going to happen to me.'

'I know. You're going to grass on me though, and I can't have that.'

'You are the worst kind of cunt.'

Lewis threw a right hook which Ronnie blocked with his forearm, throwing an uppercut underneath which would force his brother back a few steps. Trying to take advantage, he would run with his elbow and miss. They could not overpower each other. They could not allow themselves to hit hard enough.

'Take it back,' Lewis gasped as a right hook narrowly missed his head. He slipped his hand round Ronnie's head, but he wriggled free and the two men stood staring at each other, their shoulders rising and falling heavily.

'I can't.'

'Just do it, Ronnie. You know what they're going to think of me. Please.' Lewis had never sounded more desperate.

'No.'

They were stood in their mother's living room. She was out for the day, at the pub. Ronnie's bag was sat on the couch. Lewis had asked for some of it, most of it in fact. Ronnie told him no. Lewis decided then, that he was going to out Ronnie.

'You stole from an old woman who doesn't have her fucking marbles,' Lewis shouted as he slapped his brother with the back of his hand. 'I wouldn't do that. We've known her our whole lives. That's just fucking low.'

'We will see who they believe.' Ronnie was bored of fighting. He sat down on the couch, breathless. He knew how it would all play out now that he had called 999. 'I don't think it will be you, funnily enough.'

'What did I ever do to you, Ronnie?' Lewis was holding his arm where Ronnie had bitten him. 'I've said anything bad to you.'

'You're going to try and tell me that?' Ronnie laughed obscenely. 'You're the one who called me a cunt when I was only a kid. You never respected me the whole time I was alive.' Ronnie shook his head. 'You didn't need to treat me the same way she did, but you did. You chose to be like her.'

The police sirens got closer with every passing second. Ronnie's smile got bigger. He knew now, after the numerous times previous, how easy it was to manipulate the law to have his brother and mother taken care of.

'I'm not going to beg you,' said Lewis. His eyes opened wide.

'It wouldn't matter, I wouldn't change my mind.'

Lewis would hit him so hard that he fell against the wall. Ronnie felt the back of his head trickle slightly. In a moment that shocked even Lewis, Ronnie would proceed to bang his head so hard against the wall, that the circle of blood grew.

'Oh dear,' said Ronnie. 'I'm bleeding, Lewis.'

Lewis would pick him up and throw him across the other side of the room. He would try to rub the mark from the wall, but he would only end up with Ronnie's blood on his own hands.

'Is that because you decided to hurt me?' Ronnie asked.

'I didn't.'

'The blood on your hands though, what does that tell you?'

'You're sick.'

'No, I'm not sick.' Ronnie felt his wounds nip and he smiled. 'I'm clever.'

'They won't believe you.'

'What, they won't believe me over you? Think of what you've done, Lewis. Think of who you are and who everyone else knows you to be. I'm a good guy. You're a registered sex offender.'

'Mum made me treat you like that,' Lewis said. 'She hated you, and if I didn't treat you the same way then she'd hate me too. I'm not like you, Ronnie. I have… issues. Problems.'

'Yeah, like what?' Ronnie asked.

'I can't talk about it.' Lewis sighed. 'If I could tell you, I would.'

'Come on to fuck, Lewis.' Ronnie slapped him in the face cheaply. 'We're brothers, there's nothing that you should hide from me.'

Lewis said nothing. He just punched Ronnie as hard as he could. Ronnie's eye socket almost splintered with the veracity. 'Piss off,' said Lewis.

Ronnie stood back up from the wall and laughed. Lewis could see it all happening, and he wasn't smart enough to stop any of it. In a flash, Ronnie ran at the glass cabinet which sat at the corner of the living room and jumped into it. The glass shattered, and Ronnie fell flat on his stomach, covered in glittery shards. Lewis did not expect that.

'You're fucking mental,' Lewis gasped.

The front door opened.

'*POLICE!*'

Five officers would run immediately to Lewis and pin him to the ground. Behind them, would appear one of the senior detectives. James Barge. He would pick up Ronnie Macleod and help him to his seat.

'You should have tried to get out,' Barge said, gripping Ronnie's hand and checking the bruises and cuts over his face. 'You shouldn't have tried to fight him.'

'I know, Barge. I tried. I'm sorry.'

'Don't be sorry... it's that monster over there that should be sorry.'

Lewis did not appreciate any passing comment of Jim Barge. He would kick and scream and that made it more obvious that he was a guilty man, arrested again for another crime. It would be added to the very long list. Nobody would question it, and nobody would ask him why he was the way he was. He was a wrong'un.

'I need to tell you something, Jim.' Ronnie held the back of his head, wincing. He looked at him, trying to be as honest as he could. 'You won't like it, though. It's about Seonaid.'

Though he were only acting, Ronnie tried to play off Barge's cringes and shock at the information he was relaying to him. He considered crying, to make it more believable, but then he remembered that the entire moment of time was dead to him. He finished his story and put his head into his bloody hands. He felt Jim's hand on his shoulder. Signed, sealed and delivered to the next Sheriff.

Barge stepped out from the house and walked down to the Police van where Lewis now sat. The two men stared at each other for a long time. Lewis wanted to know what the fuck Barge was going to blame him for now. Barge looked deeper, he wanted to know if he seen someone capable of what it was he was certain that he did.

'Lewis, could you explain something for me please.' Barge sat down so that he was at eye level with him. 'I have a report from your brother which suggests that you may have been responsible for the unsolved crime relating to the rape and assault of a young woman in the forest behind this house.'

Lewis reacted the same way he always did. Even he realised there was no point trying to testify his innocence. He just took it as an opportunity to kick out and hurt as many people as he could. Some professional people had questioned if there were more to why he acted in the way he did, but Lewis wouldn't allow those people in. They were just another monster in the system.

Nobody is perfect. Nobody is purely evil. Nobody is one dimensional.

You will have started this story thinking Ronnie was a pour soul in an awful situation. Only, from what we have gathered, Ronnie is the reason that most of these situations happen. His mother's drug habit? His brother's crimes? They likely would have happened, but a catalyst will trigger the reaction much faster. Ronnie pushed things to happen faster. He made it so for him to succeed with whatever he wanted. He took advantage of what was in front of him to increase the odds in his favour.

Just like Charles.

He was evil too.

So, why should any of us care?
You need to break a hero to make them.

SIXTEEN

Now, every time I witness a strong person, I want to know: What dark did you conquer in your story? Mountains do not rise without earthquakes.

Katherine MacKenett

Ron sat quietly as they raced northwards towards the lighthouse. His grandson had mumbled one or two words to him, which he ignored. Ron was in his most special place. He allowed nobody to know about it or enter. It was much too sacred to be shared.

'I need your help,' he begged, sitting upon a white bench which looked out to marble hills in the distance sitting under a peaceful white sky. 'I am scared. I don't know what to do anymore.'

'You always told me it was human to be scared.' replied the voice. 'It would be foolish to try and understand him. There are too many secrets between you now. He is buried in this and you cannot help him. You will die if you do.'

A teardrop fell from Ron's eye and smashed into the white luxurious oak upon which he sat comfortably. There was a smell of rain behind the horizon. Ron knew, when smelt rain, something bad was about to happen. He smelt it that night his own happiness ended. He had smelt it every heartbreak since.

'Do you think someone is going to die?' Ron asked.

'Yes.' His son sat beside him now and held his hand. He was dressed in white, and his beard was shaved perfectly. Upon his brown hairline, every strand laid perfect. Just as it had the day his funeral came. He gave his father a reassuring smile. 'Sorry, dad.'

'Better being prepared, I suppose.' Ron had a chuckle. 'He's not been right for a while, to be honest Fin. I just can't seem to pull him back out whatever mess he's in. He's convinced that Charles is going to help us when he finds it. He won't.'

'You sound like you know the answers he needs?' Fin asked, but he spoke as though he too knew the answer. 'How do you stop him from finding what he is destined to find? You can't fight history.'

'I hope he's killed,' Ron said painfully. 'I don't want him to die, but I don't want him to become what it will make him. I'm fortunate that we just can't find anything to solve it. Yet we are stumbling closer and closer to something that will show him where it is.'

'If he finds it, what do you do then?'

'I hope I'm dead.' Ron sighed. 'Nobody else but one family on that island knows what it is Charles wants. Charles doesn't have a clue what it is. If Ronnie finds that family, then he will find it. When he finds it, there is no chance of him giving it to Charles.'

Fin looked at him cautiously. 'You're lucky this is all in your head, Ron.'

Ron? Why would Fin call him that? 'It's dad to you. I need somewhere to be able to talk about this since you died.'

'Put it down, or you'll be dead too.' Fin shook his head and for a moment, Ron saw another face. He was a bald man. He was angry. His accent was not familiar; somewhere from the West Coast. It was impatient. It was biting.

'Sorry,' whispered Ron. 'I'm not holding anything though.' He opened both his grey hands to prove it.

'You don't need to apologise to me, dad.'

Ron checked twice. It was Fin's face, and he did call him dad. He looked up into the sky, where there were dark skies and thunderstorms now. There had only been peace and sunlight. There were cracks, like shadows, poking through the ceiling. Everything was starting to fall apart. Raindrops came tapping down above them.

'The end is coming,' Fin said sadly.

'Will I lose you?' Ron asked.

'It is the end,' grimaced Fin.

'I've lost you and now I am losing Ronnie. When does this pain stop?'

'When you lose yourself.'

He took a sharp breath and jumped in fright. He was no longer sitting beside his son but stood beside Ronnie in the dark. To his right stood the Butt of Lewis lighthouse. Ron doubted David Stevenson imagined his red-bricked timepiece would be the showdown for two psychopaths and a cripple. It had survived the harsh Atlantic wind and swell. There was no promise it would survive this.

'I don't think he's well,' Brian said as he gestured an open hand. 'Help him back into the car before he falls over.'

'I'm fine,' shouted Ron. His right hand gripped tightly on the black handle of his walking stick. 'My name is Ron, sir. How are you?'

'I'm good, pal.' Brian spluttered his words as he tried to bite the corner of his thumbnail. 'Sorry to have you out here so late after your day at the hospital. I'll try to be quick.'

'Thanks. I appreciate it.'

Ronnie stared wild-eyed back towards his grandad. 'Why the fuck are you being nice to him, have you lost your head?' He turned, but only for a second before his scowling face returned to his grandad. 'I need you here, but you're lost in your fucking head talking to Fin, whoever that is. How about you stop pretending to be some made up man and you help me out a little, yeah?'

The old man looked around him. The grassland was now dirt with the heavy traffic each day and the constant moisture made the ground beneath them very slippery. Apart from one long brick wall which extended around the lighthouse, there were sharp cliff edges to all other sides of Ron. He gulped. There was a lot at stake.

'Is this the man you beat up on the ship? Ron asked, nervously pointing a finger out towards the gun. 'I think you should apologise.'

'He won't,' muttered Brian. 'I don't mean to try and pretend I know him better than you. Lord knows that would be impossible given how much you've volunteered for him. You are going to think this comes from a bad place, but genuinely, I have massive respect for the shit you put up with to get this waste of space to work.'

'I appreciate the sentiment,' lied Ron.

'You're such a little darling, aren't you?' Ronnie asked. 'Fancy a game of dollies?'

Brian smiled to Ronnie's belittling humour. 'There are hundreds of men just like me that work for Charles. Yet they all forget the most important part of this job. Its respect. See, I have a lot of respect for the man behind you. Mr Macleod. Whilst I don't have any for you, I must still respect the balance of probability. You are unlikely to do anything serious, but, as we've seen, you are likely to try.'

Ronnie screwed up his face laughing. He looked to his granddad who looked petrified and immediately wrote off his opinion. 'That is some of the worst patter I have ever heard in my life, please.'

'I look into the eyes of a lot of men,' Brian said, the sarcasm removed. 'I can tell within moments if they are a coward. I have seen men fail to even blink as they had their head cut off.' He lowered his head. 'Do you want to know what type of man you are, Ronnie?'

Ronnie, rather than move to protect his grandad, took three steps forward until Brian reminded the two men he was armed with a handgun. He swung it into Ronnie's face and tapped the barrel.

'You're terrified,' whispered Brian. 'I can help.'

'Where did you find the weapon?' Ronnie asked jovially. 'Out that dusty fucking gift shop on the main street? If you're going to kill me with that thing, then do it right now. Don't waste time I could be better spending dead.'

Ron heard, for the first time, words of defeat from his grandson. He wondered if he really meant it. Ronnie wasn't the type to give up. Perhaps everything was too much. Perhaps he knew what he had to become for all of this to stop, and it was too much… even for a monster.

'You won't believe me, Mr Macleod,' Brian looked to Ron. 'I want you to believe me that I don't want to do what I need to do. There are a lot of things I do that are questionable. This is the worst. For me. You though,' his glance turned to young Ronnie. 'You need to listen to what I am about to say and learn that no matter how *brilliant* you think you are, you will always be taken down by someone greater.'

'You?' Asked Ronnie. 'You said it yourself, you're a thug. You do bad things for bad people.'

'Perhaps, but I don't do bad things because I'm a bad person.' Brian sighed. 'Do you tell your grandad everything? Or just the things he'd like to hear?'

'If my grandson has done anything to upset you, then I fully take responsibility.' Ron outstretched a hand, but he quickly fell back onto his walking stick for support. 'I am truly sorry for the upset that he caused you. I can have words.'

Brian pointed the gun at Ronnie. 'You see that? He's taking the blame for everything you've done to me. Why can't you say sorry?'

'You don't deserve it.'

'I appreciate your gesture, Mr Macleod, I do. I know a gentleman when I see one and you are of the highest calibre. There is no doubt of that.' Brian raised a smile to the old man. 'Do you keep many secrets from your grandson?'

'I don't,' said Ron. 'We are very open with each other. About everything.'

'He'll have told you who I am then,' Brian responded quickly. 'He'll have told you how I met him?'

'You work for Charles.'

'Yes, but I don't think he told you that.'

'Does that matter?' Ronnie interrupted.

'To me,' Brian replied.

'It doesn't matter how I know it,' Ron replied. 'What is you are trying to do with us here this evening? We have had a very emotional day as it is, sir.'

'When I was young, my grandad passed away.' Brian lowered the gun slightly. He looked up to the night sky. 'I found out the day after his funeral. My father told me that I didn't need to know about it. He told me that, for reasons he never declared to me, I couldn't possibly understand the whys, or the when. It's interesting really, when I think about this… what we are doing right now. Did Ronnie ever tell you that he knows who killed your friend, Jim?' Brian lifted the gun back up, aiming it straight at Ronnie. 'Did he tell you anything about that?'

'He didn't,' Ron said.

'That's right,' Ronnie added.

'Don't you find that odd, Ron? Why hasn't he told you? He was a close family friend. If you were my grandfather, I would be sure to tell you everything the second I found out myself.' Brian rubbed the barrel of the gun as it remained pointed at Ronnie. 'Anything to say, Ronnie?'

'I don't wish to repeat myself, sir.' Ron struggled for his walking stick. 'My grandson was there when he died, and I was there too. It was a terrible night that I don't expect he will want to relive. I certainly don't, thank you.'

Brian shook his head and tutted. Ronnie's eyes hadn't moved. The whites had darkened as his attitude soured. Ron, meanwhile, well, he was playing the part. He knew what the bald man was doing to them. He was testing their resilience. He would question Ronnie about these things later. He was not letting Charles' man win.

'Ronnie recognised him,' Brian shouted. 'Charles came into the hospital, dressed as a nurse, and your boy knew that. He let him inject Barge with a drug that would kill him. Ronnie seen all of that, and still let Lewis go to prison. Don't you think that's crazy?'

Ron looked to his grandson. 'You knew that was him?'

'You didn't?' Ronnie blurted the words out before he could think. 'You've known him for longer than I have.'

'Aye,' said Ron. 'Years ago, lad, when he had some colour in his hair.'

'I just can't work out why Jim's life meant less than his will, being that Ronnie was the sole benefactor. To think Jim trusted your grandson when he promised to be the single point of safety and security against your family... then when it came to it, he fucking ignored his phone. What kind of monster are you?'

'It's not like that,' Ronnie said, turning his head slightly to his grandad, but not enough to be able to look him in the eye.

'Did he tell you about his mother?' Brian continued.

'No...' Ron stuttered. 'What about her?' He didn't want to hear anymore, but he was now too deep into Brian's game. Something was going to break his heart. He knew it. This was their game. They might not get Ronnie, but they can punish him through his grandad.

'Well, you know that Morag was attacked by her drug dealer all those years ago, don't you? There's Ronnie, defencelessly sitting in that house whilst she's beaten. Tragic, don't you think Ron?'

Ron nodded. 'I never had much time for her and that habit of hers, but it didn't need to lead to her being beaten for it. She only needed to ask, and I'd have helped.'

'Ronnie beat her,' Brian said.

'What?'

'You punched her senseless, didn't you pal?' Brian almost laughed. 'Ronnie punched her in the throat. Kicked her until she was out cold. She'd shat herself.'

Ronnie felt his grandad's eyes bury into the back of him, pleading him to turn around. Instead he stood with his eyes closed. He didn't have anything to say to either of them. He just wanted to punish Brian. The ache behind his eyes drummed the beat of war.

'You tell me that he's lying, lad.' Ron's voice shook in the wind. 'You tell me that none of this is true.'

The Truth Hurts

Ronnie wouldn't. He couldn't.

'Lewis caught our Ronnie stealing from the old neighbour with Alzheimer's. You'd think he'd pay him off or something, but no… Ronnie isn't like a normal criminal like me. No, Ron, you see… Ronnie passed off a false story to the Police.'

'When?' Ron interrupted. 'I don't remember any interview by the Police.'

'There is clear proof that Ronnie was with Lewis on the morning his ex-partner was sexually assaulted. Yet, Ronnie needed something to deflect away from his crime… and he thought nothing less of having Lewis go back to jail for a crime he never committed. Seonaid still doesn't even know who raped her, so why would Ronnie know who it was?'

Sobbing clouded the cliff behind Ronnie. 'You can't have, lad.' Ron forced cough after cough to stop himself crying. 'Sir, you can't be right. Our Ronnie wouldn't do something like that.'

'I'm sorry, Ron.' Brian's eyes pleaded with Ronnie to admit everything. 'He did. Lewis caught him stealing from Morag's old neighbour before she passed away. It's a relief she didn't remember it. Who knows what would have happened if she did.' Brian squeezed lightly on the trigger. 'I could kill him, just out sympathy for you Ron. You quit your job for this piece of trash.'

Ronnie's head hadn't raised since he lowered it. He just looked deathly past his brow towards Brian. He knew that he was enjoying breaking the old man. Charles had expressly told him not to hurt Ronnie physically, but he gave no instruction about mental pain. Ron was crying louder now. He wobbled, almost falling over his walking stick. Ronnie heard it. He did not turn around.

'We sat down just the other day to try and figure out why our friend Ronnie wouldn't say anything about Barge's killer. It's only when you know the things I've just told you, Ron, that you realise it's not because he's rude, and it's not because none of this has made sense… it's because this shady figure is a bigger crook than the rest of your family. If a different copper comes in sniffing around, your Ronnie is going away for a very long time.'

Brian laughed. 'You're a piece of work, aren't you?'

It was all true. Ronnie had lived a life knowing that Jim Barge would never prosecute him, because like his grandad, he could see no wrong. But someone new? They would find all of this and more. Ronnie would go to jail longer than either Morag or Lewis put together. Brian didn't even know the half of what he'd done.

Ron cried louder now. He couldn't stop. For most of his life now, he had pleaded with every God and deity that Ronnie would not turn out like his mother, and he would be thankful for every day that it was true. Now, he looked at him. It was so obvious. Ronnie wasn't as bad as them. He was worse.

'You're an angry man, Ronnie.' Ron shouted at first, took a breath, and then shouted even louder. 'There's no excuse for the things you have done though. No excuse.' He wiped the tear from his cheek. 'Can we go now?'

'Ronnie, do you feel like you've let him down yet?' Brian shook the gun at him. 'Why did you do it? Why did you pretend you were a good bloke? Did you get a kick out of him ruining his life? Was it nice to watch a man be beaten? Why are you a monster?' Brian waited for a response. 'Silence says it all, don't it grandad?'

The wind began to pick up wilder than it has before. The men could barely hear each other from the flapping of their clothing.

'You've let me down, Ronnie.' Ron took an enormous breath. -

'I'm hurt,' said Ron as he shut his eyes and found himself next to Fin. 'Ronnie's lost his mind, son, he's not thinking clearly. I need him to...'

He stopped.

There were lightening strikes littering the sky now. The marbled paving was cracked and uneven as the earth beneath it shook and rolled under Ron's feet. Through the ash and cloud in the far distance, embers glowed.

Ron couldn't remember why he came here anymore. His lungs filled with an awful taste that he couldn't breathe out as easy as he took it in. They felt like they were getting smaller each time and a subtle panic shuddered through his body from the tips of his toes to the wrinkles on his forehead.

'I'm beginning to die,' he whispered to himself. He couldn't even barely hear his own voice.

The wind was ferocious now as it screamed round the lighthouse to Brian who stared at Ronnie and to Ronnie, who stared back at Brian with the strongest contempt he felt for anyone in his life. How dare he destroy the only thing his grandad held dear to him. No longer was he Ron's boy, he was Morag's. Ron just had one more vile reason to have lived his life the brave victim. He deserved an apology. Even if it meant nothing.

Ronnie turned to his grandfather to say the word, but he was gone. The black sea roared below as it thudded against the cliff, and whatever it had taken with it.

FLASHBACK VIII

'What is it you intend to do once you leave school, Morag?'

Her parents regularly invited their esteemed colleagues for dinner and she would be encouraged to join them. She didn't mind. It was nice to speak to people who had really achieved something in life, to be able to learn from them and chisel her own future from their advice.

'I want to do something with children,' she mumbled with a bread roll twisting and crunching in her mouth. 'I don't think its teaching, but I don't specifically what it is. I still have plenty time to decide though, thankfully.'

She was intelligent enough to develop the conversation onto something that the adults would carry on for hours into the night. Yet, they still found her very endearing. Her mother's friend – an educational psychologist – had commented that she was the nicest fourteen-year-old you could find. She was thoughtful and keen to learn. For her parents and their backgrounds, they could not be more blessed to have her.

Sure, she made one or two silly choices. Her dad was the angriest when he found out that Fin had gotten her pregnant. He didn't mind that she was doing… whatever it was she was doing, he just had a problem that she wasn't being clever enough in the way she went about it. Still, she would give birth to Lewis. Her relationship with Fin would end quickly after that. They were incapable of raising a child together and so he run away to the Navy until he realised that choice was never for him either.

Morag made the best of it. She refused to let her son put an end to her own life. So, she learnt to be the perfect mother. Or at least, as perfect as she could be. Whatever he needed, no matter how hard to find it, Morag would get it. She would never be the world's best mother, and he would never be the greatest son. Yet, they had each other and providing they were healthy, it was all that mattered.

Her grandad brought over their family from the Isle of Lewis in the late twenties. They settled in Hawick, finding jobs in the mills and falling back into their working-class lifestyles and attitudes until her parents went to University and sought professional careers. Morag understood you didn't get anything unless you worked for it. Her parents made sure of that. They always told her that if she didn't work hard like they did, she would end up like her uncle.

It makes no sense then, that Morag would become so hideous and violent. She had no reason to wake up one day and decide that her world forevermore would exist of hatred and vitriol. There was no clear breaking point that any mental breakdown could be pinpointed to.

Not unless, the truth could become too much to handle for Hawick's bright-eyed lass.

Lewis was no older than four. He should have been picking things up like every other child, but he wasn't. He still wore nappies, and he still wasn't talking. Morag found her having to feed her son every meal of every day. He just didn't seem to understand. He was incredibly lethargic too. Doctors just assumed he would get better, but he never would. He would only get worse.

'He will improve as he gets older,' said Dr Machiavelli. 'He's still got a lot of developing.'

'You've said that to me before,' she shouted. People told her that Lewis was special, but it had only recently occurred to her how special he was. 'He's a retard.' There was only one reason why his development could be stunted, but the doctors didn't want to tell her.

She was angry enough without a doctor confirming her suspicions. She'd done her own research and she knew exactly what was wrong with her son. There were a few natural ways for

Lewis to suffer as he did, but only one way guaranteed he would suffer from the number of defects that he had.

They didn't trust Morag to look after her son's complex needs alone, not after she was stupid enough to fall pregnant with him in the first place and then keep him despite the number of worrying tests. So, they entrusted her uncle, who stayed only when both had to travel for work.

She hated when her uncle came to stay. He was a loner. He didn't work, he just studied, and he liked to tell everyone everything that he learnt. She presumed it made him feel important for the short amount of time he was lucky enough to have company. He would even force her to dry the dishes so he could tell her the final drabs of pointless knowledge he picked up. She hated it, but she had no choice.

And anyway, the worst was yet to come.

She would be asleep when it started. She knew it was better that way because she wouldn't know it was about to happen. She wouldn't need to let the anxiety build her in her head as he would run his cold hands down her sides and into her pyjamas bottoms whilst her son lay sleeping in the cot beside.

She would feel the bedsheets flutter, and his cold, rough hands move over her thighs. She would shudder, but it wouldn't put him off. If anything, it would add to the excitement. You'd have to ask him why. She would just keep her eyes shut and her mind on other things.

Then, once he was unable to hold back, he would rape her. He would do thing that nobody need experience, far less read. She was, at the beginning, an innocent girl. Her uncle put an end to that. Eventually, it became normal. In a way it angered him. He couldn't orgasm the same way if she didn't wriggle at least a little bit.

Why did nobody know it was happening? She wasn't allowed to tell anyone; her uncle would kill her if she did. She lived with the secret in the hope that one person would look at her and realise that Morag had been repeatedly raped. She begged for someone to ask, just so she could tell the truth and stop the abuse.

In the end, after the months and the years, she would be so desensitised by the entire situation, that she figured she was asking for it. She was, after all, a woman. What the fuck else was she useful for? He could fuck her if he wanted. It didn't matter anymore.

In the times that it hurt too much to think about, heroin was there. It would kill the pain and let her, just for those short minutes, pretend she was happy and forget anything horrific had ever happened to her. She didn't need to face the consequences of her actions, to allow her uncle to force himself upon her.

That's why Ronnie would always anger her. He wasn't like her little Lewis. Lewis didn't deserve to be different, but he was. Ronnie came out and everyone told her how perfect he was, and how lucky she should feel. In the same breath, they'd try diagnosing Lewis' continual bad behaviour. People thought he might have ADHD. Yet, Ronnie was a 'wee star'. No. Ronnie was embarrassing for her little diamond.

With everything, there's a breaking point.

Morag decided to face the horror of her past. It was the only way that Lewis would get the help he needed, and he was the only thing that mattered. If she got the chance, she'd tell her uncle what the years of horrific abuse had left them both with. She hoped she could finally punish them for every second he punished her.

She invited him into the trees. The text message alone made him hard. It was all he could think about. Finally, after all these years, *she really wanted him*. She grabbed his hand and took him deep into the woodland, and her uncle – no longer regretted by the way he felt about her – reached in to kiss her softly on the lips.

'What are you doing?' Morag shouted as she pushed him as hard as she could into an old Oak. Leaves fell down around the two of them.

'I thought,' he stuttered over his words, rubbing his aching back.

'You thought what?' Her line of sight chased his as he frantically looked for a way out of the situation, embarrassed by his desperate mistake. 'You thought I was going to invite you here for a shag? You won't touch me ever again.'

Her uncle took a step back. He was shocked. This was not how it was supposed to go. She was supposed to embrace it. They would do it here, one more time. That was why she had invited him.

'Why not, my dear?' His voice made her shudder, and she closed her eyes. 'One more time, surely? We can spare the time for each other? I'm going away for a while. I can't return, and I don't know when I will be able to.'

'You don't fucking get it, do you? I've told dad. He knows.'

Her uncle looked dead inside. He wondered if he should just murder her and run away. Yes, it would look bad that an uncle would kill a niece for no reason, but it would be easier on the stomach than the world finding out an uncle had spent every night babysitting his niece, fucking her in her sleep.

'You know what will happen if you tell people,' he reached out for her hand which she snapped back. 'You know that nobody will understand.'

'I don't fucking understand.' Morag felt tears run down her cheek. 'You don't fucking get to do that. You don't get to ruin my entire fucking life over something that you couldn't hold in. Who would think of touching a child?'

'I loved you,' her uncle said softly. 'I only did it because I loved you.'

'Don't.'

'Morag,' he tried to open his hand to her, but she slapped it away. 'If you didn't want this, then why did you invite me here? I feel like there's still a chance for us. We could go together, if that is why you have come to meet me.'

'You need to know the truth,' she said, ignoring yet another seedy advance.

'The truth?' Her uncle asked.

'You raped me,' Morag said indignantly. 'You raped me time and time again. You clearly thought it was the perfect crime. You didn't think there would be any evidence and you certainly didn't think that the nice little girl with the west end would tell anyone about her dirty uncle. Well, you fucked up.'

'I don't understand,' he said. His hands were shaking. He was already very late for his lift to the airport. He needed to go away, not for this, for other things that had gone wrong. People were looking for him, including the Police, and he couldn't afford to go away to prison. 'What are you trying to tell me?'

'Lewis is your son,' she said. 'What the fuck are you going to do about that, Uncle Charles?'

SEVENTEEN

The left hook came before a right hook smashed his skull. Furious jabs to the body followed, at least one per second and two if he could force it. The flurry of violence knocked his sight around as he got closer and closer to the ground. One knee at first, then the other. His skull was next to smash into the stones.

Ronnie had lost it now. Silence swarmed around him, but he could hear only the buzz of his internal anger. His skull vibrated and the heavier his mood became, the tinnier the bone inside his head sounded.

His eyes struggled to see through the night. He could barely see his hands, as they fluttered in and out of the darkness. Ronnie wasn't sure if his eyes were deceiving him, and that was worrying. He had to be able to trust his own body. He tensed his leg one final time and drove it as hard as he could into the soft stomach of Brian's lifeless body.

'I'm going to find whatever the fuck is I need to find.' Ronnie kneeled to whisper into Brian's ear. 'You're going to want to be there when I have it. I'm to kill that old little cretin with my bare hands, and then I'm going to punch you in the head until you stop breathing. You're not going to want to miss it.'

Ronnie had felt anger in the past, but nothing like this. His veins burned. His eyes popped from his head. This was all his fault, but he didn't want to take the blame. He couldn't. There had to be another reason why his grandad died.

He turned to his car. He was going to run it straight over the top of Brian's legs. His mind was playing tricks again at first. Then the Porsche picked up speed. Ronnie had only made it a few feet before the car flew off the cliff edge. The hard wind held the sound of the metal crashing against the rock below.

He couldn't fucking believe it.

The road away from the lighthouse was dark and still. As he began his long walk, he relied slowly on continuing to hear tarmac slap against the sole of his shoe. It annoyed him that he had to concentrate on this. He had so many other things he needed to process.

Mainly, his grandad. The entire journey had been about curing him. By that reasoning, he should be trying to find his way home. The plan to help Charles didn't matter now that he was dead because Ronnie had nothing to gain from it.

But he could become the most powerful man in the world.

Charles would probably try and hunt him down like he did with his grandad. It didn't particularly bother him. He was an old man, what could he do? Ronnie had lost everything. Dying, though he were terrified of it, didn't seem like much of a surprise. He had seen enough death.

But he could become the most powerful man in the world.

'Why did I have to be like that with you?' Ronnie screamed into the air with his hands outstretched. 'I loved you. Only you. I'll never hear you forgive me,' he barked. 'I'll never be able to *apologise.*'

He took one more step forward and he stared across the fields. His eyesight was a bit better now. He could see the moonlight glisten across the landscape. Sure, he could just lie down here and wait to die. Or he could take this entire situation by the balls. He could think about himself for once. *He could become the most powerful man in the world.* Charles would pay for what he did to his grandad, to Jim, to Lewis. He would suffer for all the other people he would have hurt, who's story would never be heard.

People weren't going missing for something worthless. The people on this island, and by association Charles, knew what it was his ancestors were hiding. At least, they knew of its power and they knew it was worth fighting for.

Two single LED headlights burst through the darkness just

past the brow of the hill far in front. Ronnie quickly darted into the long grass in the field and lay down. He knew that Brian would not be alone. Charles would not be silly enough to allow Brian and Ronnie to be together knowing their history and what they had already done to one another.

Ronnie's breath fluttered the grass beneath him. His breath quickened as the car slowed down only feet from him. They couldn't see him, surely. He reached down to his phone, the battery was out and in a separate pocket to the phone. They weren't tracking him.

The car stopped.

Ronnie's heart quickened only slightly. He wasn't nervous. He was excited. He knew what he wanted. He was desperate for Charles to climb out of the car. He closed his eyes, and fully let himself go. Inside his mind, the thought of hurting someone excited him. He could taste the feeling of beating someone. When he finally killed Charles, he would be sure to rip his head off and smash it off the ground.

The car drove off.

He was almost angry. More angry than disappointed, that was for sure. He only got to imagine that sensational feeling. He didn't even get to make a fucking threat.

Then his mind seized. His brain felt as though it was about to burst from his head. It was the only way he could imagine this getting better. He punched the ground, hoping pain in the rest of his body would take away from that his mind. He had broken his leg once. He could deal with that. This was a pain that was dissolving his grip of reality, and he was struggling to cope.

He stood up, and carried on down the road, occupying his mind with his fantasies. I honestly think, if those who knew him, seen him now, they'd struggle to recognise him. His eyes sunk into his head and black bags now lined the bottom of his eye lids. He hadn't shaved, and for the first time in his life he had an actual black, murky beard as opposed to the classy stubble he normally wore. You'd wonder if he was fully aware, if he wasn't beginning to lose his mind.

Nobody else walked by him. He walked for around twenty minutes before he arrived at the town of Eoropaidh. He hadn't noticed until a second car passed by and broke his trance. He looked at the name of the village and tried to work out why he recognised it. When he tried remembering, the back of his head pulsed with pain.

Eoropaidh was a tiny village of houses. You would blink and miss it, and most people did. There was nothing here but the people who were born here, raised children here and died here. Nobody moved to Eoropaidh. It was a village steeped in its own history.

Ronnie was bursting on a piss, and he was thirsty too. He needed a drink, and he needed one now. He was a couple of feet from one of the homes where someone was awake. He stood outside for several minutes and watched two people walk in and out of the front room. They looked concerned.

He considered bursting in, demanding what he needed. Then he remembered that a rational person might phone the police. So, he politely knocked the door, and tried to remember the version of him which could be nice and mean it.

'Good evening,' Ronnie said as the door opened. 'I hope-'

'*Leòdhas*,' interrupted the young lady. She shouted it twice more, louder and louder. She frantically opened the door into the living room and stood pointing at Ronnie.

'Sorry, I didn't mean to-'

'I cannot believe this,' said the girl. She was around five-foot-tall, her hair brown, her eyes green. She held her hair in a ponytail which stretched her forehead to the back of her head. 'I cannot believe you are here.'

She dragged Ronnie into the house, by his own surprise, and threw him into the living room. Inside, sat two others. The older man sat beside an even older lady. They looked deep in thought. They were talking Gaelic, but they paused in Ronnie's presence.

'*Leòdhas*,' they all said together. 'You have come.'

Ronnie didn't know what to say. He tried to think of something, anything, but the result was him opening his mouth and no sound coming out.

'You must forgive us for looking so concerned,' the man said. 'My daughter was due home many hours ago. She has not returned.'

'I'm sorry...' Ronnie couldn't help but recognise the young girl. 'I've just come from the lighthouse. My car... it fell off the cliff.'

'She wouldn't have been there,' sighed the old lady. 'She's a doctor in Stornoway. We're worried. We heard reports of men by the hospital, looking for someone.'

His eyes went white, and his tongue became so dry it stuck to the roof of his mouth. 'I... it must be hard to suffer this. Can I do anything to help?'

'What is your name?' The old man asked again. 'Your real name.'

'My real name?' Ronnie asked. 'I only have one name.'

'Yes, Leòdhas.' The old lady's eyes stabbed into him. She was angry.

Ronnie suddenly remembered back in the church, when Ainslie showed him the photograph. He remembered how convinced she was that he was a dead man. He hadn't thought for a second that this family had also seen this photo. They too would see the similarity.

'I'm sorry,' Ronnie said. 'My name is Ronnie Macleod, but I cannot help you.'

'You can't?' The old man asked, standing up to walk to their side dresser. He bowed his head and looked to a photo that Ronnie guessed was of his two daughters. He could only see the younger embraced with another female. 'Why not?'

'I just came from the lighthouse, like I said.' Ronnie slowly took a step to his right, towards the old man and the door out of the property. 'I haven't seen anyone else.'

He had just closed his mouth and turned to smile to the rest of the family and make his excuses to leave when everything went black. He wondered if the pain in his head had gotten worse.

EIGHTEEN

Ronnie's eyes were blinded by the light that entered them. His vision was lost to him. His hearing echoed. He was paralysed now, or his limbs were either tied together. Whatever the case, he was in a lot of trouble. Every one of his broken senses told him that.

'You are in a very serious condition,' a voice said to him from his right. Ronnie's eyes rolled into the back of his head as he tried to control them. 'How long have you been bleeding?'

'I've not,' Ronnie whispered. 'There's no blood.'

'You are bleeding inside your skull,' the man said. 'We probably made it worse when I hit you with our iron, but not to worry.'

'Not to worry?' Ronnie asked. 'I've had headaches… bad headaches.'

'You will. It's putting pressure on your brain.' Ronnie felt the man's hand touch the back of his head, and his eyes shot open. His vision shot back inside of his eye sockets and he could see the man from Eoropaidh.

'Ainslie's dad is supposed to be dead,' said Ronnie. It was though he had come back to himself in an instant. 'She told me that.'

'I thought you didn't know my daughter,' said the man. 'Not dead, by the way. Just a retired doctor. Taught that girl everything she knew. Where is she?'

Ronnie shook his head. He was laying down, tied to something hard. He was in the back of their car. It was an old estate car. He could tell that from where he lay. Ainslie's father stood by the boot door. Dawn was rising behind him.

'Why am I tied up?'

'We'll get to that,' the man replied. 'I want to know where my daughter is.'

'How do I know?' Ronnie asked. 'Wait!'

The man dragged Ronnie out of the boot and he crashed onto the ground. The sound of wood splintering behind him. He was tied to wood. He could move nothing but his neck. 'This is lovely, it really is.' Ronnie strained to look around. 'Where are we?'

'Callanish,' said the man. 'We're going up to the stones.'

'You what?' Ronnie asked, when suddenly he was flipped upside down and his face met the gravel beneath. A moment later, he was lifted a few feet into the air.

'Come on now, Marjorie.' Ronnie heard the old man from the other side of the wood. 'Keep the door straight, we need him there in one piece.'

Ronnie thought for a second, and then realised he had been strapped down to the living room door. 'Who decides to kidnap someone, and then tape them down to their fucking front door?'

'Gods do not swear,' the old lady said, tutting.

'Was he ever a God?' The man cursed. 'He is the devil.'

'We find out where Ainslie is first.'

'I know. We'll crown the bastard, then gut him.'

Ronnie looked from underneath the door, trying to see his first glance of the stones. It was nice to see some of the tourist attractions, even if someone died every time he arrived. Like St. Clements Church, the Callanish Standing Stones had been converted into another Historic Scotland site. It did not seem to bother the family that an organisation now owned the land they were about to kill him on.

'Smashing idea this,' Ronnie shouted. 'Kill someone beside a museum. Do I need to give you money for the fee?'

'They can't even work out what the stones are for, so they have no right to tell me and my family that we cannot access it for its rightful purpose,' said the old man in a passionate statement about Lewis' history. 'Today we bring the island it's next Chieftain. It's next king. They cannot stop us from enacting what history requires of us. Oh goodness, no.'

'Smashing of you to pay me in,' Ronnie smirked before lowering his head. 'What the fuck do I do now,' he whispered.

'Still nothing from Ainslie,' said her sister talking for the first time since Ronnie had met her. 'Her phone rings, but there is no answer.'

'Keep trying,' said her father. 'She is a strong woman, Marjorie. She fought this cause so brilliantly for us all. She believed in this all so much more than we did. You know how much she taught us all.'

'That bastard took it away,' barked the old lady. 'I'll gut himself myself, Artur. He cannot take my grandbaby away from me.'

'She might have been making all this up,' said Ronnie. A second later, he was dropped face first into the long grass. The door was lifted, and Ronnie seen the Callanish Standing Stones for himself.

He could see far across the island, until the hills devoured the north and the curve of the earth took the south. The sun was beating down, illuminating the heather and the peats, the waters and the rocks. For a moment, Ronnie forgot he was strapped to a door. He was speechless at the beauty.

'It's beautiful,' he said.

'Silence.' The old lady hissed at him. She was very short, now Ronnie thought about it. Short people were always angrier. 'Where is Ainslie?'

'Right now?' Ronnie asked. The woman nodded. 'No idea.'

Artur now had thrown a brown, ragged gown over his head.

'Where did you pull that out of?' Ronnie shouted, laughing. He looked to the others, but they did not find it funny.

'I would have hoped we would be able to welcome the heir on better terms.' Artur growled when he spoke. 'We thought we would never see the day that he would return, but here we are. Now, I implore you. Where is my daughter?'

'I can't tell you anything different,' said Ronnie. He was never

The Truth Hurts

admitting to the truth. The situation was strange enough.

'Your grandad,' said Artur, as he plucked one of Ronnie's heartstrings. 'My daughter called me, to tell me about him. She cannot believe that someone told you he could be cured. Imagine losing him. Imagine him dying, and you never being able to say goodbye. This is how we feel. We need to see her again.'

For a moment, Ronnie held it together. Then he wept. He felt the raw emotion of his grandad's passing. His heart had been stabbed. It was a pain thousands of times greater than his head. He couldn't bear to realise that he would never get to talk to him again. 'If my head is bleeding, how long do I have?'

'The bleed won't kill you,' Artur said plainly as he rooted into his bag. 'Murrin will have killed you long before it gets the chance. Have you hallucinated yet?'

'Have I what?'

'Hallucinated. Have you seen anything you would consider to be abnormal?'

'A family of three roasters with a grudge against me, but other than that.'

A glint of metal put Ronnie off making anymore jokes. The knife appeared from a bag and its blade stretched for ten inches at least.

'That's a belter,' Ronnie said with his eyes wide open. 'That'd tear you open.'

'Oh,' Murrin, the old lady, said. 'It will. It'll rip right into you.'

'They thought Leòdhas had left his secret here by the standing stones. We know this can't be true. Too many people walk by.' Artur patted the rock. 'It will be good to find his secret.'

Ronnie looked at the three of them and felt stupid. Ainslie had wanted to kill him because he was the true heir. What would they do to him before they finally let him die?

'One final opportunity,' said Artur. 'Ainslie. Tell me, where is she?'

Ronnie didn't even answer.

'The work of Leòdhas derives from the work of the Pagan traditions. More notably, the divine work. He is godly. We today commit you to him as his true heir and ask him to devolve to you the secrets of his kingdomship.'

'This has got really bloody weird,' said Ronnie. He looked around them incredulously. The family gave no answer.

The old man walked to Ronnie and the other two just stood, smiling towards them. Ronnie looked behind him, in the hope that someone else would walk up and interrupt the whole thing. They didn't. They wouldn't.

'In the ceremony, I hold here today upon the Callanish Stones we commit our friend here to the higher state to sit with our brother, Leòdhas. We transform him from a man to a deity. We commend him to those above and ask Leòdhas to provide him with guidance.'

Ronnie winced as the man threw water towards him from a silver cup which was handed to him by Ainslie's sister. The grandmother was crying. Behind her tears sat anger. Ronnie could taste her emotion. She was about to taste his blood.

'I look up to you this morning, Leòdhas, with my witnesses and our head of family. I look to you, right now, and I ask... make this man our God.'

The old man took a sharp step to the right, and the old lady spoke for the first time. She whisked both hands as high as she could and pushed the air in front of her with both palms.

Ronnie didn't have the time to blink. The wooden door behind him seemed to shatter, crack and splinter. His mind had shot itself to bits once again as the thudding beat in his head overtook any sort of emotion. He felt as though he was thrown up into the air, sent flying down the Celtic Cross of stones. The family applauded. He lay for a moment and tried to catch his breath.

He rolled onto his front and looked at the family as they took steps towards him. He felt very ill, as he got back to his feet. The world spun around him, and no matter how hard he shook himself he could not shake the reverberations around him that he now felt.

'What happened?' Ronnie asked. 'I can't see.'

He has returned.

Ronnie stopped moving. He was almost certain that inside of his head, someone other than himself had whispered.

He is back. I cannot believe it.

Another voice. In fact, numerous voices inside his head were calling out to him. His ears were still ringing. He could not be sure that these voices were not coming from around him. He could not yet see.

Tell them that he is back. Tell everyone. Leòdhas has returned.

'Who are you?' Ronnie asked to the voices inside of his head.

'You don't remember?' Artur asked.

Ronnie had forgotten that the family were there. His vision was only starting to come back to him and he had to squint to make out the three figures in front of him. 'I... I can't see.' He reached out both his hands for balance.

Don't trust them.

Ronnie's head buzzed whenever the voices in his head spoke. There were four now. They spoke together, and apart. They spoke continuously.

You are about to die.

'I... I can hear voices now. What did you do?'

The old man smiled and whispered something to the old lady. She too smiled in turn and they stood to look at Ronnie in a way they had not looked to him before. 'Hallucinations,' the old man whispered as he grinned wider.

They know who you are. They know what you did.

'I know she's dead,' Artur spat. 'We know you killed our daughter. You evil monster.'

'How do you...' Ronnie was cut off as his head began to burn with the voices. He could no longer distinguish reality from that which happened in his head now. He could not decide what he was imagining, and what was very real.

She has the knife.

Ronnie couldn't be sure if there were people inside his head now, but he knew he couldn't afford to take a chance. 'You tell that wee granny of yours to put that knife down right now. I'm the King. I command you.'

Real charming. Good effort.

'You are disgusting,' the old man replied. 'You sit and learn about these deities for your entire life, and then you come to learn that it's just as bad as every other person told you. God's are supposed to be good people, Leòdhas.

'I love this island. I love everything about. I don't love the people who stayed here. I don't love the people, particularly like you, who scarred this land for gain. We knew you were here the minute you arrived on this island. I don't know why Ainslie tried to help you. She thought you would be different. Murrin knew exactly who you were, though. A killer. Scum. You deserve this.'

'He didn't care about Ainslie,' spat the woman. 'He won't care about us. We need to act Artur. We need to act *now*!' She began to scream so loudly that her voice became hoarse. Her granddaughter held her, as she writhed in anger.

Tell them. Tell them you killed her.

'You're right. I did kill her. I punched her in the throat and I watched her die. She bled to death, and I caused every single moment of pain. It was slow.' said Ronnie. 'I'll kill you too. Stay back.' His vision was almost with him, but his ears still needed time. He could only hear echoes, and he hoped that he wasn't confusing the voices in his head with the voices in the field behind him.

'You didn't kill her, Leòdhas.' The old woman spoke for the first time. She was croaky. She sounded like she might die at any second herself, without too much effort. 'You sacrificed her.'

We're coming.

'No, I definitely killed her. She came at me, and I ended her life.' Ronnie was looking for time now, but he was going about it the wrong way. He had no idea. 'You don't know what I'm capable of, but I'm telling you right now, if you don't back off, I'll show every one of you.'

'She came at you because she bloody well knew who Leòdhas was.'

Ronnie could finally see without the blurry shadows disguising the family. 'She told me that your side was the worst, the most shameful. She said to me that the last one of yours to be buried was faced down, her own choice. Even she couldn't face being related to you. How does that feel?'

'No.'

'Yes.'

'No,' screamed the old woman. She ran for Ronnie and the large kitchen knife appeared from under her robe.

Ronnie was sure that his time was up. The knife went to pierce his chest and slice his heart. He didn't have time to stop it. He closed his eyes. He didn't want to watch himself die. He hoped that wherever he would end up, that his grandad would not be there. He didn't want to have to spend the rest of eternity knowing that he hated him.

He shut in on himself, allowing the pain inside his head to take over. That way, he would remove himself from reality and not be in his body when it happened. It would mask dying, of that Ronnie was sure. Blood was filling his skull. He was as good as fucked anyway.

However, nothing happened.

Ronnie opened one eye, and gasped. The entire family lay dead, lying in pools of their own blood many feet from where they stood just a moment previous. The old lady lay by the tip of the cross. The old man lay far to the right of him. Ronnie's stomach turned. His mind was still full of static. He could not remember moving, yet the entire family were brutally dead. Each person looked up to the sky, never to blink again. The knife lay between them all. It was drenched in different shades of blood.

We protect you, Leòdhas.

He would get the biggest fright of his life and stumbled backwards once again. Ronnie turned to see the most astonishing creatures he had seen in his life. He felt threatened by them, but he knew deep down that they were the ones talking to him. They were the ones who saved his life. He looked up, to meet their eyes.

'Are you the people who are talking inside my head?' Asked Ronnie.

Some of them. We're not people though.

Four stood before him. They were at least six-foot-tall to their shoulders, and another foot or so for their large heads. They were white, almost ghostly. They were wet. They looked like horses, but they also looked like men. Ronnie could not describe the perfect mix of the two of them.

We are the Blue Men of the Minch. We protect Leòdhas and his land. It is good to see you again.

'I'm not… I'm Ronnie.'

You were Ronnie. You are now the protector of this land. We will all protect you.

'You will all?' Asked Ronnie. 'This is a bit far-fetched if I'm being honest with you.'

There are more than just the Blue Men who live to serve you.

'Like who?'

It's not our place to say.

'Convenient,' said Ronnie as his doubt increased. He was more certain now, than he had been for some time, that he was dying. Brian had knocked him out twice, and he was more certain than ever that this caused the bleed on his brain. He wondered if his grandad's death had been too much for his subconscious.

'I'm bleeding inside my skull,' said Ronnie. 'This is all in my head.'

You were bleeding.

Ronnie looked at them all, and slowly raised his hand to his head. The pain was gone. The bulge, which he felt back by the lighthouse, had vanished. 'That can't be possible.'

Perhaps.

'What is all of this?' Asked Ronnie.

You are the new Chieftain of Lewis and Harris. You have been summoned by Leod to rule over this island. To help you, you have friends. Not human friends, but, friends nonetheless. We will all play our part to save you before the day is out. Then you can save your people.

'Why would I need saving?' Ronnie scratched his head. 'If I'm this fucking King, then I can save myself, no?'

You'll find out before the day ends.

Before he could ask anything else, the Storm Kelpies began to march away from him. They did not take long to speed out of view, leaving Ronnie standing beside three dead bodies. He closed and opened his eyes for five minutes. He hoped that he would wake up in the B&B. He hadn't slept since the morning prior to that. Everything that he thought of just led him to believe that none of this could be real. He had just imagined that this family existed. He had to have. After all, Ainslie said herself that her father had been murdered.

Yet, as he kneeled and touched him, his blood was warm, but his corpse was cold. He had begun to stiffen already. He stood for a moment or two more as he slid the battery into his phone, just for a second, to check the time. It was 8:57.

They would be opening soon. Charles would now have tracked where he was too.

Ronnie was stood by three dead bodies.

He ran.

He jumped over the fence, but his lace caught onto the barbed wire and he tumbled down the hill quicker than he could have run down it himself. His shoulder hit off a boulder, and he came to a stop. He knew he would still be caught from here, so he stood and ran even further. He would not look back, and he would not concern himself with public paths and roads. He did not wish to have anyone ask him who he was or where he had been. He could not be sure that he hadn't just invented them, like he had everyone else. That was the only explanation.

He stood now in a field, alone. He looked around. There were no roads. No houses. There was nobody that could see him now.

'If you can hear me...' said Ronnie, aloud. 'If you can hear me, show yourself. I command you.'

Suddenly, werewolves surrounded him.

NINETEEN

'This has all gone far too quickly for me to take this seriously. You're werewolves?'

'Dead ones,' said the tallest one in the strongest Northern accent that Ronnie had ever heard. 'Angry ones too, if bastards get in our way.'

They didn't look like they did in the books. They were more wolf than man. Their skin was dark, leathery and grey and their eyes were bloodshot. Their teeth, pearly white, shone in the morning sun. Their fur was bedraggled and smelled awful.

'Some horses told me-'

'Wow, lad. They're kelpies. Don't mistaken them, they'll get angry.' The middle one spoke. He was Glaswegian. How on earth was a werewolf Glaswegian?

'I've lost my mind,' said Ronnie. 'I'm stood with wolves, and I've just been with a couple of *kelpies* who murdered a family I've clearly just imagined. Now I'm stood in a field. This is completely crazy. I had a bleed on the brain up until five minutes ago. I've probably got a concussion.'

'A concussion? You wish, pal.' The taller one spoke once again, but they all laughed together. 'You were daft enough to go up to those standing stones and you stood there long enough for them to send Leòdhas down. Anyone else would have been lucky enough to be killed. You're the bugger whose luck turned out that you were the true heir.'

'I was kidnapped, you might have missed that.'

'Same thing,' the Glaswegian wolf said again.

'I'm arguing with a wolf,' Ronnie said. He sighed. He shook his head and looked up into the sky. He could not believe what was happening.

'Yup, and you're never getting out of this one.'

Ronnie was sure he was making all of this up. 'Can you talk inside my head too?'

You're fucking right we can.

'Please don't do that when you're here.' Ronnie scowled. 'Why am I the heir, then? What am I here to do?'

'He doesn't know, Angus.'

'I'm not surprised.' Angus was the taller one. 'Do you know who Leòdhas was?'

'Some... great God?'

'Oh, fuck no,' said the shorter one. 'Angus, get him fucking told. I can't be putting up with this shite.' He was angry, just as Ronnie had thought about the shorter ones.

'Leòdhas,' said Angus, 'was the worst and best leader you've seen. He was an awful man, but I'll tell you what, he looked out for the people he cared about, and he got things done. You got anyone to look after?'

'No,' said Ronnie. 'Well, not anymore.'

'You've made them think they hate you.'

'Worse than that.'

'Tell us.'

'No.'

'Listen, if I'm going to serve you for the rest of fucking time immemorial, you're going to tell me what the fuck is going on here.' The short one panted. He was aggressive.

He looked at each creature, as it looked back to him. He still wasn't sure this was real, but at the same time, he couldn't control them with his mind. Surely, in a dream, you could do that?

'Stop asking me to sit down, eh?' The smallest one shook its head and barked.

'I've done some terrible things,' said Ronnie. 'I've hurt the wrong people. I don't even know why. I've grown up angry, and I've hid it. Since I've come onto this island, I've just lost why I hid it. Last thing my grandad ever said to me before he died was that I was a disappointment to him. He always thought good things. I think now I've just lost my way, and there's nothing to bring me back now.'

'Must be tough,' said Angus. 'This is Charlie, the wee one over there is Bill. Have a seat. Talk to us.'

'You think you've got problems,' said Bill. 'We're the ones who fucking died and can't leave this bloody world.'

'Bill, don't be so coarse.' Charlie seemed to be the one most averse to swearing. For a dead wolf, he also seemed to be the neatest. The less deathly looking.

'How did you all die?' Asked Ronnie.

'We can't remember. Can't even remember being dead, to be honest with you.' Angus stopped, choked up flesh, and then continued. 'The only thing each of us remember is giving our afterlife to Leòdhas if our graves were disturbed.'

'You must be old,' said Ronnie sympathetically.

'My foreskin is older than half of those trees,' said Bill. 'It's seen less action as well, I'll tell you that.'

Ronnie laughed. It had been a long time since he found someone with the same dark humour he had and willingness to share it. He still wasn't sure, though. There was nobody who knew his humour better than himself. His own subconscious.

'Was your grandad your only relative?'

'No,' said Ronnie quickly. 'I have a brother and a mother. A few weeks ago, I would have said I have nothing in common with them. Now, the only thing I see different between us is that I wasn't stupid enough to be caught and thrown in jail.' Ronnie sighed. 'I'm such an idiot.'

Now he had calmed down from his anger, he felt incredibly stupid and awful about how he thought about the people who had cared for him. In all honesty, he couldn't remember what he had thought, said or did, and though it wasn't an excuse, he still regretted it.

'I wish I could fix it.'

'Too fucking late now, pal. Bigger fish to fry.'

'What do you mean?' Asked Ronnie.

'People are coming for you, my son. The people on this island

The Truth Hurts

aren't going to wait too long to find out that Leòdhas' heir is here. They are going to tell their people and they are going to want to kill you, or use you.' Bill took this notion very seriously. 'You are going to be the most wanted man in the world.'

'I don't understand,' said Ronnie. 'Why?'

'You control the undead,' shouted Bill. 'For fuck sake.'

'All the undead?' Ronnie asked.

'No,' said Bill. 'For hundreds of years' people have shared stories of Outer Hebridean Myths. I am sure very much like others, you have seen them only as fairy tales.

'The issue is, they're not stories. They are real creatures and they live to serve Leòdhas… who, by the way, was a real bastard too. You're in good company, if you are who you say you are. You should be chuffed.'

He wasn't. Ronnie tried to believe what they were saying, but he was still convinced the entire conversation was happening inside of his head.

'You can call on us, just by talking to us. Leòdhas was just a man, it was his servants who gave him his power. You too have that power.'

'Aye, but don't fuck about with it,' said Bill. 'I'll eat you myself.'

'We can't kill Leòdhas,' said Charlie. 'Nobody can.'

Angus stood and stretched all four legs, and then his back. He appeared to be becoming restless. Perhaps that's what all werewolves do.

'When did your grandad pass away?'

'Yesterday,' said Ronnie.

'Only yesterday?' The three werewolves asked, turning to each other with confused expressions.

'Did he die on the mainland?' Asked Angus.

'No, here.'

'Where?'

'On the island.'

'Shit for brains, where on the island?' Bill was very sharp when he wanted to be, which was every single second of every single day.

'The Butt of Lewis Lighthouse. He fell from the cliff.'

The three of them began to whisper, and then they turned and walked away to talk some more. Ronnie tried to look over, without appearing to be too obvious. They were werewolves, and he didn't know how far their supposed loyalty would stretch. He found it frustrating that he couldn't listen into their thoughts, but they had front row seats to every single one of his.

'I know that you probably think this is all a bit weird,' said Angus. 'You probably still think it's in your head. It's not though. We're real, and everything around you is real too. Whether you like it or not, you're a God now and people are going to look up to you for advice and guidance.

'However, with that comes… benefits. See, we are creatures from the dead. We died, and we clear up the things that death leaves lying around. What I'm saying is… we know things.'

'I don't get you,' said Ronnie.

Angus would sit back down in the long grass, and he would tell him what he meant. The conversation was meant for only Angus and Ronnie. Even the other werewolves would step away. Whatever was said though, made Ronnie very angry. For the first time in forever, he cried hard. He punched the grass, and he screamed out familiar names about Morag and his father Fin, that he had never known of before.

'We need to go, Leòdhas, but trust me… should you need us, we will be there.' Charlie bowed. 'You only need to ask for us, and we will save you.'

'Thanks,' said Ronnie awkwardly. 'I thought you said I needed to save this land, though?'

'Oh, you will. The danger will come. It will be up to you to destroy it… though, it will destroy you first.' Charlie paused. 'I fear it already has.'

'Your grandad didn't die, by the way.' Angus said in an almost supportive manner, interrupting Bill who now looked very annoyed.

'I seen him fall off the cliff,' said Ronnie.

'He can't have died, is what I am telling you. It is *impossible* for him to have died.'

Ronnie stood, and he was more certain than ever that everything that had happened since walking into the wee cottage in Eoropaidh was in his head. There was no way he was stood talking to werewolves, and there was no way his grandad was alive. 'Listen, this is all in my head... I want him to be alive.' Ronnie waved them off. 'Thanks, though.'

'Wills-o'-the-wisp,' said Angus. 'That is how we know your grandad can't have died on the island.'

'I don't understand.'

'When someone on this island is about to die, there are lights... they summon upon the soon to be dead and they glow brighter when they die. If you're telling me that your grandad died at that lighthouse, I am telling you that no lights shone that far North that night. You can't die without them appearing.'

Ronnie was already sprinting up the field, North to the lighthouse before he'd heard it all.

He thought back to Charlie's comment, that he had already been destroyed by whatever was on the island. He tried very hard to be a better person, to hide from who he really was. Angus had told him more about himself and his past than he had ever learnt from his mother or his grandad. Suddenly, he felt an undying urge to be that better person again. It didn't matter who he was, that wouldn't define him. What mattered, was who he saved and why he saved them.

Even if you hear a bad story, you need to understand there was a time when you were good to those people... but they will never tell you that. Morag, Lewis, Fin. They were all good people. Good people he couldn't save, but he would save Ron.

TWENTY

Ronnie had run far enough. By that, he hadn't run very far at all. He wanted to prove the wolves right and see his grandad alive next to the lighthouse, but he could not find the energy. The last two days had used up everything he had, and all he now lived on was hope. Hope that something good might come of all of this.

He stood by the road, and he looked across the road to the loch opposite him. It was peaceful. Too peaceful. Ronnie thought back to where everything began, and he remembered how peaceful the water was. He couldn't help but think it was foreshadowing to the war ahead.

He realised he hadn't turned on the mobile for some time. He slipped the battery into his phone, and he turned it on. For a few seconds, it did nothing. It sat peaceful. Then, though, it burst into life. There was message after message for missed calls. Ronnie presumed that was Charles. He had been off grid for a very long time.

He opened the first message.

WHERE ARE YOU? CHARLES.

Ronnie's first thought was, why did he write the entire thing in capitals? A man with so much authority, so much money, surely had learnt how to use a phone and write in proper English.

BRIAN HAS CONTACTED ME. I WARNED YOU.

He deleted the message. He didn't want to worry himself with warnings. He had done enough bad things in his life to warrant that. Though, he could do more if he needed to. He was sure he could kill again.

We can kill him too.

His phone pinged in a different tone, and this meant a number was contacting him that he did not have in his phone. He looked, and it was a third text message. He opened it up, and he could feel the heat of the anger.

CHEAP SHOT AGAIN? I WILL KILL YOU.

He hoped it wasn't his grandad. Maybe he was angrier than he looked. Charles' tone tutted again. Ronnie looked at his phone.

RON IS DEAD. I HOPE YOU ARE HAPPY.

Thanks for news update, Ronnie thought before throwing his phone into his pocket and turning on its 'Do Not Disturb' function. That way, he would not be bothered by the phone again, but should anyone come looking for him, they would know exactly where he'd be. He was ready for the fight.

He took another look out to the loch, and he wondered what he should do next. Part of him wanted to believe that his grandad was alive, but he was also sure that he could just be imagining it like everything else. His main worry was that Charles might expect him to go back.

Ronnie heard a purr, and when he looked to his right, a car was purring down the hill towards him. He squinted, and he seen an elderly couple in the car. He stuck out a hand, and he hoped that they would stop.

Luckily, they did.

'You ok, son?' The elderly, wrinkly man was American. He wore a cap upon his head which bore a white Nike tick on a black background. His polo shirt was as white as his skin. His wife, sat beside him, looked like his twin. They both wore wedding rings. Ronnie guessed they were married.

'I thought it would be a clever idea to come out for a walk, but I've got lost,' said Ronnie. 'I just want to get back to Stornoway.'

The old man tutted. 'Hard lines, partner. We're going in the wrong direction.' His wife nudged him. 'Tell you what, the good Lord hasn't seen much of a helper in me this holiday… we're heading South, but we're staying in Stornoway. Come with us, and we'll take you home?'

Ronnie wasn't sure.

'I don't think you're going to get much more help out this way. It's a lonely road.'

'Where are you going?' Ronnie asked.

'Luskentyre,' said the old lady. 'We'd be happy for you to join us. God hasn't sent us this way for no reason.'

Ronnie was getting a little bored by this point of hearing about Gods and deities. He, according to the family whom he apparently murdered, was now a deity. He wondered if this family felt his Godly presence.

He climbed into the back, and the car strummed down the road at an incredibly slow pace. The car would take twice the time as the sat nav would tell them, but they would get there in one piece.

'So, you from here, sir?' The old man moved the mirror to look Ronnie in the eye.

'I... no. I live on the mainland.' Ronnie stuttered.

'Ah, a tourist like us. We're from Texas. You heard of it?'

'I think so,' said Ronnie. 'It's... America?'

'We understand sarcasm too,' the old man said as they two of them laughed. 'You a Christian?'

'Not really,' said Ronnie, wondering why that would be an appropriate second question. 'I would say I believe in myself, but I don't want to offend you after your kind offer this morning.'

'It's not us that you offend, but you're in luck... God will always look to forgive you, if you let him. My wife here, she never thought that he would–'

'He did,' said the wife. 'He took my hand and he forgave me.'

'Do you... is it possible that God isn't all good?' Asked Ronnie. He hadn't thought when he had asked, and almost immediately he knew the question was extremely offensive. The two elderly Christians seemed unaffected, though.

'Oh goodness, child. He's as evil as he is good. He's as scary as he is loving. He knows what he wants from us, and he can punish us... but in the end, he does everything for us. He does it because he loves us. You must have relationships like that, no?'

'No,' said Ronnie. 'My mother beat me. My brother beat me. I grew up in that environment and I got too used to it.'

'If you were to ask him to forgive you, he would,' the old man smiled to him in the mirror. 'I'm Ted, by the way. This is Shirley.'

'Nice to meet you both,' said Ronnie. He was honest for the first time. 'I'm Lewis.' He couldn't stop himself. He *had* to lie.

'Like the island,' said Shirley. 'That's very sweet.'

The conversation ended. It started very vaguely, had drowned itself in the depths of Ronnie's personal life, and then burned out just as quick. In fact, they stayed silent for the rest of the journey. Shirley had stopped for a moment to pray, but not another word was said.

Luskentyre is a beach that one cannot forget. Its beauty is scarring. You may not believe you were in Scotland. In fact, Thailand had once found itself in bother for using Luskentyre to attract people to its country. As much a selling point, as a crime.

From a distance, the beach was golden and white. The sea was deep and blue. Up close, it was brighter. The water was clearer. Ronnie walked on, leaving the two pensioners to enjoy a flask of tea by their car.

He stood on the grassy knoll standing above the beach and was taken by its beauty. Wind dragged the sand across itself, keeping it smooth. Its beauty was untouched, and Ronnie was the only person there.

He slid down the hill to the sand and pressed his left foot into the pristine floor, and then his right. He could not believe, for its beauty, that he was the only one there to share it.

'I wish you were here,' he said to his grandad in the sky. He spoke to him for the first time since his passing. 'I wish I hadn't been that person. Yet, I know I'll be him again. It's a good thing you're gone. You won't know it now.'

He walked down to stand on the corner of Luskentyre beach. To his left, he seen Lewis. To his right, he saw the island of Taransay. He wondered who lived there, who visited there, who had spent time there questioning their life and wondering if everything that they did was worth it.

'I don't know how, but I want to make it right. I want to make sure you forgive me.' His voice quivered. 'If you only knew.'

It's tough, isn't it.

A new voice appeared in his head, and Ronnie flipped his neck, almost causing whiplash. Nobody was there.

I hate losing someone.

Ronnie looked to his left, there was nothing.

I hate realising it's my fault.

He turned to his right and fell over, jumping back as far as he could. He felt the soft sand cushion his head, but this was not his focus. In front of him, towering over him, stood a... wolf? He did not know what it was.

'You're a werewolf?' Asked Ronnie.

No.

It was the size of a large bull. It was shaggy like the werewolves, but it smelt enormously fresher.

'What are you, then?'

I'm Cù-Sìth, of Luskentyre.

'Do I... Am I...'

Do I respect your honour? Yes. Do I support you in your fight? I have to.

'You have to?'

I don't like what you've done.

'You surely don't know what I've done.'

You'd be surprised.

Ronnie looked around him, disinterested in the criticism. Ted and Shirley were holding hands at the other end of the beach, pointing out the same scenery that Ronnie had just taken in. Their love did nothing for him. He was not interested in how deeply they respected each other, or how God had come to bind them.

'If you know so much, what is it I've done?' Ronnie squared up to the giant dog.

You've killed.

'So, did Leòdhas.'

Only when he had to.
'I had to.'
No, you didn't. You had a thousand other options, but you chose to take the easiest one because you were angry. You didn't think about how you could save her life.
'You can't know that.'
I know about death.
'You've died?'
I know about death, is what I said.
'Every other creature that I've spoken to is dead.'
Not me.
'What do you mean, then?'
I am Cù-Sìth.
'I think we've covered that,' said Ronnie. 'I mean, how do you know about death if you haven't died?'
I take souls.
'Where?' It annoyed Ronnie how bitty the conversation was becoming.
To the afterlife.
Suddenly Ronnie's eyes shut, and he was back in the church, back in the roof, back in front of a very sullen Ainslie. Her manic stare drilled through him. He had not noticed at first how much this moment had broken her. Something had to have triggered it. There was no way she had travelled with the intention of losing her mind.
You knew there was something wrong.
Ronnie noticed he was not stood back in the spot where he stood originally. Another version of himself stood there.
You could have walked away.
Ainslie pulled the knife much sooner than Ronnie thought. He looked back towards himself. Nothing. No awareness. Why did he not see the knife quick enough to be able to do anything about it? Or did he just choose not to?
It would be obvious if you had taken the time to care about her.
Ronnie ignored *Cù-Sìth*, and he carried on watching as Ainslie ran towards him, and he took his fist and drove it into her

throat. She would collapse, and she would suffocate. He had not noticed, until now, that he stood and watched her die.

Did you enjoy it this time round?

'No,' said Ronnie. He twitched as the other version of himself turned. He remembered turning. He heard a creak. 'Can he hear me?'

Sort of.

In the distance, Ronnie heard a baying voice of a dog. He noticed that once Ainslie stopped moving, that the other Ronnie was no longer in the attic.

A second bay was heard. Ronnie followed himself, down the steps. He was rushing, looking behind himself. Ronnie could not remember looking so worried. He remembered feeling calm.

'I wasn't worried,' said Ronnie. 'I remember that.'

You remember wrong.

A third bay sounded, but Ronnie was inside his car and he had already raced well away from the church. Ronnie turned, now in the graveyard again, and noticed that *Cù-Sìth* was with him again.

I bay three times before I collect the souls, dead or alive if they haven't escaped.

'You are a murderer too then,' said Ronnie sarcastically.

'You alright?' Asked Ted.

Ronnie was back on the beach.

'Yeah, you?' Asked Ronnie. He had butterflies in his stomach.

'You're talking to yourself there... you hungry?'

Ronnie looked to Ted, Shirley and then to *Cù-Sìth*. The dog was stood to his left. Surely, he could see him.

'I... I think I'm tired.' Ronnie wanted to give nothing way. He did not want to worry Ted.

'Here are the keys to the motor,' said Ted. 'We're going to be a while here, so if you want to nap, you head back to the car and lie across the back. It's comfy.' He and Shirley walked on down the beach.

I don't murder. I collect the dead. You don't think people die when they kill? You don't think they cease to be human?

'I didn't say that,' said Ronnie.
You made it clear in your thoughts.
'I regret what I did, ok?'
Right now, perhaps.

Cù-Sìth was right. Ronnie didn't know how he would feel the next time he was angry. Right now, he was calm, and he felt horrifically sad for the acts he had committed. Yet he could remember not even a day ago when he was angry and enjoying the torture.

You really are the true heir.
'What?'
Leòdhas was just like you.
'You don't really explain much, do you.'
I don't need to.

Ronnie was annoyed by *Cù-Sìth*. He didn't like that, for a creature who was supposed to serve him, he was very critical.

I don't need to like you, to serve you.
'Stop reading my fucking thoughts,' said Ronnie.
Stop killing, then.

Ronnie looked past the dog, and as far as he could see, bright lights appeared. He then remembered it meant death.

'Do you see the lights?'
Yes. Another death.
The dog bayed.
You're about to face a difficult decision.
He turned.
I don't think you'll make the right decision.
He ran.
Good luck.

Huge footprints were all that were left. It was pointless, just like all the other weird creatures who appeared before him. He was no further forward on whether or not he was actually crazy.

He reached down into his pocket, and he took out his phone to check the time. There were no more text messages... but there was a voicemail. He looked at the contact several times, before he believed it was the number it said it was.

MACLEOD, RONNIE (WORK)

He had a thing about keeping every single contact in his phone as formal and as accurate as possible. Even his grandad was listed as Macleod, Ron. Not grandad.

He tapped into his voicemail. He would never believe what he was about to hear.

'Son.'

'Shut the fuck up.'

'Help.'

One voice was very clearly Brian.

'Ronnie, help me!'

The other was very clearly his grandad.

'I will rip your fucking throat if you don't give me that fucking phone.'

There was ruffling, and then a deep, long breath.

'We both warned you that nobody wins when they go against us. Yet, despite my very best advice and my most esteemed colleague supporting your endeavours... you still go against me. I can't understand why, but there is clearly a reason. Either you think too highly of yourself and you need to realise where you stand in this world or... you're an idiot. You're certainly no match for what I can send after you. Brian may be the best, but he is the beginning and he will be your end. I don't fucking care anymore. You've driving me to swear and I never, ever swear.

'Yes, I do have your grandad here. I didn't know the little bastard had a phone with him. He fell beside the wall of the lighthouse from where I was standing, watching, and I thought... I'm going to pay back years of misfortune that this idiot caused me. Brian is hitting him and then he remembers you and well... his rage consumes him, and who am I to say no?

'We didn't account for the fact that you are too selfish to come back and look for your grandad. So, we've been sat waiting here for you to come back and I'm still fucking waiting. I don't care if you have the secret any more. I hope you do. It will make my afternoon less worthless.'

There was another kerfuffle as the phone was wrestled

around. Ronnie could hear Charles in the background, shouting orders. Then a deep, full breath released down the microphone and chilled Ronnie's ears.

'I've let you beat me three times now just so Charles can get whatever he wants. It's not about what Charles wants now. I want to slit your throat and drink your blood while you die watching. I want to knife every organ out of your body and watch the pulse faint from you. We're at the lighthouse. We have your grandad. For every hour you are late, I will cut another limb from his pointless fucking body.

'You have one hour.'

The line went dead.

TWENTY-ONE

The car park was empty when Ted and Shirley finally stumbled back after an hour of prayer. They had never believed in mobile technology and the night was rushing it. Ted looked to God for advice, but he gave no reply. He was too busy racing to save his flesh and blood.

In the day that Ronnie had been summoned to whoever by whatever, he had caused death, heartbreak and sadness. He began to have sympathy with Christians. People were always challenging their God to do what was right by the bible. Ronnie couldn't make one person happy, never mind millions.

The little Rover Metro, borrowed from a pen pal in Kilmacolm, could go far faster than Ted had given it the chance. It reached ninety, as the steering wheel began to shake violently. By ninety-five, Ronnie was almost certain that the doors would fall off. The brakes were spongy. An emergency stop would be a gamble at best.

The journey was longer than he remembered, but it would be the growing anxiety which made it worse. He was trapped in his mind, desperately trying to reach for a plan which would save his grandad and their relationship..

What would define him would be the day to come. How he acted, and the actions he took up by the lighthouse, would show the real Ronnie. Of that the werewolves were certain. Even the worst of people have nice sides.

Ronnie quickly found himself stuck behind slow tourists that forced him to overtake dangerously on hills and around bends. He hoped that his new protectors would look out for him in his ventures of stupidity. He knew that he no longer mattered in any of this. If there was a chance that his grandad was alive, then every choice he made and every move forward that he took, it all had to be for him. It wasn't about making it up to him or apologising. Ronnie knew things were long past that. He just didn't want to let him die again.

The journey from Luskentyre to the Butt of Lewis takes approximately two hours. Ronnie did it in ninety minutes. He remembered the road up to the lighthouse, but it felt clearer this time. There was less static in his head.

As he approached the lighthouse car park, he suddenly turned right and bowed down a small ramp. He had arrived at the beach beside the lighthouse. Sure, Charles would make every decision up to his expected death, but he would not be allowed to decide where he died. That right was Ronnie's. He stepped out of the car and looked down to the golden sands where he would never leave.

We are here.

The voices in his head were comforting. Ronnie smiled. It didn't matter if it was all imaginary. It gave him a real confidence now, to know that he wasn't alone. If he made it all up? Nobody else would know. Nobody would be hurt by a dream.

We are ready.

He walked down to the beach and sat in front of the water. He let the sea touch his toes. Freezing. There was no chance that you could spend any amount of time in the water. There was nothing out in front of him. The world long curved off away from him and he was left looking to the horizon. There was a lot about the world and its nature that Ronnie had never considered until now.

He only tried to take his mind off what was to come. That was too real, and too painful to consider. He hoped for a headache to distract him, but in truth, he hadn't had one since the Callanish Stones. That concerned him.

His mind flickered past it for only a moment. He wondered if he would die today; if he would be laid next to his grandad and killed. He had run out of use for Charles now. What he wanted to be given, Ronnie could not give. It was hardly something he could just hand over.

A black truck reversed down the hill, but Ronnie did not notice. He was too deep in thought. He looked up to the sun and thought it was a very beautiful day to be his last. The sun beat down upon the white sands and Ronnie had to squint to see clearly. The blue ocean rolled in and creamy foam rolled up to where Ronnie sat. If he had to pick a day to die, and a place to be murdered, this would surely be it. His ancestral home would be his grave. It was hardly something he would be comfortable with, but he'd accept it. He wouldn't be aware of it in the moments to come. His hands shook with the anxiety that he would no longer exist when his heart stopped. It was upsetting to think.

There was no other reason he had been asked here. He closed his eyes, and he reached out. 'Does it hurt?'

Does what hurt?

It was Angus again.

'Dying,' said Ronnie.

Aye.

Brilliant, thought Ronnie. They could have lied to him.

There's only one thing then, isn't there? Don't bloody die.

Ronnie heard the truck's reversing tone, but he still didn't turn. He refused to give Charles the power in what would be his final day on earth. If he wanted to kill him, he would need to just do it without the speeches and the painfully depressing anecdotes.

'I don't have patience for you today, Mr Macleod,' Charles shouted through the wind to Ronnie as he stood looking to the sea. 'Turn around and get onto your knees.'

There was a long silence where Ronnie ignored the demand and Charles stood, mouth wide opened, that he was still being disobeyed.

'You don't come to the places that I tell you and you don't do what I ask. Why don't I just kill you right now?' Charles screamed loud enough that his lungs were on fire. He didn't care.

He had never felt so angry about another person. Well, man.

'I don't do what you tell me anymore,' replied Ronnie.

'What?' Charles shouted louder.

'I said, I don't do what you tell me anymore.'

'If you're going to be rude to me, Mr Macleod, at least talk in a direction where the wind won't strip you of your bullshit.' Charles bit onto the last word, and Ronnie could feel his anger.

Ronnie turned around, smiling. Charles was in a suit, like he had never broken sweat in his recent memory. His lips turned sharply as the mere sight of Ronnie turned his saliva bitter. 'If I were stand here right now and tell you I've missed you in the time I've been away, I'd be fucking lying to you Charles. I really would.'

'Did I ask you for your wit?'

'Do I care?' Ronnie looked down into the sand and slid his foot into it. 'Hold on... No, hold on. I... don't. I don't care. I don't have anything left, and you just have to accept that I'm not scared of you or your little bald thug.'

'Get on your knees, scum.' Charles pointed down to the sand. Ronnie kneeled, bored of arguing. He didn't want to talk anymore. He didn't want to give Charles the satisfaction.

'What made you think you could out do me, Mr Macleod? What was it, and at what point, did you think that crossing me and creating your own plan would give you anything but a conclusion such as this?'

Ronnie stared past him and watched Brian stumble out of the driver's door of the car. He winced and held his stomach, but then he began cracking his knuckles and swinging his fists.

'He's looking well,' said Ronnie.

The men opposite him scowled at one another. Brian wanted to finish him, but Charles still wasn't allowing it. Ronnie had to break the trust. 'I'm saying, you're looking very well, Brian. For an ugly bastard, you've really recovered well.'

'I don't get why you won't let me kill that cunt, Charles.' Brian snarled.

'I can't let you do that,' whispered Charles.

'If says another word about me, I'll slit his throat and bury him in my garden, just so I can piss on his corpse when my Julie goes to bed.' Brian turned his eyes to Ronnie. 'You think pushing me is just a joke. Don't.'

'You'd piss in your garden?' Ronnie asked. 'That's weird, pal.'

'Enough,' said Charles. 'People respect my associates. They normally don't get away with hurting them, but you've been lucky. You should really thank me, Mr Macleod. I don't want to think what Brian would do if he weren't loyal to me.'

'How loyal is he?' Ronnie asked.

Charles looked back to Ronnie, confused.

'Does he know your deepest secret, Charles?' Ronnie smiled. 'Did you tell him, or have you been hiding it even from your closest associate?'

Charles did not know how to respond, but he shook his head and feigned a laugh. He clicked his fingers to Brian who walked to the back of the car and dropped the back door of the pickup. Inside, there were six black canvas bags.

'Do you know what these are, Mr Macleod?'

'Bags for life?'

'Why are we even doing this with him, Charles?' Brian's vein across his right temple throbbed in the sunlight. 'He doesn't have anything. You can fucking see that. Just let me have my moment with him and we can be done here.'

'Do you know his secret, Brian?' Ronnie interrupted them.

'What secret?' Charles snapped.

'Excuse me, I'm talking to Brian. Allow us all the same opportunity to respond.'

'There is no secret,' Charles replied to Brian.

'What is he talking about then?' Brian stopped dragging the canvas bags out of the van and gasped for air whilst he waited for a reply.

'There's nothing, Brian.'

'I wouldn't say that,' Ronnie followed quickly. 'I mean, if you know what it is… well, it's up to you how you've processed it. I won't judge how you had to handle learning about it. If you don't know thought it might... well it changed my view on our pal Charles.'

'I did say I didn't have the patience for him, didn't I?' Charles snapped his fingers and Brian started emptying the bags onto the beach equidistant between Charles and Ronnie.

The sun was at its highest as it beat down upon the three men. Ronnie could smell something putrid fall the bags, and it made his eyes water slightly. He hoped it was the bags, and not Brian. He looked sweaty, but he was sure that not even he could smell that bad.

'You have done terrible things on this island, Mr Macleod.' Charles shook his head. 'I'm glad I was the one to catch you.'

'Funny,' said Ronnie, smiling. 'I think if we compare what you've done to what I've done, you're on a different planet. If Brian knows your secret, he can agree.'

'You have no idea. Without Barge to solve this for you, you're clueless.'

'I have. I know what you did.'

Charles looked to Brian and smiled. 'You don't believe him, do you?'

'No, boss.' Yet, Brian stopped and pondered for a moment. Then he turned his head. 'What's the secret relate to, though?'

'Oh,' Ronnie echoed. 'Now we're talking. Remember back on the lighthouse, you asked my grandad if he knew about how I knew different people...'

'Don't talk again.' Charles clicked his fingers.

'Ask Charles how he really knows Morag and Lewis Mackenzie.'

'Ignore him, Brian. He's trying to interrupt us.'

Brian pulled down the second zip, and even Ronnie could smell the death inside. Ruthlessly, he tipped the bodies out. Ainslie fell first. Then Shelagh. Ainslie's grandmother, her father and her brother. The sixth bag lay empty. Brian threw all the bags into the boot and left the bodies on the beach. They all stared at Ronnie.

'Shelagh didn't die,' said Ronnie.

'Clearly,' said Charles sarcastically. 'That'll be why she's stone cold and not breathing then, won't it?'

Ronnie looked to the people who had suffered over his questioning personality. He had let his anger transform him, and he had just rolled with the punches... which was an ironic way of putting it. 'I didn't kill all of them.'

'There's enough evidence to say that you did.' Charles brushed down the sand catching in his suit from the wind.

'Now, are you going to tell me what you found?' Asked Charles.

'I've been trying to tell Brian for the last twenty minutes, Charles.'

'Not that. What I want. What do you have?'

There was a long pause before Ronnie replied. 'Nothing.'

Charles looked to Brian, and he seemed to know exactly what to do. He went into the passenger's seat and dragged out a man. He could barely stand on the sand, and Ronnie knew him immediately. His heart jumped. His face was cut. His right eye was swollen. Ronnie's heart sunk the moment he seen his face. 'Oh grandad,' he whispered, utterly sympathetic now to what he had put him through.

'You better go stand with that wee cunt,' said Brian.

Ron's eyes seared in the light. It hurt almost as much as seeing his grandson.

As he stared at him, he couldn't help but wonder what was different. He was not the Ronnie that he recognised. He stood inches from his grandson, and he just stared. Ronnie stared back and licked his dry lips. The two men did not know what to say.

'Did you find it?' Whispered Ron, seemingly forgetting what his last words were.

'Yes,' Ronnie whispered.

'What is it?' His grandad asked.

'Excuse me gentlemen,' interrupted Charles. 'I'm not here so the two of you can forgive each other and move on with your lives. I am here because you both agreed to find me something, and you have annoyed me. Now, I would like to have my prize and have him charged for these murders. Is that ok?'

'I'm sorry, for everything. It's not good enough and I don't expect you to forgive me, but I know things now and I know about-'

'I don't need to hear it,' said Ron. 'I don't want to.'

'I'll save us,' whispered Ronnie.

'I've warned you twice now,' Charles said with increasing aggression. 'The police are well on their way here, and I want my answer. What did you find?'

'Nothing,' shouted Ronnie. 'There was nothing.'

'There was,' said Charles. 'I want it.'

'Well, I don't know what to say-'

Brian fired a shot into the air with his pistol. Ron jumped, but Ronnie grabbed him to steady him, before taking a step forward.

'Fucking try me,' said Ronnie. He ran forward to Brian, who threw the pistol to one side and sprinted even faster back at him. Ronnie swung wildly with his right hand and it careered over the top of Brian's bald head. It was at that moment, Ronnie knew he was in trouble.

A solid heel drove into the middle of his back and Ronnie doubled over backwards. As his head flipped back, his exposed throat held itself in the air as Brian's hand slapped down into it forcing Ronnie to expel every ounce of air. Brian kneeled over him and cupped the back of Ronnie's head with his left hand. He used his right to unload uncountable punches to Ronnie's head.

His groin.

Ronnie didn't even question it. He drove his knee hard into the air. Brian wasn't protecting himself and he felt the softness between his legs squidge and pop. Brian's face went white and he fell onto his backside. Ronnie stood up and cracked the knuckles of his right hand.

'I'm going to put you to sleep now, Brian.'

'You're going to go and stand over beside your grandfather before I shoot your fucking head off.' Charles was pointing Brian's gun to Ronnie. 'Now. Keep moving. That'll be enough.'

Ronnie turned back to his grandad, who stood four feet away

from him. Charles was walking over to Ronnie, gun pointed at him, until he was inches from Ronnie's face. Neither man blinked. They talked so quietly, neither man away from them could hear.

'Give me it,' said Charles.

'What?'

'The item you found.'

'There is no item, Charles. Whoever told you it was an item, they're wrong.'

'Is it valuable?'

'Brian doesn't look very good over there.'

'I don't care. I just want what I paid you for.'

'You didn't pay me.'

'I let you live.'

Ronnie rolled his eyes and spelt it out a few more times for the elderly pensioner. There was nothing to be found. Charles did not listen.

'You think you're just like that old man over there. He thinks I don't know he edited that report. There's money. There's something on this island and you know where it is.' Charles dug the gun into Ronnie's chest. 'I know you're lying to me too. I know there's gold, and I want it.'

'You running out of cash?' Ronnie asked smugly. 'Must be a tough gig, knowing everything.'

'Shut up,' spat Charles.

'You can't know everything though, can you? Otherwise you wouldn't need me, and you wouldn't need him. You're not going to kill us, Charles. We are too valuable.'

Charles stood for a moment and contemplated his next move. 'Listen, this project has been my passion for some time now. I have spent countless hours trying to solve it, and I just can't. People on this island are hiding things, and I know that.

'The Macleod's don't share their secret with just anyone. They only share it amongst themselves.' He licked is lips. 'You have been told. I know you have.'

'All I have been told, Charles, is that what you have been obsessing over does not exist. If you like poetry, then you're fine... there's a dead woman with a grave full of it. That's your fucking treasure though. Some woman's lost poetry.'

'I'll give you one more chance, Mr Macleod.'

'That would be a waste of my time, Charles.'

'Then,' Charles hooked Ronnie's leg, so he fell to one knee. 'You die.'

'Can I ask you a question first?' Ronnie's eyes fixed upon Charles now, and he didn't dare blink. He didn't, for a second, want to miss what was about to happen.

'You don't ask me questions.' Charles stared back. 'I've told you not to talk.'

'Come on, Charles. You're going to kill me anyway.'

'No.'

'Really?'

'Shut up.'

'Just answer one question for me. That's all I want.'

Charles looked past him to the sea out in front of him. He just wanted what he wanted so he could go home and move on. It had been a terrible idea to involve Ronnie. One of his biggest errors.

'I'll answer your question, but when I do, the next words out of your mouth better be my fucking prize.'

'It will be.'

'Good.'

'Are you ready?' Ronnie asked.

'Of course,' Charles replied.

Ronnie smiled, and almost laughed. He knew a secret that he knew Charles could never explain. Angus had told him. The second he knew his grandad was still alive was the second that Ronnie knew what he needed to do. He couldn't save everyone, but he could still try.

'Did you enjoy raping my mother, you fucking paedophile?'

Ronnie's ears pierced with a bang that followed immediately after the last syllable from his lips. His head buzzed louder than beside the stones. He looked down, but there was nothing. He was still in one piece.

'That's the punishment you get,' said Charles. 'Now you get to truly suffer.'

Ronnie watched Charles as he walked back to Brian, and the two men got into their car. He wondered why they had just decided to give up. Then he turned to the sea.

The sand was now red. It was wet, and scarlet. Ron had been shot. Time stood still as Ronnie ran over to him and slid on his knees in the sand.

Ronnie had finally failed everyone.

'Jesus Christ, Grandad.' Ronnie's voice broke. 'Don't die.'

'We both know it's too late for that,' smiled Ron.

He fell from his knees now onto his back, and his throat began to rasp as the air struggled in and out of his cancerous lungs. His dry tongue stuck to his dry lips as blood creeped around it and dribbled down his chin.

'Please don't die,' begged Ronnie. 'Please.'

'It's like you said,' Ron replied between shallow breaths. 'We've got a relationship where ultimately, I go long before you do.'

'I don't want you die hating me.' A tear trickled down Ronnie's cheek.

'I don't... I don't hate you.'

Ronnie would learn later that was a complete lie. Ron had grown to hate him, but you can't blame him. He was nothing to like. There was nothing, in Ron's eyes, that was bright and beautiful about Ronnie anymore. He was a creature of destruction, and Ron could not love something that he had spent so many years hating. At the same time though, he could not break his grandson. He could not let him down with his final few breaths.

Ronnie's tears rolled down his cheeks. 'You can't die.'

'Too late for that, lad. Look.'

Ronnie looked up above them and he seen the lights. He looked down, and then immediately back up again. Ron had now gripped his hand with fading tightness. The two men looked at each other, as though they were remembering the

The Truth Hurts

exact same memories. From Ronnie as a boy, cuddling his grandad, knowing he would never go home to his mother and his cycle of abuse. They would both finish with the same memory.

Ronnie was fifteen years old. They were sat on the beach of Ullapool, looking out to the sea separating Lewis and the mainland. Ron would tell him that their family's history lay buried on the island. Ronnie would ask if they would ever find it. Ron said no, hoping that it would never be uncovered. Yet, it had been uncovered, and they were both very different people because of it.

'What do I do?' Ronnie choked. 'Where do I go now?'

'You hide.' Ron was fading.

'Hide? Who am I hiding from?'

There were a few wet, clotted breaths from inside Ron as his body began to give up on him. His eyes flickered, and he gripped Ronnie's hand tighter than he had in days. 'Everyone.'

Behind the sirens, Ronnie heard a very poignant sound. The first bay of *Cù-Sìth*.

'You're dying,' said Ronnie.

'I know,' replied Ron. 'You need to go, before... you're a hated man, Ronnie.'

'What?' Ronnie could not hear his grandad. He was whispering. His eyes were firmly closed and the colour in his skin was fading out.

'You're not the only myth.'

Ronnie grew frustrated with the cryptic messages. His grandad's breathing became light. The second bay of the *Cù-Sìth* was heard as the sirens grew closer.

'Don't go looking for Charles. Just hide. You need to go. The *Cù-Sìth*. He's coming.'

The Kelpies are coming.

Ronnie shook his head, trying to ignore Angus once again.

You need to go. We are coming for you. Be ready.

The siren grew louder and louder, and Ronnie knew it was just over the hill. The black truck – with Charles and Brian – had just vanished over the hill itself.

By the water, you need to be ready.

The flashing blue lights stood by the hill. Ronnie looked to his grandad, and knew he was as good as gone. He thought he had lost him once, and it hadn't bothered him. This time, he knew that was a mistake. His heart crumbled. He looked to Charles for revenge, but he was now too far away.

The police were rushing down the hill now. Ronnie stood up.

Run. Jump into the sea.

Ronnie took one look at his grandfather. If he needed proof that he had imagined the entire thing, this was it. Voices were in his head, telling him to leave his dead grandfather on a beach. He wasn't sure. Yet, he had no other choice. He turned, and he ran. He planted his left foot into the sand, just before the water touched him and jumped as far as he could.

To the policemen, it just looked like a crazed killer trying anything to run away from them.

Ronnie, however, felt the ghostly glow touch his hands and the insides of his thighs. He smelt the salty staleness.

Hold on.

The Storm Kelpies ran deep into the sea, away from the Isle of Lewis. Ronnie turned, only for a second, and heard the third bay. Cù-Sìth was there, beside his grandad. By the time, he turned a second time, his grandad was gone.

'So,' said Ronnie. 'What do I do now?'.

TWENTY-TWO

Charles Mackenzie would go on to write of the vicious attacks of the serial killer, Ronnie Macleod. It would be transcended into the many forms of media of the world and translated into many languages. The world would know of his alleged crimes. They would never forget the face of a brutal killer. He would have nowhere to run. Not a mere mortal.

That was his story, anyway.

My version is quite different. See, I sat in the field with Angus that day and he told me the things I didn't know about. Things that would make me look at Morag, my brother and my grandad and feel guilty for the first time in my life that I had never asked them personally.

I was inconsolable after losing Ron. I tell the werewolves that he lived in vein, that he didn't do anything in his life. I tell them that he was abused by my mother and my brother who had no reason to be angry. I tell them that their misfortune was their own undoing.

Spirits talk to each other, it seems. The dead don't keep their secrets very well. So, I've written them down, alongside this story. Without those memories, then Morag and Lewis are just flat characters in a story. They're angry without explanation. It takes a strong character to survive years of abuse. I'm not saying she was right, but she wasn't wrong. She was wronged.

This is the story that Charles McKenzie might not want you to hear, but you're going to hear anyway. You're only weak when you don't know. Well, now you know everything. If this is all a game to know as much as possible, then we are on a level playing field.

I know what he did to my mother, and I know what he did to my brother. My dad lies in peace now I know. Charles' actions to my mother only lead to my father taking his own life. Of that, I hold him solely responsible. There is only so far you can push one man, and he was pushed over the edge.

I'm not angry anymore, just determined. My anger was a creation of a situation I was forced into. I was only a product of who Charles wanted me to be. I'm far wiser now. Writing down this tale helped me see that.

I write the tale so that people feel how I felt and thought how I thought. I give no apologies for the anger and acidity in my words. It's a memoir of my darkest days, and my darkest achievements.

It is time for me to rise.

See, Charles has gone into hiding now. Nobody seems to know where he is. I suspect he now knows what I know... what you all know. He won't stay hidden for long. His passion is revenge, and he will want nothing more than to bring me down.

You can't kill Leòdhas, though. So, what do you do?

Find the bastard. Make him pay.

I'm coming to get you Charles. I believe you're coming to get me too.

Good luck.

Ronnie McLeod.

ABOUT THE AUTHOR

A.K. Scott lives near Glasgow with his wife and two children. When he's not working or washing baby grows, he likes to write stories which become darker than he ever imagined or wasting time playing his PlayStation. He has previous career experience as a stand-up comedian. He is available on Twitter @iamaaronks, feel free to say hello or ask any questions you may have.

Printed in Great Britain
by Amazon